SINFUL KNIGHT

KNIGHT'S RIDGE EMPIRE
BOOK 16

TRACY LORRAINE

Editing by Pinpoint Editing

Proofreading by Sisters Get Lit.erary

Photography by Wander Aguiar

Models - Zakk Davis & Evan Keys

1
———

EVIE

A month ago...

I wince as a loud crash fills the flat before their shouting starts up again.

My fingers curl around my pencil so tightly, I'm amazed it doesn't snap in my hand.

Every single word that's thrown at my sister pierces through me, causing me just as much hurt as I'm sure they are her.

But there's nothing I can do about it.

A few years ago, I'd be rushing in there and trying to fight her corner. But I quickly learned that that only makes things worse.

As much as it pains me, I've promised Blakely that I'll keep out of it. No matter how vicious it sounds.

Movement across the room catches my attention and I look up to find our father rolling toward me. As per usual, he's got an empty bottle of vodka between his thighs and a mostly burned-out cigarette hanging from his lips.

"She causing trouble again?" he asks, his voice rough from years of abusing his lungs.

My brows pinch as anger continues to burn within me.

"She's sick, Dad. Something I thought you might understand," I spit.

He tsks, continuing to roll toward the bin to deposit his empty bottle.

"Recycling," I bark, making him pause.

"It's just one bottle," he mutters under his breath.

"So far," I add. "One bottle so far today. When you're the one who takes it down to the bins, you get to have an opinion."

He stares up at me with cold, shocked eyes. But I don't care.

Gone are the days that I used to shut up and put up. I'm done with that shit. If I get an opportunity to point out what a shitty father he is, then I'll do it. I still might feel guilty as hell about it afterward, but he doesn't need to know that.

"What's crawled up your arse and died today?"

There's another bang across the flat before a door is pulled open and heavy footsteps thud this way.

My stomach knots, my grip on the pencil tightening again.

"Afternoon, Derek," Dad grunts, studying his oldest friend as if he wasn't just threatening his firstborn in the bedroom.

"Jeremy. And little Evie," he coos, his expression morphing to one that has disgust rolling through me.

He studies me as if I'm not little at all. Which, of course, I'm not. Not anymore.

"I have something for you," he sings suggestively, shoving his hand into his pocket.

Dad studies us with interest, but I ignore his attention. I'm too desperate for what Derek is about to hand me.

Excitement stirs in my belly the second I see the wad of notes in his grasp.

"Here you go, sweet pea." The way his fingers brush mine makes goosebumps race up my arm, and not the good kind.

"Thank you," I say politely, trying to take it from him.

"You do know you could make more, though, right?"

"Derek," Dad growls, unimpressed by his suggestion. Although to be fair, he's unimpressed by all of this. He may never have had an issue with Blakely selling herself to ensure we all have enough food to eat, but he's never had the same opinion of me. Well, screw him. If he can't get a job and support his kids, then his bullshit opinions are meaningless.

"When I change my mind, you'll be the first to know," I tell Derek, finally pulling what I'm owed from his fingers.

It's nowhere near as much as I could earn, I know that. With his hefty cut taken out and the fact I have some hard rules for what I will and won't do means I earn a hell of a lot less than my sister. But so be it.

It's more than I used to make at the art shop in a year, and it's going to ensure university happens for me come September. I'm beyond caring what people think.

"While we're talking about jobs, you're not busy tonight, are you?"

My brow lifts as I glare at him. He knows full well I wanted this weekend off.

"With your sister out of action again," he drawls, rolling his eyes as if Blakely is faking her illness to get her out of work. "I'm a girl down for tonight. I'll pay you double," he offers.

Silence lingers as I consider his offer.

Dad glares at me while Blakely crashes around in our bedroom doing God knows what.

"Does it break any of my rules?" I ask, keeping my eyes focused on Derek's haggard face. He's the same age as Dad, but you'd never believe it from looking at him. His skin is wrinkled, his lips thin and showing evidence of years of smoking right along with his yellow teeth. His hair is grey and well overdue a cut. The only thing he has going for him is the money he blatantly robs from all his girls. But seeing as he preys on the desperate, it's unlikely that any of them will complain about the ridiculous cut he takes out of our pay cheques.

"You know I'd never put you in a position like that," he says, trying to make it look like he cares.

Dad scoffs, also putting on the same act. If he cared, he'd be out busting his arse for our family instead of rotting inside this flat on a daily basis, drowning his sorrows in vodka.

"Fine. As long as you come good on the double pay, I'm in."

"Good girl." He winks and my stomach turns over. "There will be a car here at seven-thirty. I'll get your outfit dropped off this afternoon."

Happy that he's got what he came for, he backs away from us and disappears out of the front door.

"I don't like this, Evie," Dad complains as I march to the fridge for a bottle of water. I hate spending my hard-earned cash on the stuff, but like hell am I drinking what comes out of the tap in this place. It's brown on a good day.

"Well, it's a good job your opinion on my life holds no weight then, huh?"

There was a time when I'd never talk back to my father. But that ship sailed once I discovered what a lazy wanker he is.

"You're going to regret agreeing to all this," he warns as I take a step toward where Blakely is still hiding.

"You only regret the things you don't do," I point out before disappearing around the corner.

He's very fucking judgy for someone who barely exists.

"I'm sorry," Blakely says before I've even walked into the room.

I find her lying on her back diagonally across the bed with her legs dangling off the edge.

"It's okay. Money is money."

"I hate this."

"I know, B. But there's not much you can do," I say, dropping down beside her and taking her hand in mine.

"I miss it," she says with a wince. "There's something I never thought I'd say. But... dancing. It's... I don't know, therapeutic."

"You'll get back to it. You just need to give your body time," I say softly, taking her hand in mine.

She lets out a heavy sigh, which makes my heart hurt for her.

What we thought was a cold at Christmas turned into the flu, and then as time went on, that morphed into glandular fever. Blakely was so ill. So weak and lethargic. She's always been such a beacon of strength and energy to me, and to see her suffering and existing as only a shell of the person she used to be has been hard. And not just on me. I hate seeing the way her health has affected Zayden, our little brother. Well, not quite so little anymore. He turned eleven two weeks ago, and he's going to be moving up to Lovell Academy in only a few short months.

It's been a long road to recovery for her. She's frustrated, and Derek is beyond impatient that his best girl is mostly out of action. And she's more than ready to get back to it.

"I can't believe he convinced you to go tonight."

I shrug. "It's no big deal."

Twisting her head to the side, her light blue eyes bounce between mine.

"Really? I thought you said that you never wanted to go back there so long as you lived."

"Go back—" I suck in a gasp. "No," I breathe. "He never said. He just— shit."

"It'll be okay," she tries to assure me, although it's not very convincing. "I'm sure the guy won't remember you. If he's even there."

My stomach knots, the lie I spun my sister about that night tasting bitter as if I just spilled it.

I told her the reason I returned home a mess of nerves was because of the old guy who touched me up without permission and planted me on his lap.

Obviously, that's far from the truth.

The real reason I stumbled into the house later that night, my make-up smeared down my face, my body trembling from the cold, was *him*.

The guy with the silver eyes who taught me more about myself in those few minutes together in his bedroom than I thought possible.

So much has changed about my life since that night.

I hate that it was because of him, but there's no way around it.

By doing what he did, he opened up something inside

me that was begging to get out. And it gave me the confidence to step up and be the person my sister, my family, needed while she looked after herself.

Hell, I barely even recognise the innocent girl who walked into that massive house all those months ago.

Squaring my shoulders, I suck in some confidence.

"You're right. Screw him. Derek offered to pay me double, and I fully intend on banking that cash right alongside this," I say, pulling the money from my back pocket to show her.

"I know I probably shouldn't be proud of what you're doing but... I'm so proud of you, Evie. And I can't thank you enough for what you've done over the past few months."

A shy smile pulls at my lips.

"I've enjoyed it." She quirks a brow. "Most of it. And it's going to give us the life we've always dreamed of in no time."

A genuine smile pulls at her lips before it grows so big, her dimples pop.

"I can't wait. Just you, me, and Zay." Her eyes glaze over as she imagines it while both of us ignore the elephant in that scenario.

"The car is coming at seven-thirty, right?"

"Uh... yeah. Are you—"

"I'm going," she interrupts. "Just serving, though."

Relief floods me that she's going to be there. Nothing bad can happen while I've got my fierce big sister watching out for me.

"Come on," she says, pushing herself to sit up. "We're going to get ourselves party ready."

I glance at the clock, seeing that we've got a few hours before Zay gets back from school, and jump to my feet.

"Let's go."

Without a word to our father, who has once again disappeared back to his room to hopefully drink himself into an early grave, we head out of the flat, arm in arm.

The prospect of spending a few hours with my best friend is almost enough to make me ignore the evidence of just how shitty our lives are here in this building. The walls are covered in graffiti, evidence of drug use has been kicked to the corners, and the stairwell smells like piss.

One day... one day, we're going to walk out of here for the last time. And that day cannot come soon enough.

2

___

EVIE

Just like last time I prepared to enter that house, Blakely follows my orders to make me look like anyone but myself. It's something that's been happening more and more recently. She tugs the blonde wig onto my head with ease and I quickly fall into the role I've created.

Evie is the art nerd who'd rather spend her life with her head in a sketch pad than socialise with people, but this version of me, this… vixen… she's entirely different.

She thrives on interaction, on attention and praise from men. She eats up that expression on their faces as they roll their eyes over her body, wishing they could have that little bit more than what she's offering. Hoping that they'll be the lucky one she breaks her own rules for.

It won't happen. I've drawn a hard line in the sand for what I'm willing to do. And I fully intend to stick to my morals, even if they are hanging on by a thread.

"Well, that's… worse than I was expecting," I confess when Blakely pulls two outfits from the bag she just collected from the front door and reveals two black corsets.

"Men are scumbags," I mutter, reaching for my dress—if we can even call it that—when she hands it over.

"They're rich and think they can have anything they set their eyes on. It's good for our bank accounts. Our future."

"But not our virtue."

She studies me, a small smile curling at her lips. "Virtue? What's that? I think I lost mine a while ago."

Laughing at her, I pull the outfit on.

"It looks cute," Blakely muses as I faff about with the trim on the stockings.

"I'm not sure that was what they're trying to achieve. I'm meant to be hot, sexy, and irresistible."

"Evie, you are all those things as well."

She drops to the edge of the bed and lets out a sigh.

"Are you sure you're going to be okay?" Blakely might have had a nap during her facial at the beauty spa earlier, but she still looks exhausted.

"Of course. I'm going to be right there with you tonight. Any problems with any of those dickheads and you come and tell me."

"You actually sound a little terrifying right now."

"As I should. You've no idea the pain one can cause to a stuck-up wanker with a tiny penis who thinks he's something special."

"Oh, the images," I complain, picking up my perfume and spritzing myself and my outfit.

"The tales I could tell you, Eve," she teases.

"There are some things a sister never needs to know, no matter how close we are."

Pushing to her feet, Blakely takes a step toward me and gently cups my cheeks, careful not to mess up my make-up.

"This won't be forever," she promises. "As soon as we

can, we're taking all the money we've stashed and we're restarting our lives."

I nod gently as tears of hope begin to pool in my eyes.

"I know. One day."

"It will happen. Me, you, and Zay. We can have the life we've always dreamed of, anywhere in the world we want."

It's a pipe dream. Despite saying the words out loud, Blakely has to know that.

But I'm happy to hop on and dream right alongside her while ignoring the obvious issues in our plan.

Maybe she's right. Maybe there will come a time when we can just disappear into the sunset and leave all this behind.

There has to be, right? Or all of this is for nothing.

***

My legs are like jelly as I step out of the car, my eyes locked on the house that had such an impact on my life only a few short months ago.

I was so scared to walk in there that night. Terrified of the eyes on my body, of the men's opinions of me.

I'd never left the house before wearing so few clothes. Every single one of my insecurities about my body was screaming at me to run. But I couldn't. And as Blakely steps up beside me in her own trench coat to cover her outfit, I'm reminded of why I put all of those fears aside that night and stepped through the door.

"Ready, kid?" she asks, her eyes twinkling with a weird mix of pride and mischief.

I stare into them, hating the exhaustion and shadows I

can see within them. No one else would; she's doing a fantastic job of hiding the truth, but I see it.

"Yep. Let's go take this party by storm."

As we close in on the mansion together, that fear still wracks my body. But it's different from that night. I no longer care about having the eyes of strangers on my body, it's almost become second nature. I'm only scared about one person.

Him.

The devil with the silver eyes and sinful smile.

Butterflies take flight at just the memory of that night.

I should look back on what happened in his bedroom with disgust and regret. The way he overpowered me and took exactly what he wanted with zero regards for my agreement. But that's not how I feel about it at all.

He unlocked something in me that night. Something I subconsciously knew was there but had never acknowledged.

But after I ran and finally got myself into a cab home, I had the realisation that my body was buzzing with excitement, my thighs were clenched with desire, and just the memory of feeling his powerful thrusts, his cock hitting deep in my throat had me slicker than I think I'd ever been before.

His dominance. The way he took away my free will and forced me to play his game.

Fuck. It was such a turn-on.

Feeling how hard he was just from looking at me, from having me close. It taught me the kind of power I have just being myself. Okay, I may have been flaunting my best bits, but I did nothing to seduce him. Nothing like the other girls were doing with the men downstairs in hopes of an extra tip.

I may have earned a whole heap of extra cash I wasn't expecting that night, and I probably should be ashamed of the fact he paid me like I was nothing more than a filthy whore. But I wasn't. Not even close.

I pulled that stack of notes from my dress and flicked through them with the widest smile on my face.

My sister had tried to protect me from this life since she sold her soul to the devil that is Derek when she was too young to fully understand the consequences, but I knew what I needed to do. And there was no talking me out of it. Not that she stood much of a chance as she found herself bedridden and unable to move, let alone put up any decent argument about me stepping up to help our family.

In those moments on my knees for him on his bedroom floor, I never could have imagined just how much he was going to change my life.

I might be grateful to him for helping me to find my inner vixen, but that doesn't mean I'm happy about walking back into that house and finding myself locked in his intense stare again.

The threat he issued me... it was real.

He never wants to see me again, and despite everything I feel about that night, the danger that laced his voice makes me feel the same way.

If he's here tonight, if he recognises me—hell, if he even remembers me—then I fear that my life might just change all over again.

And all because of the devil dressed in sheep's clothing with the glittering eyes.

"Evie?" My sister's voice cuts through my thoughts and I look over, meeting her concerned eyes. "Where did you go? I said your name about five times."

"S-sorry. I just—"

"I won't let him anywhere near you. I promise."

"I know. Come on." Threading my arm through hers, I march toward the side entrance of the mansion where we're permitted to enter.

The kitchen is a flurry of activity. There are girls everywhere getting prepared for the night while the caterers finish up their canapés and tidy up the mess they've made.

We're quickly sucked into the chaos and after a few minutes, Charlie finds us.

Before long, men start appearing, the keen beans who want to get their night started early.

Charlie rounds up her team of dancers, and after a few supportive words from Blakely, she leads me into the main room and helps me up onto one of the tables. My home for the night, dancing for the wealthy arseholes who are going to be hoping to get lucky. Not with me, though. The only thing they're allowed to lay on me is their eyes. I'm not one of those dancers who will be stripping down and giving out extras. Although, I've been assured that this poker night won't be as wild as the Christmas one. We'll see.

With the heavy beat of the low music that pumps through the room, I roll my body temptingly and keep my eyes on the room.

More and more men appear, their eyes going to the girls long before they find their acquaintances who are already here and start their night.

But at no point do I see that sleaze who thought he could put his hands on me. Nor do I see the guy with the silver eyes.

As the night goes on, the relief that floods my veins makes all of my movements easier. I soon lose myself in the music along with the constant hum of conversation around me, and I almost forget where I am.

But that all changes when a violent shiver races down my spine and my skin prickles with awareness.

It's ridiculous. I've had eyes on me all night. But none have affected me in any way. Okay, that's not entirely true. The men who look old enough to be my grandfather send a wave of disgust through me as they eye my body like I could be their next meal. It's gross.

Spinning around, I scan the room, trying to find who might have caused that visceral reaction within me. But there's no one new.

He's not here, Evie. It's just your imagination.

But as my body continues to burn up, I find it hard to believe myself.

He's here. He's just not showing his face.

Rolling my hips, I spin around once more, trying to appear natural and scan the room. But still, there's nothing. He isn't here.

That's it, Evie. Keep lying to yourself.

Three other girls dressed exactly the same as me step in the room together before splitting up, each one heading for the tables we're dancing on.

"Shift change," the girl who closes in on me says. "Give us a hand here, gentlemen."

As she flirts with the drunken men at the table beside me, I try to get off the table as elegantly as I can, not feeling as confident to ask for help as she is, especially as my skin continues to prickle with awareness.

But unable to resist, 'helping' hands reach for me and I'm guided from the tabletop without falling on my arse, and much to my surprise, without being groped by the rich dicks.

Maybe they only let the real sleazebags out at Christmas.

With my head held high, I take off across the room, my hips swaying with every step, and I make a beeline for the exit.

With freedom, or at least a respite, within reach, my feet move faster in my ridiculous stripper heels and I'm almost free of the room full of debauchery when I look up and come face to face with the one person I was hoping not to see tonight.

My heart jumps into my throat, my stomach knots, and my stupid, traitorous body burns up as I remember just what it was like to be at his mercy.

His eyes flash with recognition a beat before anger swallows the glittering silver, leaving two dark, dangerous orbs staring right back at me.

Swallowing harshly, he licks his bottom lip as if he's considering eating me for his next meal.

Is it wrong of me to hope he is?

"You," he hisses, the strong scent of alcohol on his breath washing over my face. "You shouldn't be here."

His fists curl at his sides as his eyes drop to my lips, and then lower. His face morphs into one of disgust that makes my stomach sink.

My need to escape takes over and I stumble back, needing to put some space between us.

He lets me move, but that disgust quickly morphs into something else.

Amusement.

He stalks forward, making my heart pound even harder and my head begin to spin.

My back collides with a door as a gasp of shock rips from my lips.

The heat of his body burns into my front as he leans

closer, trapping me between him and the unforgiving wood at my back.

Reaching out, the door clicks open and I stumble back. Tripping on the thick carpet of this room, I almost end up on my arse as he crowds me, giving me little choice but to continue backing up.

I gasp when my back hits the cool wall and he closes in on me.

There's nowhere to run, nowhere to hide. And I highly doubt that anyone is going to come to my rescue.

Do I want them to?

"Do you remember what I promised you if I ever saw you here again?" he asks, leaning close enough once more that I can almost taste whatever he's been drinking tonight.

My chest heaves as I try to suck air into my lungs. Every breath is laced with his scent, making my head spin and my inhibitions leave my body.

I should be scared. I *am* scared. But there's also excitement fluttering in my belly.

I shouldn't want him to force me to my knees again. I shouldn't want him to take from me without any thought for what I want.

But I do.

I crave that sense of powerlessness. The relief of someone else taking over my decision-making as everything I spend most of my days worrying about disappears from my head.

His eyes bore into mine, waiting for an answer.

I'm so lost in his orbit that I've no chance of finding any words. All I can do is swallow nervously and nod.

I remember those words as if he only just spoke them. They've haunted me ever since. Teasing me, taunting me, making me crave to know exactly what he meant.

"Good. It shouldn't come as a shock then," he growls before burning hands land on my body.

I blink, preparing myself to buckle under his strength. But my knees never hit the carpet.

Instead, he shocks me in an entirely different way.

3

———

ALEX

I t's been months since I laid eyes on this vixen. But there hasn't been a day since that night I found her in my bedroom with my watches in her hand that she's hasn't infiltrated my thoughts.

Never has a girl taken up so much space in my head. And I don't even know who she is.

The only things I know about her are her job and the fact she's a thief. Oh, and yeah, she's hot as fuck and sucked me like a fucking goddess.

Wrapping my hands around her hips, I dig my fingers in hard enough to leave bruises, making her gasp in shock before I move them upwards.

"There aren't many places you could hide your stash in this outfit," I mutter, skimming my hands over the indent of her waist before climbing up her ribs toward her tits that are barely contained in her sinful corset. "But I know you better than that, don't I, thief?"

"N-no," she gasps when my hands cup her breasts. But while she reacts to my rough treatment, I'm left disappointed. Her corset is too structured to give me what I really want. Handfuls of her. It's the ultimate tease, and it's driving me to insanity.

"I bet those men out there love this little get-up, huh? How much have you made tonight shaking this pert arse in their faces?"

"No, I—"

My hands lift, my fingers twisting in her blonde wig as she tries to deny my words.

"Don't lie to me, Vixen. We both know what you are," I sneer. "Using this hot little body to make men bend to your will and pay your bills." Gripping her hair tighter, it starts to move, revealing her darker, red hair I remember all too well beneath. "You're a whore, thief. A whore who's only good for one thing."

"Screw you," she gasps as I pull her wig free. Seconds later, the net that's holding her usual dark locks captive hits the floor, allowing her loose curls to fall around her shoulders.

"There she is, my little thief."

She blinks up at me, her blue eyes dark and hungry as she chews on her bottom lip nervously.

"What's wrong? You're not scared of a little attention, are you? I'll pay. You know I'm good for it." I wink and her face burns red. I've no idea if it's in anger or embarrassment, but I fucking love it.

Moving forward, I press the length of my body against hers, pinning her against the wall and allowing her to feel exactly what she does to me.

Finding some strength, her hands lift, her palms pressing against my chest.

"You need to back up."

"And you need to not be here, remember?" It's a lie. All

I've wanted since that night we first met is to find her here again.

The guys ripped me for not moving into my new flat when they all did over New Year. But as much as I wanted my own space and to finally get away from Dad and the ever-revolving door of housekeepers he keeps fucking and chucking, I was also desperate to find her again. And other than hoping she'd return here despite my warning not to, it was my only hope.

I'd visited as many of the places the girls who Dad hires for his events work. But I came up empty every time.

She was a ghost.

This perfect figment of my imagination.

I'd been watching my friends find these insane girls that they were intent on keeping for themselves, and I was desperate to find that kind of connection. To experience what they were. And then there she was, walking around in that sexy Santa outfit and tempting me in a way not many others do.

Her shriek fills the room as I wrap my hands around the back of her thighs and lift her from the floor.

"What the hell are you doing?" she screams, her fingers digging into my shoulders, her nails piercing my skin through my shirt, sending the most mind-blowing bolt of pleasure through me that ends right at my cock.

After the night I've had, the last thing I should probably be thinking about is sinking so deep inside this mystery ghost I don't know where she ends and I start. But it's the only thing in my head.

Fuck Isla and Ant. They were just a bit of fun, a way to pass the time. Hell, if I knew she was here, I never would have bothered going to my own birthday party. I'd much prefer to celebrate here.

"Coming good on my threat, thief. Isn't that what you wanted?"

Without releasing her, I sweep the contents of Dad's desk to the floor and lay her out on it.

"That's why you decided to show your face tonight, isn't it? Or did you really think that wig was going to fool me into thinking you were someone else?"

I stare down at her as she writhes on the tabletop.

Her corset pushes her breasts high, her cleavage making my mouth water as her chest heaves. Her tiny thong sits low enough on her hips to give me a nice view of her smooth stomach, and as I run my eyes over her flawless skin, I can't help but imagine what it might be like peppering every inch of her with kisses before sucking and nipping, marking her all over as mine.

A maelstrom of possession and desire collide within me as she tries to fight.

"I don't fucking think so, thief. Do you know how long I've been waiting for this?" I growl, looming over her, capturing her wrists before she does anything crazy like slap me and push me right over the edge.

Lifting her arms over her head, I lock her hands together in one of mine, leaving her stretched out over Dad's desk.

Knowing my father, I'm sure she's not the first woman who's been laid out over it, but I can fucking guarantee that no one has ever looked this good.

"Look at you," I purr, my eyes darting all over her sinful body. "Is this what you hoped for when you walked back into this house tonight? Were you hoping that I'd be here? That we'd be able to finish what we started all those months ago?"

"If I wanted that, don't you think I'd have come and

found you before now?" she sasses, making my cock weep in my jeans.

"Scared, maybe?" I taunt.

"Yeah, maybe," she gasps as I drag her to the end of the desk, allowing my aching length to press against her burning pussy.

"So desperate for me. Just like that night at Christmas. Tell me, thief. How much for full access to this body, huh?"

"Fuck you. I'm not for sale," she snaps, jerking violently on the desk, trying to free herself. But all she achieves is rubbing herself harder against me.

"So it's just your services I can buy then."

"I'm a dancer, not a whore, you wanker."

"Hell yeah, I am. And can you guess who I've been imagining as I get myself off?"

A growl of frustration rips from her lips.

"Need a clue?" I ask, leaning over her until I'm pinning the length of her body against the desk and my lips are brushing her ear. "She's a little thief who gets off on men watching her flaunt herself in these tiny little outfits."

"I don't give a fuck about those men. Don't pretend that you didn't fight for my virtue that night. I saw your knuckles, your split lip."

I can't help but chuckle in her ear. As my breath rushes out, she shudders against me.

"You think I was fighting to protect you from that scumbag? Silly, silly little thief," I taunt. "I was merely ensuring he wouldn't be the one to get you on your knees first. Imagine my surprise when you came to me instead of me having to corner you."

"I didn't come for you," she argues venomously.

"No," I agree, pulling back so she can see the wicked

smirk playing on my face. "And I think we should correct that, don't you?"

"No, I need—"

"To do as you're told. Now, wrap your fingers around the edge of the desk above your head, and don't fucking let go," I demand, holding her eyes firm so she can see just how serious I am.

The vodka from earlier still pulses through my veins, spurring me on. But since my eyes landed on her, I'm surprisingly sober and aware of every single one of my actions.

She continues to search my eyes, trying to find the joke in my demand. She can look as hard as she wants. I'm serious as fuck about what's about to go down here.

"Now, thief. I don't have all night." Total lie, and if I get my way, I'll be spending all fucking night with her. Just... maybe in my bedroom instead of my father's office.

Dragging her red-stained bottom lip between her lips, she lies immobile.

"And what if I don't follow your orders?" she asks bravely.

"Doesn't matter. The outcome will still be the same."

"You know, I was never actually—"

"I'm waiting," I snap, digging my fingers into her hip once more and grinding against her barely-covered pussy.

Silently, she continues to fight for another three seconds. But the moment the rough seam of my jeans rubs her clit, she loses all her fight. Shifting her wrists beneath my hand, I grit my teeth and release them, praying she's going to be a good girl for me.

I need what's going to happen next more than my next breath.

I've regretted not getting a taste of her that night since the moment my door slammed shut behind her.

I should have chased her. I should have dragged her back by whatever means necessary and shown her just how real my threat was.

If I had any fucking clue that I wouldn't find her again for months, I wouldn't have let her leave for days. Until she was fucking ruined and sporting more than enough evidence to remember exactly who owned her when I finally let her leave.

Desperation has me pushing her knees wide the second she follows orders and wraps her fingers around the edge of the desk.

"What are you— fuck," she gasps when I sink to my knees. "Are you— shit," she moans as I press my nose against her soaked knickers.

"So wet for me, thief. I knew you fucking loved taking my cock."

"Oh God," she whimpers as I begin licking her through the fabric, her sweet taste spreading across my tongue.

Everything else I've done tonight, all the other people I've spent time with vanish as if they don't exist. They may as well not. The only other person I need right now is this temptress before me.

"Have any of those motherfuckers out there touched you tonight?" I growl, continuing to tease her as my cock aches painfully behind the confines of my jeans.

"No," she moans.

"Good. And they won't, either. The only man who touches you from here on out is me."

"Oh, Jesus."

"He's not going to help you. You're mine now. Do you understand that?"

Her body trembles as she thrashes her head from side to side, refusing to accept my words.

"Huh, let's see if I can make you understand another way," I mutter, dropping my eyes back to her soaked pussy.

Tucking my finger beneath the fabric, I drag it aside, exposing her.

"Fuck me," I grunt, taking in the perfection of her cunt. "If I knew you were hiding this down here, then I might have searched even harder for you."

"Please," she whimpers so quietly I'm not even sure if I imagine it.

"With fucking pleasure."

Leaning forward, I lick up the length of her swollen pussy, letting her taste flood my mouth.

Jesus fucking Christ. I have no idea who this woman is, but I'm fucking addicted.

Her back arches and her legs try to close around my ears as I circle her clit.

"OH MY GOD," she screams as I force her legs open and spear my tongue deep inside her.

I eat her like she's my last meal on this earth, licking, sucking, nipping her tight little bundle of nerves with my teeth as if it's the last thing I'll ever do.

Her cries and screams for more bounce off the walls around us as she closes in on her release.

She does exactly as she's told, her fingers not releasing the desk as I push her higher and higher.

Releasing one of her thighs, I tuck two fingers deep inside her as my tongue focuses on her clit.

"Shit, you're so tight," I groan against her, bending my digits to find her G-spot and finally sending her careening toward her release.

Her muscles clamp down on me, her cries getting

louder and louder, and just before I'm convinced she's about to fall, a female shout hits my ears a beat before the door swings wide open.

"Oh my God," our intruder gasps.

Before I know what's happening, my little thief has practically catapulted from the desk and runs toward the open door.

"No need to stop on my account," the blonde who has her back to us to give us privacy says with amusement.

"That did not happen. You never saw anything," my vixen snaps before she disappears from my sight without so much as a look back in my direction.

Fucking rude if you ask me, while I'm sitting here with her juices smeared all over my face.

Lifting my fingers to my lips, I suck them into my mouth, savouring her lingering taste.

So fucking sweet. And nowhere near enough.

Getting to my feet, I rearrange myself in an attempt to make my boner look a little less obvious before I stumble toward the door, ready to start my search.

There's no fucking way I'm waiting months to get my hands on her again.

4
—

EVIE

"Eve, wait," Blakely calls as I take off through the lavish house toward the bathroom I know I can hide in.

Shame burns through me, making my blood boil in my veins and turning my face a mortifying shade of red.

"There's nothing to be embarrassed about. I'm... proud of you."

Her bizarre words make my steps falter, and I spin around to look at her.

"What? What the hell is wrong with you?" I bark. "Just... be normal for once."

If she's offended by my angry accusations then she doesn't show it.

"That is normal, Evie," she argues, gesturing back to where I just ran from. "Do you know who that was you had on his knees?" she asks, her brow quirking in intrigue. She's way too invested in this already. It's weird.

"I'm not talking about this with you," I mutter, continuing down to the bathroom.

"Evie, come on. I've been so worried about you

distancing yourself from everyone. Not making friends or connections."

"Jesus, Blake. Do you even hear how fucked up this is?"

I glance over my shoulder as I slip into the room just in time to see her shake her head.

"I want you to experience life. You spend so much time with your head stuck in a sketchbook or your tablet, I was concerned that—"

"I don't like people?" I snap. "I don't. That..." It's now my turn to gesture toward the office. "That was a mistake. It never should have happened." I suck in a breath. "I never should have come back here," I wail before finally slamming the door and locking myself in the massive downstairs bathroom. It's at least double the size of the one we all share in our flat. It even has a fucking chaise lounge in it. Ridiculous.

Pulling my uncomfortably wet thong down my legs, I lower my arse to the seat at the same time my head falls into my hands.

What even was that?

I don't do that with guys. Hell, I don't get that close to people full stop.

But him...

There's something about him that peels back all my neatly placed layers of armour, and he strips them away one by one until I'm nothing more than his puppet. And he achieves that in only minutes, with barely any words and just those heated eyes.

Blakely doesn't say a word on the other side of the door, but I know she's still there. I feel her presence. And as much as it frustrates me, I also love that she doesn't shy away from the hard stuff. She's not only my sister, but my best friend, the mother figure I lost a long time ago, and the best fucking person I know.

I just wish that sometimes she didn't see me quite as clearly as she does. There are times that I think she knows me better than I know myself, and it's unnerving.

Frustration pulls my muscles tight as I stand and face myself in the mirror. My cheeks are flushed and my pupils are dilated from the release my sister stole from me.

It was going to be mind-blowing. I already knew that, and I now hate that I'm mourning the feeling of his lips and tongue against me.

I shouldn't want anything from him, not after the way he's treated me.

But there was something so right about him between my thighs. And not just because he owed me.

I could have experienced that with anyone. I'm sure there are plenty of guys who would be willing to give me my first taste of pleasure that doesn't come from my own fingers or a vibrating little friend. But no. It had to be him.

Sucking in a breath, I attempt to do something with my hair and I turn toward the exit, preparing to face my inquisitive sister.

The second I pull the door open, she's there with a smug, knowing smirk on her lips.

"I'm sorry," she says, although, from the glint in her eyes, I don't think she's apologising for what she walked in on. "I really fucked up the timing of that, didn't I? You should totally go back and finish—"

"Can we go home yet?" I ask, talking over her.

"Uh..." She glances down at her watch. "No, not yet. And you're expected back up on that table in ten minutes. Your break is almost over."

"Brilliant," I mutter, turning my back on her and marching to the kitchen.

If I'm expected to get through the rest of this night, then I'm going to need a drink. A strong one.

"Give me whatever you've got," I demand of Charlie, who's manning the bar.

Her eyes narrow in suspicion before lifting to Blakely, who's followed me. Thankfully, she doesn't question my request and instead just grabs a glass and sloshes a more-than-generous measure of vodka into it.

"Thank you," I mutter, immediately throwing it back.

"Has something happened?" Charlie asks, concern oozing from her pores.

"Nothing you need to worry about," my sister answers for me as I fight the burn that erupts down my throat.

Charlie still eyes me suspiciously. "The men are loving you tonight, Evie," she praises.

"Great," I mutter. "At least they're all behaving."

"All of them?" my sister whispers in my ear.

"If we can never talk about it again, that would be great."

"You should have stayed put and let him finish you off. Apparently, you turn into a right bitch when denied an orgasm. Who knew?"

I glare at her, my cheeks blazing once more.

"I hate you," I hiss, the alcohol already starting to warm my belly.

"Love you too, Sis," she calls as I head back into the main room to retake my post.

Much to my irritation, I'm helped back up onto the table with more than a couple of pairs of willing hands, although none of them overstep the mark. Clearly, the invitations for tonight's poker game went to slightly more upstanding gentlemen than the last one.

I've barely stood to my full height before that all-too-familiar tingle of awareness races down my spine.

"For the love of God," I mutter under my breath, my eyes discreetly scanning the faces around me.

I don't find him at any of the tables, or laughing with the men standing around deep in conversation. But the second my eyes land on a darkened corner, I get my answer.

I don't need to see him to know he's there. The second our eyes collide, the air becomes charged. My muscles tense, my thighs clenching as the feeling of him between them slams into me once more.

Fuck. Why couldn't my sister just have waited two more minutes to barge in?

No, I chastise myself. None of that should have happened, and despite missing out on it, I know all too well that if I'd experienced the crescendo, I'd be craving a repeat even more than I am right now.

Swallowing my desire and my need to jump off the table and right into his lap, I force myself to focus on the job at hand. But while I tell myself to ignore him and entertain the visible men around me, it's not long before everyone else blurs into the background and I find myself dancing just for him.

It's a heady experience that ensures my nerve endings continue to tingle with desire and my clit pulses to the beat of the music.

None of it is enough to return to the position I was in earlier, though.

"Are you really sure this is what you want?" Blakely says from behind me the second I bolt for the exit.

I grit my teeth instead of replying.

What's the other option? Find my way back to his bedroom and finish what we started?

Desire seeps through my veins as I consider for just a second that it's an option here.

It's not.

I'm not the girl who spends the night with the prince of this castle. I'm the girl who's paid to stand up on a table barely dressed and entertain his father's dickhead friends.

I'm the girl he paid for a blowjob, for fuck's sake.

I know my place here, and it is not with him right now.

He got his kicks when I parted my thighs for him. It's just a shame I didn't get mine.

The car to take us home sits with the engine running in the colossal driveway, and without looking back, I make a beeline for the back door.

"Evenin'," the driver greets, his eyes studying me in the mirror.

"Hey," I grunt, hoping my tone is enough to put him off from attempting to make conversation. It's not.

"Good night? You sure look like you've enjoyed yourself."

I've no idea what he sees, but something tells me that if I were to look in a mirror, nothing but exhaustion and regrets would stare back at me.

I mutter some kind of half-arsed reply as my sister's footsteps close in on the car.

"Evening, Phil. How's it going?" she asks, her happiness

despite the tiredness darkening her eyes making me groan internally.

She's suffering, I know she is. How does she just keep going?

"Better for seeing my favourite customer," he flirts back, his eyes twinkling in delight.

"Seriously?" I mutter under my breath. "The driver."

"Oh, shut your mouth," Blakely chastises lightly, falling into easy conversation with Phil as he drives us home.

One of the perks of working for Derek, I guess. He always ensures his girls are delivered home safely. What an upstanding citizen.

Staring out the window, I block out the chatter around me and instead focus on the passing lights of closed shop windows and the hustle and bustle outside the pubs and clubs.

As we head across the city, the landscape changes from one of wealth to one of poverty, and it only gets worse the deeper we drive into the Lovell Estate.

This place really is the pits of hell, but still, it's home. The only one either of us has ever known.

The people outside the pubs are no longer just standing around enjoying themselves. Now, they're smoking, fucking, or fighting, not giving a shit about the others around them watching on.

The corners are filled with working girls trying to earn their next fix, and the dark alleys are lined with dealers, waiting for them to get their hands on that elusive cash.

While I might not love what my sister was forced to do before she was old enough to really understand what she was agreeing to, I have to be grateful that she has never been forced to the streets.

Derek might be all kinds of fucked up and corrupt, but

he's always found her work that's safer than those girls out there.

The car pulls to a stop outside our building, and the second it does, I pull the handle, ready to make my escape and shed the pathetic amount of clothes I'm wearing in favour of my pyjamas.

Blakely says goodbye to Phil before her heels tap against the stained old concrete of our entrance behind me.

"Evie, stop running."

"I'm not."

"Yes, you are," she helpfully supplies as I dig around in the plant pot beside our front door for the key.

The safest idea when the most important person in both our lives is sleeping inside this flat? No, not really. But while this part of town might be all kinds of dangerous, there's one fundamental rule. We don't hurt our own. That and Derek Matthews is kind of terrifying, and everyone around here knows him as our uncle and wouldn't dare lay a hand on his family. I might hate everything about it, but I'll take anything I can to keep those I love safe.

Pushing the door open, I just about manage to stop it from slamming back against the wall and storm to the bathroom.

"Evie, come on. Just talk to me," Blakely begs, but I don't stop.

Before I do anything else, I need to get out of these clothes and wash tonight and his scent from my skin.

I can deal with Blakely later. She's not going anywhere.

In seconds, my stripper heels go flying across the room, colliding with the wall with a satisfying crash before my coat, corset and thong hit the floor. I never bothered going in search of my wig, so at least there's one less thing to strip from my body.

Turning the water on as hot as it'll go, I step into our old, battered bathtub and move under the pathetic spray. I want to say it's the worst shower I've ever been in, but sadly, I don't have any experience of any other.

The dribble of water burns as it hits my scalp and runs down my neck, but as hot as it might be, it's not enough to rid me of the memories of tonight.

I'm hardly surprised when a soft knock sounds out on the bathroom door.

"Evie," Blakely breathes, poking her head into the room. "I'm sorry. Are you okay?"

Hanging my head, I continue to hide behind the rubber duck-covered curtain.

"I'll be fine. I just need…"

"I hate that you're in the middle of all of this. I tried so hard to keep you out of it." Regret and pain lace through her voice, making my stomach knot uncomfortably.

I agreed to this life to help her. It was the only thing I could think to do when she was sick to help our family. And mostly, I enjoy it.

Okay, not so much the bits that involve other people and leery old men. But thanks to that night, to him, I've found a part of myself I didn't know existed. It's that freedom I enjoy. I get to explore things I'd never opened my mind to before, safely away from other people and able to set my own rules.

"I made the decision, Blake. You don't need to feel guilty. This is our family. We do what needs to be done together."

"But you should be—"

"Stop, Blake. Please," I beg, the water dribbling down on me already turning cold.

"I just want better for you, Evie. I've always wanted so much more for all of us."

"This is our life. For now, we need to make the best of it."

She mumbles some kind of disagreement before moving from wherever she is. "I'll leave you to it. Just... are you really okay?"

"Yes. I'm okay," I lie. "I'll be right out. The water's cold already."

I regret my words the second a pained sigh falls from her lips, but she's gone before I can say anything to reassure her.

Yeah, our life isn't great. But it could still be a hell of a lot worse.

5
———

ALEX

I lay in my bed with my phone resting on my chest and my cock tenting the sheets that cover my waist.

Unlike the first time I met her, I didn't hang around at Dad's after she left. There was no point. She wasn't coming back to find me; she made that more than obvious when she ran from the house the second I turned my back.

All I did was go for a piss, and by the time I returned, she was nowhere to be found.

Charlie, the woman in charge of the girls Dad hires, refused to say a word about where she'd gone. It was fucking infuriating. But other than throttle the bitch, what the fuck was I meant to do? She was immune to my sweet talk.

She's escaped me once. I don't know why I thought tonight would be any different.

Without thought, my tongue sweeps across my bottom lip, craving another hit of her sweet taste. But it's long gone, washed away by the bottle of vodka I swiped on the way out of the house in my need to get away.

My head pounds steadily as memories from the night before play out in my mind like a movie.

I was so fucking desperate for some kind of connection last night, and while hooking up with my brother's best friend and the guy who's meant to be our fucking enemy was hot as hell, I can't help but wonder how they're both feeling about it this morning.

It might not have been my first three-way, and despite what some might think, it also wasn't my first experience with a guy.

Love is love, right? Pleasure is pleasure.

It's been drilled into me for a long time that both can get you what you want if you come at it right, and it doesn't matter the sex of your opponent; hitting their baser desires usually ensures the answers you're looking for.

Throwing my arm over my eyes, my past flashes behind them, making me want to sink into the mattress and never reappear.

My friends think they know me. I'm the happy-go-lucky guy who's always in search of a high, whether that comes from drink, drugs, or sex. And while that might not be too far from the truth, there's so much more to it.

They think Daemon was unlucky and drew the short straw when he was born the weaker twin. But that's not it at all.

The truth is, Daemon and I have different skill sets. Skill sets that our grandfather saw long before we had any idea about the kind of world we'd been born into. And being the helpful fucking grandpa that he was, he honed our skills in the only way he knew how.

He trained us, turned us into the soldiers both he and the family needed, fucking us both up beyond repair in the meantime.

I always hoped our dad would put a stop to it. That he would see what his father was doing to his boys and would save us. But he never did.

It took years for me to understand why, but when realisation hit me one day that the reason he was allowing it to happen was because he'd been conditioned, trained just like we had, pieces started falling into place.

Dad wanted us to follow his and our grandfather's footsteps and become Cirillo soldiers. He wanted us to make our ancestors proud and to help carve out the future of the city he loves so much.

But at what cost?

The only thing I do know for a fact is that the Deimos' reign of terror will end with us. I've no idea how many generations the abuse has gone on for, but it stops here.

My soon-to-be niece or nephew, and any more that follow, will never endure the shit that Daemon and I have. I don't care how much Dad might insist on our children having the training they've been born for. It will not happen. I'll kill him with my own bare hands to protect them if needs be.

While Daemon and the others are transfixed on Calli's bump being a boy, and the next heir to the Cirillo throne, I can't help hoping her belief that it's a girl comes true. If it is, if both of us only have girls, then it will all end.

It might be old fashioned, and proven wrong with Stella and Emmie's appearance, but female members of the family aren't trained to be soldiers. They have other roles and responsibilities in the family. And while I might not believe in that sexist bullshit, if it protects those that come next, then I'll happily toe the line.

My phone buzzes on my chest, dragging me from my depressing thoughts. Lifting it, I find an Instagram notification. One of my usual followers commented on a photo I posted last night before we started partying.

My hair was on point, my eyes clear and excited for the night ahead despite knowing I was going to be third-wheeling my coupled-up friends.

Hell, even I can admit that I looked good, and it seems from the hundreds of comments I've received on my selfie that my followers agree.

A comment asking to see if I'm looking as fresh this morning catches my eye, and before I think about it, I shove the sheets a little lower—not *that* low—tense my abs, and snap another photo.

Uploading it and adding my favourite filter, I tap my thumbs against my screen as I type in a caption to go with it.

TheOneAndOnlyAlexD: Wild night, but woke up to an empty bed. *sad emoji*

I only have to stare at my screen for a few seconds to see the likes and comments begin to roll in.

A boost of dopamine shoots through me as I'm noticed, as people stop whatever they're doing in their lives to react to me. It's a fucking heady feeling. One that I became addicted to very quickly once I discovered social media.

The others all think I'm crazy for taking snapshots of my life and posting them online for the world to see. Maybe I am. For as much as I love the praise I receive from my followers, I've also got a toxic obsession with the hateful comments the trolls leave as well. I like to think their hate balances out the love and keeps me humble. Probably an incredibly fucked-up way to deal with it, but what the fuck ever. At least I'm not a crack addict.

The biometric scanner turns green as I press my hand to it and push the front door of the flat beneath mine open.

A female voice immediately hits my ears and my brows rise.

"Well, well, well. I didn't think the infamous Isla Kallis did the morning after. I heard she was a hump and dump kinda girl."

"Fuck you, Deimos. Fuck you," the woman in question snarls the second I round the corner into the kitchen in Ant's temporary home.

I can't help but chuckle at the scowl that covers Isla's face.

"Ah, morning, Pest. Good to see you again."

My eyes hold hers for a beat. Unsurprisingly, there's no shame or regret shining within them. Isla is a self-confessed party girl. I'm pretty sure that what we did last night barely scratches the surface of what she gets up to.

My confidence that everything is going to be okay here shrivels up and dies the second I rip my gaze from her to the guy who's standing like a fucking statue across the kitchen. He's hugging a mug of coffee and staring at the island in the centre of the room like it's a TV or some shit.

Unease ripples through the room as I study him.

"Right, well, this was fun and all that, but I gotta be heading out."

"Need to replenish your supplies ready for tonight?" I ask teasingly.

"Something like that."

Spinning on her heels, she places her mug on the counter and bounces up to Ant. She smacks a kiss on his cheek before whispering something in his ear that doesn't reach me before she's across the room again.

She smiles at me as she approaches, but it doesn't meet her eyes. If I was under any illusion that hooking up with her last night would change the mutual hate thing we've had going on for years, then she's just confirmed it hasn't.

"See you around, loser."

"Later, Pest. Don't let the door hit you in the arse on the way out."

"I hope it does. It'll be a better fuck than you were."

I throw my head back and bark out a laugh. "Try telling me that when I can't remember just how hard you came with my cock inside you."

Heat flickers through her eyes, letting me know that she remembers just as well as I do.

"Have fun, kids. Don't do anything I wouldn't do."

My scoff quickly gets swallowed up by the slamming of the front door.

Tension quickly descends around us.

"You want a refill?" I ask, marching across the kitchen, refusing to give in to this bullshit.

I get it, he feels awkward. We kissed and I made him come all over his stomach, but so fucking what? We were drunk and craving a high. It's not like I want to turn him and drag him down the aisle.

"Uh…" he stutters, still refusing to look at me.

"I meant what I said when I left last night," I say confidently, ripping the mug from his hands and placing it under the machine. "It was one night. I don't want more or even a repeat."

Silence spills between us as the machine kicks into action.

"Not sure my ego can take that," he whispers as I pass him his fresh coffee, his eyes finally lifting to mine.

I snort a laugh. "Not due to poor performance," I confess. "Just... a wild night."

I shrug, turning my back on him again to make my own coffee.

"So..." he starts behind me. I can't help but smirk, knowing what's coming. "Are you bi, or?"

Grabbing my mug, I jump onto Ant's counter and look at him.

His hair is still a mess from all the activities last night, and while he might be wearing a t-shirt, it doesn't cover the hickeys that are littered all over his neck.

"I dunno," I say honestly. "I'm not a fan of labels. I'm just... me."

He nods thoughtfully, a soft smile playing on his lips.

"Well, you are quite unique," he confesses.

"Being normal is overrated."

"Dude, look around. None of us are fucking normal."

I don't miss the sadness that darkens his eyes.

He might be safe from his uncle's wrath while he's locked up here with us, but there must be people he misses. Family.

"It'll be over soon," I say, hoping that it's true. "You'll get to see them again."

He lets out a pained sigh and takes a sip of his coffee.

"So," I start, needing to turn the conversation back to something less depressing. "Isla was still here this morning and you look like you haven't slept a wink. Wanna spill?"

A laugh tumbles from this throat. "Sure. But I'm not hanging around in here to do it. My legs are barely holding me up."

Pushing from the counter, he passes me in favour of his living room.

By the time I join him, he's laid out on the sofa.

"She reminded me that I'm still alive, that's for fucking sure."

"Looks to me like she might have tried to kill you all over again," I quip.

"You might not be too far wrong there. Damn, man. She's fucking insatiable."

"Just what you needed though, right?"

"All right, smart arse. It had been a while."

"You really fucking liked her, huh?" I don't need to ask the question; I can see it still in his eyes whenever he looks at Calli.

"Yeah, but she's where she's meant to be. I was just... I dunno, a way to help pull his head out of his arse or something."

"You're a good friend, Ant. A good person."

"Even with my Italian blood?" he teases.

"Couldn't give a fuck whose blood is pumping through your veins as long as you're not trying to kill me or those I love."

"So what about you, then? Where did you fuck off to last night?"

Slumping lower in the chair, I rest my head back and look up at the ceiling.

The need to spill everything about my vixen burns through me.

But for some reason when I open my mouth to tell all, no words come out. Or at least not any about my sexy ghost.

"Dad had a poker night."

"You left us for poker?" he asks, looking almost disappointed.

"Well, no. I didn't know until I left and looked at my phone."

"So why did you leave?" he asks, his brows pinching.

"Careful, you're starting to sound like you didn't want me to go," I tease.

Lifting his hand, he scrubs it down his face.

"I mean, I didn't hate it, if that's what you want to hear."

I can't help but laugh. "I already knew that, Ant." I'm not sure if that's the response he's looking for, but he was all in last night. He might have hesitated to start with, but once he got over that, he was fully on board the pleasure train. "What's the issue?"

He shrugs. "I... I just wasn't expecting..."

"To enjoy it?" I ask when he trails off, breaking our eye contact.

He doesn't respond.

He doesn't need to.

"It was pleasure, Ant. Just a bit of fun. It doesn't have to mean anything." My words are meant to be reassuring him, but as I hear them, my stomach knots.

Was that all I was to her last night? A bit of fun?

Has she forgotten me again already?

I wake to the steady pounding of my head. I only had a couple of shots last night, but being a lightweight who hardly ever drinks, it's enough to have been feeling the effects this morning.

My need for the bathroom ensures I'm unable to pull the covers over my head and try to block out the world for a little longer.

Rolling over, I swing my legs off the bed as the room spins around me.

I hang my head, willing it to stop. But the second it begins to improve, I'm slammed with images of the night before. Or one image, to be exact.

Fuck. I never should have let him touch me. Let alone...

I shake my head and glance behind me.

Blakely's side of the bed is empty. It's hardly a surprise. No matter how late she goes to bed, she's always up before me. She's been taking care of me and Zay for so long that it's ingrained in her to get up first and play the part of mum.

She doesn't need to anymore. We're both old enough to look after ourselves. Zay might only be eleven, but with all that we've experienced in our lives, he's much more mature than I'm sure he should be. We both tried to maintain his innocence. But when you live in a building with more drugs than a pharmacy and more sex than Pornhub, it's hard going. And that's not even mentioning the other kids. His primary school might be okay... ish. But the second he starts at Lovell Academy... A shudder rips down my spine. I've spent the past seven years there. I know exactly what goes down and what the kids are up to. We just have to hope that he doesn't get swept up by it all. That, or our miracle happens and we manage to get the hell out of here.

The sound of Blake and Zay chatting in the kitchen makes me smile as I pad toward the bathroom. Nothing makes me happier than being at home with my family. Even if our flat is a dive. Who cares when there's love, right?

"Jesus Christ," I gasp when I look up after loading my toothbrush and take in my reflection.

My make-up is everywhere, reminding me that I didn't properly remove it after my shower last night. Instead, I dried off, pulled some pyjamas on and fell straight into bed with wet hair.

Blake was already snoring by the time I got to our room, proving just how exhausted she really was, and all I could think about doing was the same in the hope slumber would banish thoughts of him from my head.

I want to say it worked, but I'd be lying. My dreams were full of dark and dangerous eyes, the scent of the sexy man that made my mouth water and my thighs clench.

Grabbing a wipe from the packet on the side, I attempt to fix my face before heading out once more.

Saturday morning is one of two favourite parts of my week.

Family time.

Every Saturday morning and Tuesday evening is when we shut out the rest of the world and just focus on us. On what's important.

Zay's laugh lightens my mood as I walk back to the bedroom to get dressed ready for breakfast.

My head still continues to pound, but I ignore it in favour of looking forward to what's to come.

I'm pulling my skinny jeans up my legs when the bedroom door opens and the scent of strong coffee fills the room.

"Good morning," my sister sings happily, making me wince inside.

She's always been a ray of sunshine. No matter how shit life gets, she's always got a smile on her face.

It's something I've always admired about her. Something I wish I could embrace. Unfortunately, I struggle to see the good in everything the way she can. While she's smiling, you can usually find me with my resting bitch face being grumpy at the world and the hand it dealt us.

"Hey," I grumble.

"Oh, feeling that good, huh?" she chuckles, lowering her arse to the edge of the bed and holding one of the mugs in her hand out for me.

"Thanks."

"So," she starts, making me roll my eyes.

"Seriously. Can we just forget everything about last night?"

"Evie," she sighs, tracking my movements across the room.

I stop in front of the window and stare out at the depressing view before me.

Rain runs down the rotting window, making the depressing, grey streets of Lovell blur.

"You had Alexander Deimos on his fucking knees for you," she states, making me wish the ground will swallow me up whole.

"Blake," I groan.

"Do you even know who he is, Eve?"

"Some good-looking rich prick who always gets what he wants?" I snap.

"Uh... well, yeah," she agrees. "But he's so much more than that, and you had him on his *fucking knees.*"

I cringe. "Please, can you stop saying that? It was a moment of madness. I—"

"Tell me what really happened the last time you were there. And don't even start with the bullshit you've been spinning for the past four months. I know it was him."

Lifting my mug to my lips, I take a sip, hoping it'll help to calm me.

"Okay, fine," I sigh. "It was him," I confess, spinning around, resting my arse on the windowsill while keeping my eyes on my coffee.

"Go on," she encourages.

So I do. I tell her every dark and dirty detail. And by the time we're interrupted by our hungry little brother, I'm not entirely sure if she's more shocked or proud.

Weirdo.

"**O**h my God," I moan just like I do every time we come to this place.

Waffle On is Zayden's favourite place in the world. Well, this place and The Taco Lounge.

The smoky bacon mixes with the sweetness of the waffle and the maple syrup, making my mouth water and my hangover finally subside.

Looking to my left, I find Zay shovelling food into his mouth as if it's going out of fashion. He's paying us zero attention as he focuses on filling his stomach.

"You know," my sister says, watching me curiously, before lowering her voice. "Alex could come in useful in our quest for a new life."

My brows pinch in confusion as I study her, trying to hear the words she's not saying.

"No," I hiss, not willing to even discuss whatever idea is churning behind her eyes.

"Evie, just think about it. He's loaded. Has everything. Those watches are just the beginning. You wouldn't even need to—"

"What the hell, Blake?" I snap. "What's got into you?"

She shrugs, not looking guilty at all.

Zay looks up, sensing the tension between us. His blue eyes that are so similar to the ones that stare back at me every time I look in a mirror dart between us.

He hates when we argue. The look of disappointment on his face makes my stomach knot.

"I need the bathroom," he says quietly, sliding out of the booth and disappearing across the café.

"Aren't you fed up with this?" Blakely asks. "Of doing anything we can to scrape the money together we need for a fresh start?"

I puff out a breath. "Of course. But all of this," I say. "It's about more than money. We could have millions stashed away, but that doesn't mean we can just take Zay and start over. It's not that easy."

"But it could be with the right connections. And money talks. We've just never had enough to make it say anything."

"You're clutching at straws. He just wanted to bang a dancer. An easy hook-up. There's nothing more to it."

She shakes her head. "You didn't see the way he watched you all night." *No, but I felt it.* "He wanted you. And," she adds before I get a chance to say anything, "the feeling was mutual. You wouldn't have done what you did for just any guy. He's special and you know it."

Special. Yeah, that's one way to describe him.

"It doesn't matter, Blake. None of it matters. It was a mistake. If I have anything to do with it, I'll never go back to that house or see him again."

"You're lying."

"Am I?" I counter, anger beginning to burn through my veins.

Pulling her phone from her back pocket, she opens up Instagram and types something in.

"Look," she says, holding it out for me.

The second my eyes land on the phone, my mouth waters and I swallow nervously.

"You're really going to turn that down?"

Inches upon inches of Alexander Deimos spread out before me.

"He posted this picture this morning. Bet he was thinking about you. I bet that beneath those sheets he's ha—"

"Everything okay?" Zay asks as he rejoins us.

He nervously looks between us, trying to assess if we're still mad.

"Yeah, little man. Everything is fine," Blakely says, trying to reassure him.

A smile twitches at his lips as he hesitantly slides back into his seat.

My heart sinks as I watch him. He's terrified that something will happen that makes us abandon him.

Reaching out, I snag his hand under the table and squeeze supportively.

"Love you, Zay," I whisper. His cheeks heat as he looks around to make sure no one else heard me.

It's easy to forget that our little brother is quickly growing up. It won't be long until he's too embarrassed to even be seen with us because we're so uncool.

"You too, Evie."

"Eat up. You're going to need your strength for the skate park after," Blakely says, finally making Zay's face light up.

"For real?"

"Yeah. For real."

While Zay might be shy, that all changes when he gets a skateboard under his feet. The second he drops into a halfpipe, all his fears and anxiety over our living situation seem to melt away and in its place is this confident, skilled skater.

"Yes," he breathes, immediately reaching for his knife and fork to finish up his breakfast.

We both watch him in silence, our hearts probably aching in a similar way.

Blakely's shoulder hits mine, finally dragging me out of my daze.

"Just think about it, yeah?"

"We don't need him, or anyone, Blake. We've got everything we need right here."

"I know but—"

I shake my head, cutting her off.

"Yeah, you're right. When the time is right, it'll happen for us."

Relieved that she's going to drop this stupid idea, I slide my plate closer once more.

"You know," she mutters quietly, "if you really meant what you just said, you should talk to Derek about only working for the Italians."

"Why?" I ask around a mouthful of waffle.

"The Cirillos and the Marianos, they've got beef."

"Beef?" I blurt. "How the hell do you even know that?"

"I hear things. But if you don't want to risk seeing him, then Italian clubs and events are the safest places for you."

"Safe," I mutter lightly. Pretty much anything seems safer than being in the middle of a frigging gang war. "Maybe I should just get a job at Foxes."

"NO," Blakely barks, making Zay startle. "Sorry. But no, that is not an option. I might not like what you are doing, but I trust Derek to keep you safe. None of the girls are safe at Foxes."

"It was a joke, Blake."

"A bad one. I'll talk to Derek for you, but in the meantime, you really should check out his Instagram, it's hot."

"Not interested," I sing, although something akin to disappointment settles heavily in my stomach.

"Okay, sure. I'll send you a link to it just in case, though."

"Surprised you wasted time on his feed, he's at least fifteen years too young for you," I tease, knowing Blakely's soft spot for older men.

"Research purposes."

"For what, exactly?" When her eyes sparkle with

mischief, I hold my hand up. "Don't tell me. I don't want to know."

"Okay, sure. But I think you've got a lot in common and would make a hot-as-hell couple."

"Seriously?" Zay says, finally interrupting. "Can you please stop talking about boys and older men? It creeps me out. It's bad enough Josh found out that you're a dancer," he says, shooting Blake a glare.

"Zay, I'm sorry. I really am. But you need to get used to it. Lovell Academy is going to be full of idiots who will have something to say."

"Brilliant. Can't wait. All my friends are going to be crushing on my sister."

"Wait," Blakely gasps. "You mean they're not already?"

7

EVIE

Despite what I told Blakely, I was only able to hold off on stalking the enigma that is Alexander Deimos for so long.

For almost two weeks, that unclicked link sat in my inbox, taunting me.

But eventually, my curiosity got the better of me and I caved to temptation.

And holy hell am I glad I did, because his feed is pure Jill Till material. I want to say that I haven't made use of those images. But that would be a big fat lie.

I might have done a one-eighty in the past few months where sex is concerned, but I seem to have an issue that's not making me happy.

I can't get off unless it's him fuelling my actions. I need the memory of him in my head or the image of his insane body filling my eyes.

It's a sickness. One I'm more than ready to recover from.

It's either that, or I'm going to end up doing something

really stupid, because I'm already becoming desensitised by his photos. And that is not a good thing.

The ringing of my iPad startles me, and I drop my phone as if I've just been caught red-handed, my cheeks blazing.

Sucking in a deep breath, I smooth a hand over my replacement blonde wig and jiggle my tits into place.

Once I've almost composed myself, I reach out and swipe the screen.

"Hi there," I purr, looking into the eyes of one of my regulars through the screen.

"Hey, beautiful. I've missed you," he says, a genuine smile playing on his lips.

I started looking into camming in the weeks that followed my disastrous first steps into this world.

Totally inspired by him, of course.

I craved the rush he gave me, but I wanted it on my terms.

And while I had agreed by then to pick up more shifts for Derek, I was still hesitant to be around people. Men.

He might have given me some confidence, shown me all these different things about myself that I never knew, but the creep who touched me down in the main room still terrified me.

Camming seemed like a safe way I could explore all of this. I could try and rediscover that inner vixen he found, and the only person who would be touching me was me. And of course, I could earn a little extra cash. Seemed like a win-win.

"How are you doing? Have you had a good day?'

"It's better for seeing you, sweetheart. What about you?"

"Yeah, it's been good. Busy," I admit. It's the truth. I

spent all day at school then did my last shift at the art store I've been working at for the past two years. Not that he needs to know all that detail.

"I hope you haven't been keeping others entertained in my absence," he teases, sitting back in his chair and getting comfortable for our session.

Obviously, I should be eighteen to be able to do this, and while I'm only a few weeks off, I couldn't get through the security checks the sites required. That was until I spoke to Derek. I guess I shouldn't really have been surprised that he had a contact who would be more than happy for me to start working on his site, so long as Derek got a cut. Can't say I was overly happy about that. He already earns far too much off his girls who are all still scraping the barrel to survive, but what choice did I have?

Do it and get the money my family so desperately needs now, or wait and suffer longer? There really wasn't a question there. My only regret was that I didn't do it earlier.

"Aw, Peter. Would I?" I purr.

Pete is sweet. He was one of my first clients and the only one who has stuck with me this long. Makes me think that maybe I'm not as terrible at this as I often wonder.

I have zero experience with men. I have no idea what gets their engines revving. I just... I remember the way they all looked at me that night. It was terrifying, thrilling. And I figured I could make use of that.

"Talk to me, tell me what's been going on with you," I encourage.

Pete isn't just here for the sexy talk and a way to get off. He seems to really need a friend.

He lost his wife a while back, and he doesn't have any

children of his own. He seems to just be genuinely lonely and looking for someone to talk to.

There's been more than one occasion where he's paid for a session with me and nothing has even happened. We both just sit on different ends of a camera and talk. It's... nice, in a totally fucked up kind of way.

I lie there, fiddling with the lace trim of my nightie as he talks about his week, feeling like I should at least try and do something sexy seeing as he's paying for my time.

"Sounds like it's been a stressful one," I comment, noticing that our hour is almost up. He's been known to extend our time. And it might make me a really bad person, but I could really use an extra hour of money.

"Yeah, I guess."

"And what have you done to blow off some of that steam?"

"Umm... I wanted to play squash last night, but I was late leaving the office and—"

"Pete," I chastise. "You need to be taking better care of yourself."

"That's why I have you," he says, fidgeting in his chair.

"I guess it is," I agree. "Tell me what you need."

Shamelessly, I arch my back, making my tits press against the satin fabric covering them.

As if magnetised, Pete's eyes drop to them.

"You want me to take this off... Daddy?" I add, making him groan in pleasure from just that word alone.

He sucks in his bottom lip, his eyes darkening as mine jump to the timer in the corner of the screen.

"You know I do, beautiful. Let me see what's hiding behind that teasing nightie."

Trailing my fingers up my side, I pray that it looks as

seductive as it does in my head before I run them around the lace once more.

The second I pull the satin down to reveal the rosy pink of my nipple, Pete's eyes dilate.

"So beautiful," he murmurs, shifting around again as he rips his trousers open and shoves his hand inside.

Six months ago, I'd have said I'd be disgusted watching a man pleasure himself while staring at me through a camera. But now, I feel strangely liberated by the whole thing.

Never in my life have I felt sexy or beautiful. Blakely always told me that she thought I was pretty, and she repeatedly tried to enhance what she said was my natural beauty with make-up, but I was never for it. I just wanted to blend into the background. To a point, I still do.

I'm not going to turn up at school and demand to be centre of attention all of a sudden, but this, right now. I'm someone. I'm making a difference in someone's life. Okay, so, albeit weirdly. But still. I'm helping Pete right now. He needs a companion and a way to relax, and that makes me feel good.

Yeah, maybe I'll check myself in for some counselling in the near future.

"Fuck, yeah," he grunts when I finally slip my strap of my nightie from my shoulder and fully expose myself. But no sooner has he got a look at when he wants when a notification chimes that his time is up.

"Oh, no, no," he complains and briefly looks away from the screen. "I can do another fifteen. Please, tell me that you're free," he begs, sounding desperate.

"For you, Pete, I'm as free as a bird."

Blakely is out working, and Zay is already sleeping. Dad is fuck knows, probably in a vodka coma. I'm long beyond worrying about what he's doing. And if he decides to barge in randomly, then that's on him.

"Okay, good. Let me just…"

I sit there, still putting on a little show for him, trailing my fingers over my breasts and pinching my nipples for him until another notification pings and the timer in the corner restarts.

"Now, where were we, beautiful?" he murmurs.

"Tell me what you want from me, Daddy," I command. I learned in our early chats that he likes to take charge, and I'm more than happy to follow orders.

I might be all about pushing my boundaries, but being the one to dish out the orders still makes me blush like a nun at an orgy. I'm way more comfortable with this.

"Lie on your back and pull your nightie up. I want to see that pretty pussy you're hiding between your thighs."

"Someone means business tonight," I whisper as I follow orders, angling myself so he has a good view.

He groans as I part my thighs for him and finds I'm wearing knickers.

"You're a tease, beautiful."

"I think you like that about me, Daddy. You know you shouldn't be looking, and it makes it so much hotter."

"You've no idea," he drawls as I tease myself over the lace of my knickers.

Unlike what he's probably imagining, I'm barely wet. Unfortunately for Pete, the whole order man, dad bod situation doesn't get me going.

The guy on my phone, though…

I bite down on my bottom lip as I think about his photos.

"That feel good?" Pete demands.

"So good," I moan, barely seeing him on the screen before me, instead focusing on the image in my head.

Dark, messy hair, silver eyes, rippling abs and deep V lines that disappear to what I know is a much, much larger dick than the one Pete is currently stroking.

"Slip your fingers inside your panties, beautiful," he demands, and I follow orders instantly. Not because he tells me to and I'll be laughing all the way to the bank, but because this is what *he* does to me.

I don't know if it's him, or if I'm just so fucked up that the memory of sucking his cock alone gets me wetter than I think I've ever been before.

The second my fingers graze my clit, a moan of pleasure spills from my lips. It's not even fake.

Pete praises me, but it passes me by as I put myself right back on that office desk, imagining that the pressure against my pussy right now is his mouth, his tongue circling around that sensitive bundle of nerves and spearing inside me in a way that made my eyes cross.

My fingers on my free hand clench, desperately wanting to twist into his thick hair as he eats me.

Pete's deep voice continues to rumble through the room. I've no idea if I'm doing what he's asking of me; quite honestly, I don't care. I'm too far gone.

Frustrated by my restrictive knickers, I lift my hips and drag the now-soaked lace down my thighs.

"That's what I'm talking about." Pete's deep drawl hits my ears, making me cringe. I bet he thinks I'm totally into him.

Oh well, he might as well get his money's worth.

"Are you hard for me?" I ask, refusing to say his name so I can keep the images in my head.

"Fuck yeah. I'm gonna come so hard for you, beautiful."

A shudder of awareness rips down my spine.

It's not the first time I've lost myself in my imagination while on a call. But I've never been this desperate. My own fault for spending all my spare time stalking his Insta.

I should have stayed strong. I should have—

I gasp as my fingers find my clit once more. My hips jump from the bed and my toes curl.

Thinking about *him* pleasuring himself as he ate me out, I work myself into a frenzy. If the grunts and groans that fill my room, I'd say that Pete is in a similar situation.

Pushing two fingers inside myself, I up the pressure on my clit and finally crash over the edge.

Pleasure rushes through me, his name teetering on the tip of my tongue. It's so close to spilling out that I sink my teeth into my bottom lip to stop me.

The taste of copper fills my mouth as I ride my high, imagining him sitting up from between my thighs with his mouth glistening from my release before demanding I repay the favour.

Oh hell yeah, I'll get on my knees and worship you any day.

The ding of a notification drags me from my filthy thoughts and when I look at the screen, I find Pete reaching for a tissue to clean up.

"You needed that, didn't you, beautiful?"

My cheeks flame at his words.

"It's been a long week." Of staring at a guy that I can't have's photos.

"Same time next week?" he quickly asks before we're cut off.

"You've got it. But if you need it before, you know where I am."

"I sure do. Talk soon."

My lips part to respond, but the call cuts before any words fall from my lips.

"Fuck," I hiss, sitting up in the middle of the bed.

My heart is still racing, my blood boiling with desire. Pete was right, that release was needed. But it wasn't enough. It was nowhere near. And I fear that nothing will be.

What I need is a repeat of that night in his father's office where my bloody sister doesn't walk in and distract us before I can find heaven.

With a frustrated huff, I fall onto my back once more and reach under the bed for the vibrator I have stashed with a selection of other toys I've been collecting for my camming calls. Maybe I need the enhancement of batteries to itch the spot that needs scratching.

8

———

ALEX

"So, this is where you're slumming it now, huh?" I ask, marching into Ant's new home and taking in the freshly decorated flat. "I mean, it's not Cirillo Towers, but whatever."

"Fuck off, it's better and you know it," Enzo says from his seat on the end of the sofa.

"Room service," Ant shouts from down a hallway, pointing out the fact that his new pad sits above one of the Marianos' hotels.

"You've heard of Uber Eats, right?" I call back.

"Christ, you two are like an old married couple," Enzo mutters, although when I look up, his attention has been stolen by his phone.

I startle at his words, wondering if Ant has confessed to what happened that night all those weeks ago.

I couldn't give a shit if he did. Hell, he can join in next time too, if he wants. I'm game. But something told me from Ant's reaction both on the night and the morning after that he wasn't going to go off shouting his experience from the rooftops. Maybe I'm wrong and Ant shared all.

"Go check it out. See if we can impress you," Enzo says absently, jerking his chin in the direction Ant's voice has been filtering down from.

Not wanting to pass up a chance to snoop on the enemies, not that they are that now, I take off.

Since we worked together to wipe Enzo's older brother from the face of the Earth to stop his over-inflated ego from trying to take over the entire city, we're allies.

It feels good to have more people on our team. For things to be back how they used to be before Ricardo took over and started running the Mariano family into the ground.

The modern artwork on the walls is... odd, but kinda cool. The floors are all a dark grey and the walls a lighter shade. It's nice, homely in a slightly cold way. I much prefer my place with thick bouncy carpet and warm colours.

I pass a sleek bathroom and an empty guest room before I step into a large room at the very end of the hallway with huge windows overlooking this part of the city we all rule.

It's almost like being at home, the view just... slightly different.

Movement on the other side of the room catches my eye and I rip my attention from the illuminated high-rise hotel a few streets over, finding Ant walking out of what I assume is his en suite with nothing but a towel wrapped around his waist and water droplets covering his skin.

"Oh, hey," he says somewhat awkwardly. "I thought Enzo had stolen your attention."

"He sent me down to check the place out. It's nice," I say, watching him walk toward a chest of drawers and pull out a pair of boxers.

"Yeah, not sure I'd have done it exactly like this if I had

a choice, but it's a hell of a lot better than the last place my family put me."

I wince. I've only heard the basics from Ant and Daemon about what happened to them while they were locked up and tortured by Ricardo and his men. But I don't need details, the state of them when they returned and the scars they've both been left with tell a horrifying enough story.

Ant tugs on his underwear before dropping the towel and walking toward his mirrored wardrobe.

"It must be nice to be back though, with your family."

Stopping, he looks up, his eyes colliding with mine.

"It's amazing. Seeing Mum and Gessica..." He drops his head as if he's ashamed of his reaction.

"It's okay, man. What you've been through... you're allowed to get a bit emotional," I assure him, unable to stay where I am when he's suffering.

He shakes his head, his entire body jolting in shock when I press my hand against his back.

"I haven't allowed myself to really process it all. But being back here, surrounded by everyone. I-it's—"

"It's okay to break. You're safe here. All the men who tortured you both are dead, right?"

He nods. "As far as I know."

"And if we find we've missed any, we'll fucking slaughter them together."

Finally, he looks up, his eyes colliding with mine.

"We've got your back, just like we know you've all got ours. Fresh start, yeah?"

He nods. "Yeah."

"And we're going to start the only way we know how." Digging my hand into my pocket, I pull out a joint that I rolled earlier and place it between my lips.

"Get dressed, Santoro. We've got to find a way to put up with all those happy couples."

He chuckles, finally sliding the wardrobe door open to find some clothes.

"They're... a lot to take."

"That they are," I say after lighting up and taking a hit. "You want that?" I ask as he tugs on a pair of jeans.

"Yeah," he agrees. "One day. You?"

The second he asks, one face appears in my mind. Dark red curls, tempting luscious lips and a body made for sin.

Without realising it, my tongue sweeps across my bottom lip as if her taste is still there. Of course, it's been weeks since that night and I'm left disappointed.

It's not until Ant clears his throat that I realise I'm standing here staring at his crotch like a creep.

"Yeah. I want that. Just need to find the one to have it with. Want a hit?" I offer, holding the joint out.

Ant's eyes bounce between mine and the spliff before he finally reaches for it.

"Thanks," he mutters, swiping it from my fingers and sucking in a quick hit. "Something tells me that we're gonna need it to put up with that horny lot."

I can't help but laugh. "You got that right. You heard from Isla? She coming?"

"No idea. We haven't spoken since earlier in the week," he confesses.

"She been here?" I probe.

"Nah, not yet."

"Maybe she needs a tour. Help you... christen the place." Both of them have been tight-lipped about anything else happening between them, and I can't lie, I'm fucking curious.

"We'll see," he says, reaching for a shirt and pulling it on. "Come on, let's go get Matteo and get the party started."

"Where the fuck is Gus?" Enzo asks when he realises that it's just the four of us.

"Last time I saw him, he had a girl under each arm and was heading to his flat," Matteo admits.

"And you chose to hang out with us instead of joining that party?" Enzo asks, sounding genuinely confused.

"Yeah, they weren't my..." Both mine and Enzo's eyebrows rise. "They were too easy," he confesses, turning to look out the window as the Uber pulls away from their new home.

I might have only been to their old warehouse once when we ambushed the place, but one glance is enough to see that they've risen through the ranks recently.

"I see. You like a challenge, huh?"

"It's all about the chase, the fight, with our new boss. He doesn't like things being handed to him on a platter. Doesn't think he deserves it."

"You fucking done psychoanalysing me, Bro?" Matteo barks at Enzo.

"What? It's true. You always go for the hard-to-get ones who put up a fight."

"Nothing worth having comes easy," Matteo mutters. "Not that you'd know."

"What the fuck is that supposed to mean?"

"Seriously," Matteo scoffs.

I sit patiently, waiting for some more juicy gossip about the Marianos' new leader, but sadly, it never comes.

"I might want easy fucks," Enzo says eventually, "but I draw the line at paying for it."

"Jesus," Ant mutters while my mind shoots straight back to her and the way I paid her for getting on her knees for me that night—not that she had a lot of choice in the matter.

The second I think about it, despite it being months ago, my dick twitches.

At this point, I'm not even sure if my memory has twisted it all up into something it wasn't.

It was just head. From a girl who mainly looked terrified as I prowled toward her covered in blood after defending her honour against the wanker who decided to take liberties.

They'd all been watching her, undressing her with their eyes—not that it was all that much of a challenge with how little she was wearing. It wasn't just that she was younger than the rest of the girls working that night. It was her innocence. It oozed off her in waves. That was what really was getting everyone's dicks hard. Including mine.

I wanted her from the second I laid my eyes on her. But I was a good boy—what? I am—and I knew the rules.

Derek's girls were off-limits. Although, that quickly went to shit that night. It was unlike any of Dad's poker night's I'd experienced before.

Fuck knows how much he paid for the girls who turned up that night. The only one I recognised was Charlie, the boss. The others were all new. Maybe that should have been a warning that things were going to get messy. Should have clued me in on the type of woman that sexy vixen was.

But I didn't think much past my dick and wanting to make her mine. Probably why I was so shocked when I found her trying to steal anything she could find. Obviously, Dad wasn't paying that much after all.

Dragging myself back to the here and now, I push thoughts of her aside, for a little while at least.

"If it's a challenge you want, I've got just the woman for you tonight," I confess.

"Alex," Ant warns.

"What? I thought you were up for sharing," I say, dropping him right in it.

"Wait a fucking minute," Enzo says, holding his hand up to stop anyone else from saying anything. "I thought you were bored as fuck locked up in your Greek castle. Something you're not telling me, man?"

"Okay, so maybe it wasn't quite as boring as I made out," Ant admits.

"Tell us about the girl," Matteo demands.

"If you're patient, you might get to meet her."

"She hasn't said anything about it," Ant says, reminding me of what he told me in his bedroom.

"Dude, if she's not begging to be at the same party as you then you failed to blow her fucking mind," Enzo announces with a smug-as-fuck grin on his face.

"Not true," Ant mutters. "She's just busy and shit. But even if it were true, I was fucking injured. I wasn't firing on all cylinders."

Hence why you had assistance, I think to myself.

Ant looks up and our eyes collide as if he can read my fucking thoughts.

He shakes his head at me. It's so subtle that the others wouldn't notice, but I do.

One side of my mouth kicks up in agreement. If he wants it on the down low, then he's got it. I promised him that everything would go back to normal the second I walked out of that flat and I need to stand by that. He deserves it after everything he went through.

"Party at Cirillo Towers. I hope that son of a bitch is turning in his grave," Enzo spits as our car pulls up out the front of my building.

"Bitch?" Matteo snarls. "That bitch is our mother, in case you're forgetting."

"Oh, Bro. Keep your fucking knickers on. It's a figure of speech. Our mother is..."

Ant laughs. "Fucking terrifying?"

I've never met Viviana Mariano, but Ant talked about the formidable woman during his time with us, so I have a rough idea. I mean, to put up with that many members of the Italian mafia, you've got to be made of pretty strong stuff.

"Yep, that. Exactly that," Enzo jokes.

"Come on, boys. Let us show you how it's really done," I say with a smirk as we pile out of the car and head toward the main entrance.

Security has returned to normal now Matteo and Enzo's twisted big brother is worm food, so with just a handprint and a nod to the bemused soldier stationed at the door, we head for the lift.

"Pretty sure your guard just shit his pants," Matteo helpfully points out once the doors have closed on us.

"Not every day three dirty Italians walk in here, that's for sure."

"Fuck you, Deimos. I think we all know who the dirtiest motherfucker is here," Ant barks, amusement twinkling in his eyes.

"Wear my badge with pride, gentlemen," I say with a wide-arse grin as the lift continues to rise through the building.

In only minutes, I press my hand to another scanner

and let myself into Nico's penthouse. Or I guess I should say Nico and Brianna's penthouse, seeing as he's the latest member of our group to settle down.

"Shit," Matteo says, pulling his phone from his pocket.

His brows pinch as he reads before looking up at me.

"We good to hang out here a bit? Just need to—" He looks at Enzo and Ant.

"Yeah, you got it. Do your thing."

"Your VIP has arrived," I announce as I march toward the quiet living area. It's like they're not even ready to party.

"Where?" Toby asks, looking around me as if I've brought some fucking celebrity with me.

"Fuck you, Tobes, you boring motherfucker."

He flips me the bird as I march toward the kitchen, pulling my phone from my pocket to sync up with Nico's sound system and get this party started.

"Ladies," I greet, taking Jodie's hand the second she's released a bottle and spinning her under my arm. "You look lonely. Your boys not taking care of you?"

"Like Emmie would ever have that issue," Theo grunts, appearing out of nowhere. "Ain't that right, Hellcat?"

He backs her up against the wall, hooking her leg around his waist.

"And it starts already," I mutter to myself as I pull Jodie into my body and dip her low, making Toby growl over my shoulder.

"Are you fucking done?" His fingers wrap around Jodie's upper arm, hauling her into his grasp.

"Pfft, didn't your momma ever tell you to share your toys?"

The glare that Toby shoots me would have others

quaking in their boots. Not me, though. I know for a fact that I could take him. Stoned or not.

"I'm going to drag Nico out of Brianna's pussy. Don't touch what doesn't belong to you, Deimos," he warns darkly.

"Possessive arseholes."

"You'll be the same," Jodie offers.

"Like fuck I will. No pussy is good enough not to share."

"You're so full of shit. Do you even hear yourself?"

I shrug. "Pleasure is pleasure. Something tells me that sharing could be fun." I wink at her, but she doesn't return it. Clearly, she disagrees and is happy with Toby's dick. Good for her.

I grab a beer to go with the half-smoked joint that's calling my name from my pocket as voices filter over the music.

I spin around, hoping to find Matteo and his boys, but I quickly discover another couple that also won't agree with me about sharing the fun when Seb and Stella emerge.

"You're late," I state like an arsehole.

"Sorry," Stella says with an unapologetic shrug. "Busy."

Seb slaps me on the shoulder, making sure I see his smug fucking grin before heading toward the kitchen.

Pricks. The lot of them.

Behind me, Brianna and Nico make an appearance at their own party. I don't bother to turn around to see their just-fucked faces. No one needs that shit.

I've just lit my joint and dropped my arse to the couch to take a hit when the door opens and we're joined by others.

The second I see a head full of dark hair and light blue

eyes, a smile curls at my lips. I can't help it; her presence alone does something to me.

"Baby C," I cry, letting smoke plume from my lips.

I'm on my feet and pulling her into my arms in seconds, much to my brother's irritation.

"Get the fuck away from her with that poison," Daemon demands, shoving me so hard, I stumble away from his girl.

"It's just a bit of weed. I'm not making your baby take a fucking hit or anything."

"You're breathing it in Calli's face," he snarls, hiding her behind him to protect her.

"It's fine, Nikolas," she breathes so only the three of us can hear.

It doesn't matter how many times she calls him by his real name; it still shocks me.

"You're gonna take it to the balcony, right, A?" she says, poking her head around her bodyguard.

I don't get a chance to answer because Matteo, Enzo, and Ant join us, along with the only single girl between us.

"I found Italians loitering in the hall. You do know that you should all be lucky I didn't kill you," Isla teases.

"Un-fucking-likely, Kallis," I scoff. "You wouldn't know one end of a gun from the other."

She glares pure death at me, but as always, I let it roll off my back without concern.

"Whatever, cunt. I need alcohol if I'm going to have to deal with this wankstain," she announces, threading her arm through Daemon's and dragging him, and Calli, toward the kitchen. Ant quickly follows, obviously feeling at home back here and partying with us.

"So that's Isla then," Enzo says, sounding more than a little interested in her feisty arse.

"Yup. Fucking nightmare."

He shoots me a loaded look, but I don't give him any of the answers he's digging for.

Instead, we're distracted when Theo and Nico march over with beers in hand, ready to welcome our new guests into the fold.

The Greeks and the Italians at the same party without trying to kill each other. Who'd have thought it?

9

ALEX

"For the love of God," I mutter, as one by one the couples in the room begin to pair off.

I'm happy for them all, I really fucking am. But for all that's fucking holy, I'm fed up with this shit.

And not one of them will let me join in. Spoilsports. Not that I really want to insert myself into any of my friends' relationships, but an offer would be nice and all.

"Ah, time for the orgy to start," Isla jokes, watching as they all lose themselves in each other.

Ant laughs along with her, but Enzo and Matteo's eyes widen in surprise.

This is a normal occurrence for us now. I guess it shouldn't come as a surprise that it might be a little shocking to outsiders.

"So this is why you've been happy living here?" Enzo asks, elbowing Ant in the ribs. "Live porn."

"It's not all it's cracked up to be," I murmur, loneliness burning through me.

It was all fun and games when it was just Seb and

Stella, and even Theo and Emmie. But one by one, I've lost my boys. And it fucking sucks.

If it weren't for me inviting these lot, I'd once again be alone while they all enjoy themselves with only my thoughts of a certain redhead to entertain me.

I'm trying not to be bitter about it. But some days it's harder than others.

"So you two aren't going to join them, then?" Matteo asks, his eyes shooting between me and Isla.

Isla bristles, probably disgusted that anyone thinks for even a second that there could be something between us.

"I don't fucking think so," Isla grunts, her top lip peeling back.

Not one to miss an opportunity to mess with her, my lips part without instruction from my brain.

"Hey, I don't remember you saying that the last time when we—" Her hand clamps over my mouth, shutting me up immediately while her eyes narrow dangerously in my direction.

A laugh rumbles in my chest as I poke my tongue out and lick her palm.

She growls at me but refuses to release my mouth, terrified about what might come out of it next.

"Oh, I sense a story there," Enzo says, rubbing his hands together. "Do tell."

Ah, good times.

I raise my brows at Isla, while Ant shifts uncomfortably behind her.

I might be willing to tease Isla, but I don't want to hurt Ant. I made him a promise about that night staying between us, and I meant it.

"I'd rather not. I've done my best to bleach the memory

from my mind," Isla spits, frantically wiping her palm on her shorts after I lick her again.

"Pfft, it was the best night of your life and you know it," I tease.

"In your dreams." She stomps off, leaving the four of us watching her arse sway in her ridiculously short shorts that show off more than they hide.

"Damn, bro. She really hates you," Enzo jokes.

"Didn't stop me tapping that, though," I deadpan.

Ant rolls his eyes but otherwise chooses not to get involved.

I understand him not wanting to confess to the three of us hooking up, but I'm surprised he's not saying anything about him and Isla.

But hey, what do I know? Maybe he and Enzo aren't as close and overshare-y as I am with my boys.

Noticing his friend's silence, Enzo turns his attention on Ant, a smirk playing on his lips.

"We need to take this one out on the pull. He's been locked up here for way too long," Enzo says, throwing his arm around Ant once Isla is out of sight. "I bet it's so underused it's about to fall off."

"Fuck you, man," Ant grunts.

"I'm up for it if you want to head out. This lot are going to get boring really fucking fast," I state, knowing exactly how the rest of this night is going to go.

Before anyone can agree with my plan, we're distracted with the promise of alcohol.

"Shots," Isla announces, suddenly popping back up in our group with a bottle of Grey Goose and five glasses.

"Hell yes," Enzo says, immediately taking the bottle from her, or more so trying.

"Excuse me," she snaps. "This little lady is more than capable of pouring a few shots."

"Never said you weren't," Enzo says, holding his hands up in surrender, looking slightly terrified.

"Down the hatch, boys," she says before throwing her shot back and immediately pouring us all another. "So, where are we going?"

An idea that's been festering away in my mind for a while surges forward. I've checked out all the places in our territory, and the Wolves' and Reapers' to find her. But she's not been anywhere. I find it hard to believe that she'd work at Dad's poker nights but not be a dancer anywhere else in the city.

So that leads me to my last few options, and they've all been out of bounds until very recently.

"Fancy taking us to Paradise?" I ask, hoping it sounds as innocent as possible. The last thing I need is them thinking I have an ulterior motive.

"Paradise?" Matteo asks, intrigued by my suggestion.

"Seriously? You wanna spend the night in a strip club?" Isla barks.

"Problem? I thought you'd enjoy it just as much as us. A hot dancer is a hot dancer, right?"

"You're a dickhead," she sneers, making Ant laugh.

"What the fuck did I say?" Isla shakes her head and throws back another shot. "So, are you in or what?"

"Yeah, I'm fucking in. Paradise has the best dancers in the city, and it's been off-limits for too fucking long," she concedes like I knew she would. Once a party girl, always a party girl.

My point exactly. I need inside that place, because if my suspicions are correct... My dick jerks just thinking about laying eyes on her again.

I need to prove to myself that both the times we've been together weren't actually as good as my imagination leads me to believe.

She's just a girl. I've been with plenty.

The only reason I'm so obsessed is that, unlike any others, she had the audacity to try and steal from me, and then disappeared off the face of the Earth. She's turned into a challenge like I've never experienced before, and fuck if I don't want to win.

"Awesome, let's go," I announce, ignoring all my friends behind me and throwing my arms around both Isla and Ant.

"Careful. This is feeling very déjà vu-y," Isla warns, making Ant tense. "That night was already more than you could handle."

"Shut your mouth, Pest," I mutter teasingly. "Best night of your lives, and you know it."

"Do we have to?" Ant whispers, shooting a glance back at Matteo and Enzo.

"Sorry, man. Let's go find you some willing pussy."

"In a strip club full of men?" he asks curiously.

"I'm sure you can cope."

Excitement stirs within me as we leave the building and pile into an Uber I booked on the way down in the lift.

There are a few clubs in Italian territory she could be hiding inside, but Paradise is by far the best. It makes sense for her to be there.

The rest of the bottle of vodka vanishes between us on the drive. But despite the buzz I've got going on, I'm fully focused, and the second the Uber pulls to a stop, I'm out of the car and heading toward the bouncers, aware that they'll let me in the second they see who I'm with.

"Jesus, you're desperate," Matteo calls. I look back just in time to see him nod to the bouncers' approval.

I don't respond, mainly because he's right. I am desperate.

The image of her on her knees before me, her red lips wrapped around my cock fills my mind, making my legs move faster.

Fuck. I need to feel that again.

The second I step into the club, the vibrations of the music tingle through my body.

The hallway is empty, but I soon discover where everyone is when I push through the crowd into the main room.

It's packed.

I come to a halt, my eyes locked on the stage just like everyone else in here.

"Fuck," I mutter quietly as I watch the girls. They're impressive.

Too fucking good to be in an Italian club.

Shaking my head, I begin weaving my way through the mass of bodies while my eyes move from girl to girl, searching for the one I'm so desperate for. But I don't bother looking for her red hair. I already know I won't find it. So instead, I search for the blonde she tries to hide behind. I might have her wig from that night in my growing collection of things that belong to her, but something tells me she's got another.

I don't find her. And I'm not sure if I'm disappointed or relieved that she's not up on that stage.

If she were, I'm not sure if my first reaction would be to climb up there and drag her away from all the eyes or to sit back and enjoy.

Eventually, I make it to the bar where even the staff are

focused on the show while all their customers are distracted.

"Vodka shots," I shout, catching the young guy's attention. "Ten of them," I add as the others join me.

"They really are something. Why aren't they currently dancing their arses off at Empire?" Isla shouts in my ear.

"Fuck knows. But they should be."

"Boss is losing his touch. You might want to have a word."

I shake my head at her and shove a shot into her hand instead of responding.

"This was a fucking fantastic idea," Matteo admits. "But why the fuck are we here with this lot when we could be in the VIP area?"

"Lead the way, Boss," I say, gesturing to the small amount of space in front of us.

We all throw our shots back before following Matteo back through the crowd toward a set of stairs at the rear of the room. The second security sees him, the rope is pulled back and we're invited inside.

The guard's eyes lock on me, his brow creasing in concern, but the second Enzo slaps him on the shoulder and shouts something into his ear, he relaxes and nods in greeting.

The second we hit the top of the stairs, an almost empty VIP lounge and bar spread out before us. There are dancers on tables and girls waiting at the bar to deliver drinks, but still, none of them are my girl.

My girl.

I can't help but roll my eyes at myself.

My girl is a figment of my imagination, I'm sure.

I'd probably be better off seeing that therapist Nico is to

try and make me forget about this mystery woman who haunts my dreams than I am chasing her around the city.

For all I know, she's not even a Londoner.

Satisfied that she's not up here, I turn toward the railings to watch the show, the others all beside me, their eyes locked on various girls on the stage.

They might be good, but they don't hold my attention for long.

They're not the ones I want.

Movement above us catches my eye, and I find a set of suspended cages with girls dancing inside.

I don't know why, I can't explain it, but my heart jumps in my throat, and excitement explodes in my stomach.

The first cage is a bust, so is the second, and the third, but the second my eyes land on the fourth, all the air rushes out of my lungs.

She's right here. Hiding in plain sight. Just like I knew she would be.

A smirk pulls at my lips as I watch her roll her hips in her outfit that looks very similar to the one I was so desperate to rip from her body not so long ago.

My fingers wrap around the railing before me, my grip so tight my knuckles turn white.

Look out, Vixen.

I'm coming for you.

10

EVIE

While the multiple orgasms I had thanks to my vibrating little friend might have taken the edge off things after my call with Pete last week, it wasn't enough to break my new addiction to Alexander's Instagram.

I tried to go cold turkey. I did. I really, really did.

But... I lasted just over twelve hours before I got a notification to say he'd posted, and I couldn't help myself.

I was just like one of the junkies who live in our building, only my addiction doesn't come in the form of a pill or a vial, but in the form of a ripped Greek god.

I shake my head as I think of his most recent post. It was only posted a few hours ago of him getting ready for his Friday night out.

He'd just got out of the shower, his skin covered in water droplets. There was a towel tucked low around his waist, showing off those impressive V lines and his defined six-pack, but it wasn't those that really captured my attention. That was his eyes. Those silver orbs sucked me in and refused to release me.

It's why I'm still thinking about it all these hours later, willing the time to pass faster so I can get back to my phone and look again.

It's been at least four hours since I stared at it, and I'm starting to think that my imagination has twisted my memory, because one photo can't be that hot, right?

A trickle of sweat running down my spine makes me shiver and brings me back to reality.

Thankfully, my job tonight isn't all that challenging. I can pretty much do it on autopilot.

The deep bass of the music pumping through the club pulsates through me as I move my body in time.

Wrapping my fingers around the bars surrounding me, I press my back against the cool metal and drop down low.

The lights shining on me mean I can't see the people below. There could be one, or there could be one thousand. I've no idea.

As much as I might try to convince myself it's the former, I know that the reason my heart beats quite as hard as it is now is because I have multiple sets of eyes on me.

Just something else I've learned about myself in the past few months.

I like when men—okay, so one in particular—takes away my free will, and I like being watched.

I used to hate the idea of my sister spending her nights dressed in barely anything and allowing men to strip that off her with their eyes, but it turns out that I was wrong to judge because it is the most liberating thing I've ever experienced.

Especially with the hard rules I've put in place.

While Blakely might have done a little more than dance in these clubs, and other places, that is all I'm doing.

No more clothes are going to be leaving my body in public, and I'm certainly not allowing anyone to touch me.

Hence, the cage.

Being suspended up here way above the main stage provides me with the feeling of safety I need to do this. It's not all that different to camming, really. If you ignore the fact that I can't talk to anyone, or even see the men watching me. Okay, so it's really different. But it gives me the same thrill and pays just as well. I just have a longer commute home at the end of the night.

The song playing ends and the spotlights dip briefly, giving me a rare shot of the crowd beneath me.

"Shit," I breathe, taking in the packed bar.

There isn't a free seat in the house.

That knowledge makes my heart beat a little harder.

I scan the faces, looking for anyone familiar.

I hardly doubt anyone from Lovell will be here. If they were lucky enough to get past security, then the hefty entrance fee would be enough to put them all off.

The only people I'm likely to see here are the creeps from the poker nights, but it seems what my sister told me a few weeks ago is true and that the Greeks and the Italians are at war, or whatever, so there have been no familiar faces here.

And that's something I'm trying to remind myself is a good thing.

I specifically requested Derek put me in Italian clubs so I wouldn't run into him. But as the days pass and my obsession grows, I can't help but wonder if I made the right choice.

If I could just see him, even from a distance, then I'd be able to prove to myself that the connection I'm remembering is nothing but a figment of my imagination, and that really, in person, he's not all that hot.

Keep lying to yourself, Evie, and it might all magically come true one day.

Before I know it, the lights go back up, the music starts, and the doors at the end of the main stage open, revealing tonight's main act.

Not so long ago, Blakely would have been up there strutting her stuff, sending the patrons wild with her seductive dance moves and enticing body.

But instead, she's been reduced to much less exciting tasks since her body gave up on her.

She did a shift here earlier, but she was just serving drinks, something she hates. It's too close to temptation. She wants to be up here, or more so, down there with all eyes on her. But as much as she might crave it, she knows she can't do it. Not yet at least.

I really hope that changes sometime soon, because I fear that she's only going to be able to put a brave face on things for so long. Plus, I know she's worried about the drop in her income. It doesn't matter to her that between us, we're making more than she used to. She thinks she's letting the family down, and that she's failed me by putting me in this situation. It doesn't matter how many times I tell her how much I enjoy it, she still beats herself up.

One day...

One day, we'll find a way to get the life we've always dreamed of.

I have to believe that.

I keep moving in time to the music, but I keep my eyes on the girls beneath me, watching their every move.

The way they work their bodies, so sensual and

seductive. I can only hope that I have an ounce of what they do.

Sure, I'm aware that men watch me, want me. But it can't be to the level at which they desire those women.

I watch in awe as they complete their routines, driving the crowd crazy as they begin removing parts of their costumes, exposing more of their incredible bodies.

I might not want to get naked in front of a roomful of horny men, but hell, I want their confidence. They could do anything right now, literally anything, and be sexy.

Strippers, dancers, generally get a bad rep.

Honestly, when I first discovered what my sister was doing to keep a roof over our heads, I was ashamed. Embarrassed. The thought of her allowing men to use her like that didn't sit right with me at all. But I only felt that way because it's how society makes us think.

It wasn't long before I started seeing a different side to it all.

Firstly, my sister works damn hard. And not when she's actually working. But the hours of training and practice she's put in to perfect her routines and her moves have been incredible. And as she improved and got stronger physically from all the training, her confidence soared.

Okay, so she was never as shy and reserved as me. She was one of the more popular girls at school. But even still, I watched her grow in confidence to the give-no-shits woman that she is today because of this job.

And she's not an airhead, nowhere even close. She's smart, funny, caring, and loyal.

So what, she decided to take her clothes off for men and use what God gave her to ensure her family can eat? What the hell is so wrong with that?

Why can't it be liberating, inspiring, and sexy?

Shaking those thoughts from my head, I remember what I'm supposed to be doing—not that anyone in their right mind would be watching me right now when those women down there are tearing up the stage and making every straight man—maybe even a few gay ones—jizz in their pants with the sensuality they exude. I know I'm straight, but hell if they don't get me a little hot under the collar, or corset, as it may be.

Inspired by them, I add a little bit more sass into my movements, embrace my inner vixen and put on the best show of my life as I imagine all those sets of eyes on me.

My heart pounds and my chest heaves as I picture myself up on that stage. It's hot up here, really frigging hot, and my skin glistens not just with the shimmer spray I'm covered in but with a sheen of sweat. As much as I love this, I also can't wait to get into a cold shower.

With the loose tendrils of my hair sticking to my neck, I keep moving, working my way through the endless routines I've practised with Blakely over the past few years. I just never thought anyone but her would know I learned them by heart for fun.

The girls' set begins to come to an end, and the lights start darting around the colossal space around me once more, allowing me to see the crowd.

A shot of adrenaline races through me at the sight of all the men once more. As predicted, they're all watching the stage. I don't find a single one who's looking up and me and the other three girls suspended in cages from the steel rafters above us.

I get it, they're way better than us. I'd be watching them too if I were a customer.

I'm blinded by the lights once more and spin to the other side of the cage.

Wrapping my fingers around the bars, I throw my head back and roll my hips seductively, and as I stand, the lights drop. The second I look down, my heart jumps into my throat. Because there is one person looking up at me, and it's the last person I expect, but equally it's the only pair of eyes I want to lose myself in.

11

ALEX

The second she spots me, the air between us becomes electric. It crackles so fucking hot, I swear it burns me.

The club, the music, the people, they all fade into the background as she tries to keep moving.

Her eyes are wide, her lips parted, and I suspect the only thing she wants to do is run.

But she can't. She's stuck. And fuck if I don't want to be locked in that cage with her.

An image of fucking her against the bars while everyone watches below fills my mind and makes my cock hard instantly.

Fuck. It would be so fucking hot letting everyone in this place see that I own her.

My grip on the railing tightens once more.

"Going for a piss," Ant says, slapping me on the back as he disappears.

My eyes don't leave my vixen, but I sense the others move away, preferring to go and find somewhere to sit now the main show is over. Or at least, I assume it is. The music and lighting changed a while ago, but I didn't bother looking.

Why would I when she's right there?

"You know her?" an unfamiliar voice says from beside me.

Reluctantly, I drag my eyes from my vixen to the guy standing next to me. He's an older guy, probably a similar age to my father. He's dressed in a designer suit. If I didn't know he had money from that alone, then his diamond cufflinks and vintage Rolex would tip me off.

I've no idea if he's Italian. I don't recognise him, but something tells me that if he's not a Mariano, then he's one of their contacts. Which means, he probably knows exactly who I am.

The second he turns his eyes on my vixen, unease trickles through my veins.

I don't want him looking at her, stripping that tight corset off her body with his eyes and imagining how she might look with his cock in her mouth instead of mine.

"Uh... nope. You?" I ask, hoping for a little insight on my mystery woman.

"Not personally, no. I've spent quite a bit of time watching her, though. She's really quite mesmerising."

Obviously, I want to agree, but also, I don't trust this motherfucker, so I ensure my face remains impassive and wait for him to continue.

Reaching into his suit jacket, he pulls his wallet out and slides a card from inside.

"It'll cost you. Not that that's an issue for you," he says, letting me know that he's aware of who I am.

Curiously, I reach out and take the card he's passed to me.

"I'll let you enjoy the show. You looked quite captivated."

My eyes shoot to my vixen again before looking back to the man, but he's already vanished, leaving me standing there with my jaw dropped and questions on the tip of my tongue.

Shaking myself out of it, I lift the card in my hand.

Miss Vixen.

Cam girl with Elite Entertainment.

The air is punched right out of my lungs.

All this time, I've been searching for her and she's been online, showing the world everything I fucking want.

Unbelievable.

My grip on the card tightens in frustration, crumbling it. I catch myself before I destroy it, because something tells me I'll need it later.

"Deimos, what the fuck are you doing? Either book yourself a private room for some action or come and join us," Matteo shouts.

Looking over my shoulder, I find them sitting in a booth with almost all the girls up here surrounding them. I'm hardly surprised; they're Mariano royalty. It would be no different if me and the guys all descended on the backroom at The Empire.

With one more glance at my vixen, I take off across the room, ensuring I sit where I still have her in my sight.

"This is fun and all, but I want to go dance," Isla whines when the serious conversation gets too much for her. "Come with me, I'll make it worth your while," she promises Ant, loud enough that the entire table hears.

"Something you need to tell us, man?" Enzo asks, his words a little slurred from the number of shots we've all put away.

Amazingly, Isla looks the least drunk out of all of us, and she's the smallest. Guess she's just used to it.

"Oh, he's got plenty of secrets, don't you, Santoro?" she teases, dragging him from the booth and disappearing down the stairs.

"Wait up, I want to hear everything," Enzo says, racing after them.

Both Matteo and I watch as he vanishes.

"Surprised you're not going too. Thought you were down for a good time," he comments. "Ah, I see," he mutters when my eyes betray me and shoot toward her cage. "Wondered why you were so keen to come here of all places."

Ripping my eyes away from her, I focus on Matteo instead.

"I didn't know she'd be here. You know her?"

He studies my vixen for a few seconds, his eyes raking down her body and making my fists curl on the tabletop.

"Nope. Hot though."

My teeth grind as he continues watching her.

"Who is she?" he asks, finally ripping his eyes away and refocusing on me.

"I... uh... I don't know."

"But you wanted to come here for her. Seems like an

important no one."

I shake my head and scrub my hand down my face as I try and come up with something that doesn't make me sound certifiable.

"I met her once. Twice, actually. But I don't know who she is."

"But you'd like to."

"Am I that transparent?'

"Dude, you're practically panting."

"Great," I mutter.

"You've already spoken to the guy who could tell you everything about her down to her bra size."

"Who?" I ask, the vodka doing a fine job of frying my brain cells.

"Vincent. The guy in the suit with the douchey cufflinks. He's in charge of the girls. If you want to know anything about them, he's your man. Might even be able to secure you an hour or two with your mystery dancer for the right price."

"Right," I mutter. "So he's what... her pimp?"

"I guess that would depend on the kinds of extras she offers, but yeah, you could call him that."

The thought of her selling herself to men like that makes the vodka I've thrown back tonight threaten to reappear, burning up my throat like acid.

"Want some advice, though?" he offers.

Refusal is on the tip of my tongue, but I don't get a chance to say it because Matteo gives it to me anyway.

"Stay the hell away. I've no idea what they're all involved in, but it's shit neither of us wants to be tangled up in, I know that much. We make use of their services and let them run their business well away from our territory." My brow lifts in question. "Lovell."

"Of course," I mutter, pouring myself another shot from what little is left in the bottle and throwing it back.

"Sorry," Matteo says, his eyes focused on someone over my shoulder before sliding from the booth. "I need to catch up with an acquaintance."

He's gone before I get a chance to say anything, and when I turn around, he's slipping into the shadows with a suited man, although a different one from the one I now want to talk to again.

Although, if what Matteo says is true and he is her pimp, then it might just be the last conversation he ever has, because there's no fucking way I'm letting him sell her to make a quick buck.

She's mine.

Even if she doesn't know it yet.

Sitting back, I focus on her.

And I wait.

She knows I'm here now, and I like to think she's dancing just for me.

12

EVIE

My heart is in my throat as my cage is lowered toward the platform that will allow me to escape.

I'm exhausted. My feet ache from hours standing in my ridiculous stripper shoes, and my limbs are heavy, but a big part of me would happily remain locked up in my little prison if it means I don't end up running straight into him.

He won't find you. Head straight for the dressing room then get your arse out the back door and into the car as soon as possible.

My legs tremble as I make a beeline for the door marked *Staff Only* ahead of me.

There's no one other than the other girls from the cages up here, but still my skin tingles with awareness.

Since the moment I found him staring at me from the VIP platform, his eyes have barely left me.

I can't say I'm surprised that he's a VIP, but it does make me wonder if the gang war situation is over. Surely, the Italians wouldn't have allowed him entry, let alone access to the VIP section if they were still fighting?

The fact I'm even considering gang wars blows my mind.

I'm not naïve. I live in Lovell, for fuck's sake. Gang activity is as common as drug dealing and prostitution, but mafia wars are a whole other board game. They're not street gangs, they're the real fucking deal, and I'd be lying if I said I wasn't a little scared of the whole situation.

People know who I am in Lovell, thanks to my sister and Derek. But outside of that little bubble, I'm no one.

"Whoa, the crowd was crazy tonight," Alyssa says as she catches me up. "I need to go out. You're coming, right?"

"Umm..." I glance over and find her eyes blowing wide open. She's not just riding on the high of the crowd right now, that's for sure.

"Oh, come on, Evie. You never could party with us. Don't you want to blow off some steam? Find a guy to finish off the night with?"

The need to agree, to say fuck it and allow myself to be dragged along for the ride is almost too much to ignore.

As thrilling as it is to dance for all those horny men, there is always a desire to get up close and personal to one. To feel eager hands on my body, to experience just how crazy my moves make them.

But the thought of that being some random guy is anything but appealing.

There's only one guy's hands I want on me. And that can't happen.

I refuse to allow myself to be sucked into whatever that was between us. I have too many other things to focus on right now. It's bad enough that I've fallen into an unhealthy obsession with his Instagram. I don't need to turn that into an obsession with him in person.

That is not where this is going, even if Blakely thinks he could be an easy ticket out of this place.

Shaking my head, I follow Alyssa through the door and into the safety of the dressing room.

There are girls in varying arrays of dress everywhere. There are wigs, shoes, thongs in every corner of the room. Make-up and hair accessories line every counter and chatter fills the air as they discuss everything from their plans for the rest of the night, to a church event they're attending tomorrow, to the weather.

If I hadn't already had my eyes opened to the kinds of women who dance and strip for a living, then stepping foot in here really would have done it.

There are women from every aspect of life here. Some are young, faking their age, like me. Others are married, some are mothers, some do it for the money, and others do it for the love.

I'm pretty sure there isn't another place on the planet full of such fierce, determined and beautiful women. And I don't just mean beautiful with their looks. These women are incredible in all ways.

"You guys were on fire tonight," Alyssa shouts toward the girls who lit up the stage with their routines earlier.

They all beam at her praise and she quickly joins their group as she begins stripping out of her outfit in favour of the clothes she's going to be wearing to continue their night.

"Evie's coming," she announces as I try and slink off into a dark corner to get ready to leave. "Aren't you, girl?"

Looking up, I take in the expressions of the girls who are now studying me as if I'm some zoo exhibit.

"Umm... I'm not su—"

"Of course, you are. It's about time we got to know you a

bit better. You've been here now for what? A month? And we know nothing about you."

The need to refuse still burns through me, but they're right.

These women deserve for me to give them a chance. Just because I've spent my life avoiding people and keeping my friendship group as small as possible, doesn't mean it needs to continue. I'm not even sure those I spent time with at Lovell could even really be called my friends.

But I'm done there now. All my coursework has been handed in. The only thing left to do is wait for an envelope with results in it that I already know, seeing as my art course didn't have a final exam I need to worry about. So why not start over?

Thanks to this job and my camming, I have more than enough to start uni in September. Maybe now is the perfect time to fully let go of the shy introverted girl I've always been and embrace this new, outgoing and sexy woman I'm trying to be.

Plus, I've got a fake ID sitting in my purse, thanks to my incredibly responsible big sister.

"I don't have anything to wear," I say, pulling the pair of sweats from my bag I brought to change into after my shift.

Excited smiles curl up at the girls' faces before Harper steps forward and holds her hand out for me.

"Girl, you have nothing to worry about. Trust us?" Her eyes twinkle with something mischievous, making butterflies explode in my stomach.

"No. Not even a little bit," I admit.

"Probably wise," Harper laughs but still takes my hand and tugs me toward the make-up stations they're congregated around.

"Sit," she demands, pressing on my shoulders, giving me little choice but to follow orders.

My blonde wig is gently eased from my head and my own darker hair released before Alyssa comes at me with a make-up wipe in each hand to clear my skin of the face paint that was applied before I spent the night in that cage.

"Right then," Naomi says, joining the party with her hands full of make-up. "What are we going for?"

Everyone studies me for a beat before Harper dishes out instructions and they all get to work.

And I must say, when they all take a step back ten minutes later, I'm impressed. I look like... me.

I'm no longer stripper me, or shy me. I'm a new, confident, independent woman who's ready to take this city by storm. Maybe.

If I keep telling myself that, it might just come true eventually.

"Now, get naked," Naomi demands before rushing toward her locker, which I'm sure has more clothes than my home wardrobe. "We're about the same size, so..." I suck in a breath, hoping that whatever she drags out will have enough fabric to be considered clothing. I've seen the kinds of outfits she walks in and out of this place in.

"Yes," she cries, making me swallow nervously.

But to my surprise, when she holds it up for me, I don't totally hate it.

"Perfect. Grab some clean knickers and let's get this party started," Harper says, pulling a handful of miniatures out of her oversized bag and passing them out.

"Should we have these here?" I ask like the good little girl I'm used to being.

Dancers aren't allowed to drink while on shift, for more

than obvious reasons, and it feels all kinds of wrong breaking those rules.

"We're done for the night. And it's not like we're snorting coke off the side."

My eyes widen. "You do that?"

"Aw, sweetie. We're going to have some much fun," Naomi teases.

A n hour later, I'm walking out of the dressing room with my head held high and more than one miniature swimming around my veins.

The polka dot short playsuit Naomi decided I should wear fits perfectly, and it looks good. Even if I have been forced to go without a bra, seeing as it's completely backless.

My stripper heels have thankfully been replaced by my white high-tops, which look surprisingly good with the playsuit.

I feel good, and with Harper and Alyssa's arms threaded through mine, I almost feel like I belong.

It's a heady feeling.

We make our way toward the back exit where there's a car waiting for us. We're going to The Avenue, apparently. I've never been there, but I've heard Blakely talk about it.

Security eyes us with interest, although neither would dare make a move.

"Good evening, ladies. Ready to start your nights, we see?" Richie drawls in his deep Scottish accent.

"You've got it, baby. What time are you off? You should come and join us," Harper offers, giving him a flirtatious smile.

"If only. I'm on shift until five to make sure all those horny arseholes get home safe."

"Boring," Alyssa whines.

"Maybe next time, yeah?"

"Try and stop me," Richie teases back.

Both him and Steve twist around to pull the double doors open for us to exit, and the second a wave of cool evening air rushes over me, reality hits.

"Shit. I don't have my phone," I curse, tugging my arms from theirs.

"Evie," Naomi whines, sticking her bottom lip out. "I wanna party."

"Go get in the car. I'll be two minutes."

I take off running back down the hallway.

I find it exactly where I left it on a chair to pick up once I'd done my trainers up, but they distracted me with their excitement.

A few of the others watch me run in, grab it and then race back out again, but no one says anything.

The hallway is silent as I rush back to the doors, and I find that Richie has wandered off, leaving Steve alone to open it for me.

"Have a good night," he says with a nod before slamming the door closed behind me.

Darkness surrounds me, and my skin immediately breaks out in goosebumps.

There used to be a bright security light out here to allow us to see where we were going, but the thing blew a week ago, and no one has bothered to replace it.

The rumble of an engine around the corner hits my ears and I pick up speed, more than ready to be locked safely inside and away from this darkness.

Anything could happ—

My heart jumps and a scream rips up my throat, but it's muffled by the hand that claps over my mouth.

Fingers dig into my upper arm as I'm hauled backwards and slammed up against the rough wall of the club.

Fear turns my blood to ice as I fight to suck in the air I need through my nose.

A dark figure looms before me. He's huge, towering over me by at least a foot, and he's wide too. Way too big to even attempt to fight off. Even if I knew where to start with that.

Blakely has been doing self-defence classes for years as part of her training, and she's always whining about me joining her. I'm now wondering why I never took her up on that offer.

His hot breath rushes over my face as I tremble in his hold.

I want to plead, beg, anything to force him to let me go, but I'm powerless.

But just when I think the worst is going to happen and I'll be found out here when the sun rises, dead and abused, he leans forward and realisation slams into me.

13

ALEX

"Looks like I found you at last. You're not an easy girl to track down, Vixen."

The moment she recognises me, she relaxes. But I don't.

I don't release my grip on her. Instead, I do what I've wanted to do all fucking night. I step closer, pressing my body up against hers, pinning her against the wall.

A whimper vibrates up her throat when she feels the thickness of my cock against her stomach.

"Don't go acting all innocent now, thief. I've been watching you all night. There's not an innocent bone in your body. Every single fucking guy in that place was hard for you tonight."

She tries shaking her head but doesn't get very far with my hand still clamped around her mouth.

"You love it, don't you? All the attention trained on you, making men lose their fucking minds. It allows you to do whatever you want, doesn't it?

"You must make decent money doing this. I know that Paradise only employs the best, and their pay is in line with that. So do you just steal for fun? Is that it? The thrill of ensuring every man in the room wants you getting a little old and you need a new way to get your soul on fire?

"Have you even been caught before me? Do you have a little stash of prizes at home from the men who are too fucking blinded by your sinful body to notice you're ripping them off?

"Did you get on your knees for them too?" I ask, leaning closer and whispering it in her ear. "Did they get to taste you too?"

She whimpers again, her body sagging in my hold as she remembers.

"Or do you save that for the ones who catch you? Consolation prize in the hope your pussy holds magical powers and makes them forget?"

Guilt twists at my insides, but I can't stop the words that spill from my lips.

This woman. She affects me in a way I've never experienced before. And I fucking hate it as much as I love it. But not as much as I hate what she does.

I have nothing against dancers or sex workers. Nothing at all.

But the thought of her with other men, even if it is just through a screen, makes something painful and all-consuming unfurl inside me.

She stares up at me with wide, tear-filled eyes and it makes something shatter inside me.

Releasing her arm, I slide my hand to her waist, keeping her in place before I slip my palm from her mouth in favour of her throat.

Her pulse thunders beneath my fingertip as she greedily sucks in deep lungfuls of air.

I stare at her lips, desperate to lean forward and claim them in a way I didn't the first two times we were this close.

But I don't kiss just anyone. Fuck no. You have to deserve a kiss from me. And from what I've seen from this stealing little vixen, she doesn't. Not by a long shot.

But that doesn't stop me from wanting it, craving it.

And before I know what I'm doing, I've been reeled in by her witchcraft, quickly closing the final inches parting us.

There's a hairsbreadth between us when a female voice rips through the air.

"Are you fucking lost? Come on, the night only lasts so long."

She sucks in a sharp breath, her body tensing once more.

Pulling back from her a little, I look into her eyes. The blue I remember all too well glitters in the moonlight.

"Saved by the bell," I growl. "I'll see you soon, though, thief. I'd be looking over your shoulder if I were you. Now I've got you, I won't be letting go anytime soon."

Her brows pinch, but someone shouting for her again stops her saying anything in response to me.

I release her with a gentle shove in the direction she should be going and watch her disappear into the darkness.

But it's with a smile on my face, because I meant the promise I just made her.

I wait for the voices to vanish and a car door to slam before I pull my phone from my pocket and call for my own Uber.

I might have just dropped a tracker into my little thief's bag, but I don't need it. Not tonight, anyway, considering her friends were happily talking about their impending visit to The Avenue. And thanks to me, they're about to have the best night of their lives. For purely selfish reasons, of course.

Whenever we come here, we usually head downstairs to the basement. The music is better. And quite frankly, so are the girls.

But tonight is different.

I head to my second VIP area of the night tonight, knowing it's exactly where the person I followed here is.

I tipped off the bouncers to intercept my little thief and her friends before they could make their own decision about where to spend the night. Something tells me that the lure of free drinks and access to the wealthiest customers would be right up their street.

Bypassing the long arse queue that wraps around the building even at this time, I nod at the familiar faces working the door and walk straight inside, much to the irritation of the impatient, drunk cunts standing in line. I want to say I feel guilty about the special treatment, but I really fucking don't. I deserve to be able to take a few liberties after what I've been through in my eighteen years.

Ignoring the first set of stairs, I head directly for the second set and make my way down to the security room.

I have no intention of letting her know I'm here yet, but my obsession with this vixen means I need to find her. Right fucking now. And so help me God, if I find she's dancing with anyone but the girls she arrived with...

I didn't head out tonight with the intention of slitting some cunt's throat, but for her, I'd flood this place with the blood of anyone who dared look at her.

The security panel beeps, the light changing from red to green, granting me access.

Two heads spin in my direction as I step into the small room with monitors covering one wall.

"Can we help you?" the closest guy asks, sounding more than a little put out at being intruded upon.

Clearly, he has no fucking idea who I am.

"It's fine, Dan," Bas says, nodding at me in greeting.

"You can both go and take a tea break," I bark as I walk deeper into the room, my eyes scanning the screens.

"Y-you can't j-just—" Dan stutters.

I don't bother looking at him. I just keep searching.

"Can't I?" I growl.

"Dan, man. Let's go grab a drink and let Alex find what he's looking for," Bas says, getting up from his chair and offering it up to me.

"Thanks, man. Appreciate it."

"You want a drink or anything?" he offers while Dan splutters in disbelief.

I think for a moment, and while I do, my eyes land on the woman I've been searching for. She's in the VIP area with a glass of champagne in hand, just like I hoped.

Finally, I lower my arse to the now empty chair, my eyes locked on her as she dances with the three girls she left Paradise with. Thankfully, there are no men with them.

"Vodka. Neat. Cheers, man."

"I got you, bro. Enjoy."

I barely hear them head toward the door, but the sound of Dan's bitching about leaving someone else to security catches my attention.

I glance over my shoulder just as Bas warns, "By all means, make an enemy of him. But if I were you, I'd shut your fucking trap before he does it for you."

Dan's mouth opens and closes like a fucking goldfish as he stares between the two of us, trying to figure this shit out.

Bas, on the other hand, just smirks.

"Aww, so sweet and naïve," he taunts, shoving Dan out of the door. "You ever heard of the Cirillo Family, Dan?" he asks, as if he's asking if he's heard of a specific fairy tale. Grimm tales would be more like it.

The door slams closed, the beep letting us all know the locks have engaged, cutting off whatever that dumb-arse's answer was.

Shaking my head, I find the screen I want once again and sit back and watch.

Despite the screen being a little blurry, the movements of her body are as captivating as they were up in that cage.

Spreading my thighs as wide as they go with the armrests on either side of me, I tug at my jeans, giving my swelling cock some space.

The minutes tick by as I watch her, only the sound of my increased breathing keeping me company, along with the pounding bass from the club around me that vibrates through the walls.

Once she's finished her first glass, both she and her friends happily accept another from the barman who's been tasked with ensuring they're happy.

I bet he had no idea that he was going to end up being my little bitch tonight. It'll be more than worth his while if he follows orders and keeps my girl safe.

I'm so lost watching her that the unlocking of the door behind me startles me and I react on instinct, reaching for the baton Bas left on the desk before me.

"Chill out. It's just me," the man in question says, holding out a glass of vodka for me as a peace offering.

"Where's the rookie?" I ask when he kicks the door closed behind him and drops into the other seat.

"Sent him to hang out with the others. He's a fucking pain in my arse. Meant to be training him up, but fuck, man," he groans, scrubbing his hand down his face.

I can't help but chuckle, more than a little bit glad I don't have to do that kind of shit.

Thankfully, the weight of my name provides me with luxuries like not having to deal with wannabes, whether that be to work within our business or become a part of our Family. Although that does mean I get other... jobs.

"To what do I owe this pleasure? And who are we watching? Tell me something exciting is gonna go down. It's been boring as fuck in here recently."

Unlike us, the rest of the Family have been living life as normal recently. Having to keep everyone out of the loop with our war with Ricardo meant having to work without their backup. It was necessary, and mostly they understand, but equally, they're more than ready for some action of their own.

A groan rumbles deep in my throat as I watch my vixen's dance moves get more and more erotic as the four of them succumb to the bubbles I've been supplying them with.

I shift in my seat, tugging at my jeans once again.

"Oh, right," Bas chuckles. "I see."

He follows my line of sight to the screen. "Which one is your target?"

Of course, he thinks I'm here for work.

My lips part to put him right, but I quickly swallow the words.

The less he knows about my vixen the better.

"Who said it was only one of them," I deadpan.

"Dude, I swear, you're one lucky motherfucker."

I don't say anything. What can I say?

Everyone who knows what I do thinks I literally have the best job in the world. On the surface of it, yeah, I understand why they'd think that. Hell, if I were someone else looking at me, I would probably think the same thing.

But I'm not. I'm me, and I get to experience everything I do first-hand.

Yeah, some of it is fun. I sure get my kicks. But it's not everything it's cracked up to be. Far fucking from it.

We sit in silence as the barman returns with more refills. But while her friends quickly reach for the free booze, my vixen refuses.

It's the first sign that she's getting ready to leave.

Pulling my phone from my pocket, my eyes widen at the time.

How fucking long have I been here, just watching her dance?

Reaching for the glass of vodka that's sitting ignored on the desk, I throw it back and push the chair out.

"Thanks for the company, man, but duty calls."

"Anytime, bro. You know that."

Leaving Bas behind, I head out of the security office and make a beeline for the VIP bar, ready to kick things up a notch and get a little closer to my little thief.

14

EVIE

The steady beat of the music pounds through me, sweat runs down my exposed spine, loose strands of my hair stick to my neck, and the room spins around me, but I feel better than I have in a long time.

Christ knows why we were invited into the VIP section of this club the moment we stepped out of the car.

I can only assume that Harper, Naomi or Alyssa have friends in high places and that they were expecting them.

Although, no one has come over to greet them. In fact, we've been left alone to dance with each other all night.

It's kinda weird.

There are eyes watching us. My skin tingles with awareness just like when I'm dancing at Paradise, but not one man has tried it on.

I'm relieved. I don't want a man anywhere near me. I'm more than happy with my girls' night. And the others don't seem too bothered either; the free champagne that keeps being delivered stops any of them from complaining, I'm sure.

"This is the best fucking night ever," Alyssa shouts, downing another.

Her eyes are glassy, and like me, she's covered in a sheen of sweat, but she's got the widest smile on her face.

My phone vibrates against my hip where I stuffed it after abandoning our bags behind us so we could dance.

The words on the screen float around, making it hard to decipher, the exact reminder I need that it's time to stop drinking.

> Blakely: I'm gonna pass out. But I'm leaving my phone on loud if you need me. Enjoy the rest of your night. You deserve it. Just remember… wrap it before you tap it. *winky emoji*

The alcohol in my system means I bark out a laugh. The warning isn't necessary, but seriously, what big sister sends stuff like that? Mine, that's who.

> Evie: Sweet dreams. *smiley emoji*

"Everything okay?" Harper shouts as I tuck my phone back into my waistband.

"Yep."

The song changes just as I say that and Naomi screams.

"This is my favourite. But after this, we need boys. Champagne makes me horny as fuck."

"Hell yes," Alyssa agrees.

Harper throws her arms up, her body perfectly in sync with the music.

Knowing my night is over once they head out on the pull, I make the most of this song, losing myself in the beat in a way I've only ever experienced a couple of times before.

My head is spinning so much that I don't notice when the tingles that continue to race over my skin with the attention we all receive get worse.

If I were sober, then I would. I know I would.

"Oh shit, he's hot," Naomi says, staring at someone over my shoulder.

Alyssa and Harper immediately look, their eyes widening and their lips pulling up in a smile of appreciation.

I don't bother looking, although I must admit, my curiosity is piqued.

But I don't want or need a man to think for even a second that he has a chance with me.

I'll stick to my Insta obsession, thank you very much.

"Oh my God, is he..." Harper's words float off as a wall of heat collides with my back and a large hand clamps around my hip.

A fresh glass of champagne appears in front of me before his hot breath races over my ear and down my neck.

"Drink up, my little thief."

All the air rushes from my lungs as three other guys appear out of nowhere, capturing the attention of my friends.

Jolting in his hold, I make a somewhat pathetic attempt to remove myself from his grasp.

It's pointless. If I've learned anything about this man, it's that he gets what he wants.

He followed you here, a little voice says in my head.

I refuse his demand, shaking my head subtly.

"I told you I'd see you soon, didn't I? And once again,

you didn't take my warning seriously. You really should start learning from your mistakes, Vixen."

One of the other guys looks at him over my shoulder and nods sharply as silent words pass between them.

To my horror, the three of them lead my friends away and they descend the stairs to the main club.

"No, wait," I slur. But none of them hear my pathetic attempt to rescue this situation. The music is too loud and they're too excited by their new friends.

"Nice try. But it's just you and me now, and I want to make the most of those moves you've been entertaining everyone with tonight."

I jolt again, but his grip on my hip tightens, pinning us so tightly together that there's no way of ignoring how hard he is against my arse.

Heat floods my core, and my stomach tightens with desire.

"But first, it would be rude to refuse a drink, don't you think?"

He holds the glass of golden bubbles before me. And when I don't make any move to accept it, he takes matters into his own hands.

The glass presses against my bottom lip, but I refuse to drink it, forcing the cool liquid to run down my chin and drop onto my chest.

"Vixen," he growls in my ear. The deep rasp of his voice and scorching heat of his breath make my entire body erupt in goosebumps. "Don't you trust me?"

My teeth grind at his question.

I might be drunk, but I'm not that far gone.

"You should be thanking me," he tells me, pulling the glass away slightly. "Why do you think you've been treated like royalty here?"

"I never asked you for anything," I snap, unable to hold my tongue.

His chuckle flows through me, sending a violent shiver racing down my spine.

"No, you just take what you want, don't you, thief? But I need to let you into a secret..." He pauses for effect, which only irritates me further. "I don't ask either. I just take. Now drink up and I'll show you exactly what I mean."

"What have you put in it?" I hiss suspiciously.

"Nothing. I don't need drugs to get you where I want you," he states confidently.

My lips part to argue, but he's clearly less drunk than I am because he's tipped the glass, pouring champagne into my mouth before I've even realised the glass is against my lips once more.

Autopilot takes over and I swallow, suddenly parched and burning up with the heat of his body plastered against my back.

"Good girl," he praises in my ear, and I swear to God, my knees almost give in.

The second the glass is empty, he discards it somewhere, his hand dropping to my other hip.

The second his fingers collide with my phone, he reaches for it and pulls it free.

"Hey," I complain.

"No distractions, Vixen." Before I know what's happening, he's dropped it into his pocket and wrapped his fingers around my hip again. "Now dance with me, thief. Don't hold anything back. I know exactly what you're capable of."

His grip tightens until it burns, letting me know that I'm going to have evidence printed on my body for a good few days to come after this, and then his hips roll in time with the music and my head spins.

Holy shit.

Adrenaline and desire collide in a firestorm inside me, leaving me powerless but to move with him.

"See, that wasn't so hard, was it?"

"Why are you doing this?" I ask, twisting around to look at him finally.

My breath catches the second his dark, dilated pupils land on mine.

"Because I can," he answers cryptically. "And I haven't put this much effort in just to talk."

Releasing one of my hips, his fingers twist in my hair, dragging my head to the side to expose my neck.

I suck in a sharp gasp when the heat of his lips brush the sensitive skin beneath my ear.

"You've no idea how dangerous you are, do you, thief?"

If he's expecting an answer then he's going to be bitterly disappointed, because my body is short-circuiting right now to the point I think I've actually forgotten how to speak.

He peppers kisses across my skin before dragging his tongue up the length of my neck, tasting me.

My heart pounds so violently hard that there's no way he can't feel it before he sucks on me so hard it forces a scream to rip from my throat.

Lifting my hand, I thread my fingers through his hair, but I'm not sure if I want to try and drag him off me or hold him in place.

Everything about this man confuses me.

I'm at constant war with myself even weeks after seeing him last. And I fear that this right now is only going to feed my obsession.

I was already becoming desensitised to his photos online, and this isn't going to help that situation.

The hand that's still on my hip begins to slide up as we continue to dance, almost as if we're one.

Torturously, he slides it up my stomach, pausing on my ribs.

My breasts ache, desperate for his touch as his erection continues to grind against my arse.

Memories of being on my knees with it between my lips flood my head, and my mouth waters.

His hand twitches, teasing me with what I need, his thumb just nudging the underside of my breast.

"Please," I beg, unable to keep the word locked inside.

"What was that, thief?" he asks, his lips against my ear.

"Please, I n-need—"

"Why should I give you more than I already have?" he asks, his raspy voice driving me crazy.

"B... because—" I close my eyes, summoning up the courage of the girl who sits behind a screen and says all kinds of filthy things to men on the other end. "Because you want it as much as I do."

"Too fucking right, I do," he grunts, finally lifting his hand and squeezing my breast in the most delicious way.

He's rough. It borders on painful, but it's so fucking good.

"Yes," my head falls back against his shoulder, shamelessly, silently begging for more.

"Look at you," he groans. "Such a filthy little whore."

"Oh shit," I gasp when the burning heat of his hand slips beneath the strip of fabric that covers my breast.

He pinches my nipple, sending electric bolts straight to my clit.

My eyes close as I focus on what he's doing to me.

All the reasons I shouldn't allow this to happen fade away into nothing.

The good girl I've always been vanishes in favour of the woman I'm trying really hard to embrace.

"Vixen," he groans, releasing my hair so his other hand can join in the fun.

I tremble with need as his rough palm glides over my other breasts, and when he pinches both nipples I swear I almost combust right there in the middle of the dance floor.

"You have no idea how many people are watching you right now, do you?"

His words should be reason enough to stop or force me to open my eyes and find out for myself. But I don't. I can't.

"But you don't care, do you? You like being watched. It gets you hot, doesn't it?"

"Alex," I moan, unaware that his name tumbled from my lips until he stills.

"You know who I am."

"Please, more," I moan like a wanton whore.

"You want me to make you come, thief? Right here in the middle of the VIP section with everyone's eyes on you?"

I don't respond—not with words, anyway.

I roll my hips harder, grinding back against him as my hand moves behind him to grab his arse.

"Shit," he grunts. "What are you doing to me?"

15

—————

ALEX

Unable to stop myself, my hand drifts down her stomach. My need to find out just how wet she is for me is too much to deny.

I'm not sure what I was expecting when I stepped up behind her and ensured that her girls were thoroughly distracted. But it was a little more fight than I got.

I know she ran out on me before I pushed her over the edge the last time I saw her, but I didn't think she'd still be so desperate that she'd allow this.

Hell, this is everything my dreams have been made of since I first laid eyes on her over Christmas.

Her needy whimper fills my ears as my fingers breach the elasticated waist of her playsuit.

It's the perfect tease. The strips of fabric that hide her tits and tie around the back of her neck allow for the ultimate access to what she's kept hidden from me this far.

She may have been wearing very little every time I've laid eyes on her, but her tits have been left firmly to my imagination. I'm hoping I can rectify that by the end of the night.

"Alex," she cries again.

The sound of my name falling from her lips does things to me. Things that make my cock weep and my balls ache. It's so fucking intense. The need to bend her over the railing and take her right here in front of everyone is all-consuming.

She'd fucking let me too, I know she would.

Her entire body locks up when my fingers brush her clit. Her gasp of shock fills my ears before I sink lower, finding what I already knew.

"You're fucking dripping," I groan, curling my fingers and pushing two inside her.

"Oh my God," she gasps, her head finally lifting from my shoulder and dragging her eyes open.

Her fingers curl around my forearm, but she doesn't immediately try to pull my fingers free; instead, I'm pretty sure she holds me in place.

A growl rumbles deep in my throat as her nails dig into my skin.

Twisting around, she stares up at me with wide, blue eyes. Her gaze darts between my eyes and lips, making my mouth water once more for a taste of her.

She leans in, her eyes shuttering once more, and I panic.

I can't lose myself to her here.

I can't. I'm so under her fucking spell it's ridiculous. I don't even know her fucking name, but here I am, about three seconds from fucking her in public.

Reluctantly, I tug my hand from her cunt, lifting my fingers to her mouth and tracing the bottom one, painting her with her own juices.

"Clean them," I demand, pushing my fingers past her lips before she has a chance to argue.

Her eyes widen in shock, but like the good girl she's proving herself to be, her tongue laps at my fingers.

"Sweet, huh?" I ask, unable to drag my eyes away from her mouth.

Once I'm happy she's done as she's told, I pull my fingers free and dip my head. Her breath catches and her eyelids lower as if she's expecting me to kiss her, but I don't.

Instead, I drag my tongue along her lower lip, letting her taste explode in my mouth.

Spinning her around, my hand wraps around her throat and I push her backward toward the exit that's hidden in the shadows, lowering down to swipe her bag from the floor before we leave it behind.

"I'm bored of sharing you with other people. The only eyes you need on you right now are mine."

Pressing my hand to the scanner, I push the door open and stumble into the dimly lit hallway.

"What are you doing?" she slurs, her eyes darting around in fear.

"Don't worry, my little thief. There's no one back here who's going to rescue you."

"W-what are you—"

"Think it's about time we finished what we started, huh?"

"Alex, I— ARGH," her scream echoes down the deserted hallway as I throw her over my shoulder and march toward the double doors at the end of the long corridor that will lead us outside.

The fresh nighttime air rushes over us, making her shiver.

"You can't just abduct me," she squeals, her clenched fists slamming against my arse.

"Watch me, Vixen. Like I said, I take whatever I want. And right now, that's a night with you."

She continues to fight, trying to hurt me with her pathetic punches. But none of it comes close to making me consider letting her go for even a second.

Before long, we're walking in the back entrance of another building on this street and slipping into an empty lift.

No one stops us, exactly as I expected.

One look at me and they turn the other way.

Finally, I flip her back over, placing her on her feet.

She wobbles, and I place my hands on her shoulders to steady her. Her unfocused eyes land on mine. They're glassy from the champagne and full of confusion but also, most importantly, desire.

"Where are we?" she asks, although she doesn't bother to try and look, her attention focused on my lips.

I take a step closer, letting her sweet scent fill my nose.

"Trust me?" I ask again, already knowing what her answer is going to be.

Her eyes flash with determination and unrestrained heat.

"Tell me you haven't spent the past few weeks thinking about having me between your thighs again," I groan, leaning forward and brushing my lips against the corner of her mouth.

It's not a kiss. But it's oh so close and so fucking tempting.

She doesn't respond, but she doesn't need to. The violent tremble that rips through her body is enough.

"You want my face back between your legs, don't you, thief? You want me licking, sucking and fucking your cunt until I finally push you over the edge."

"Oh God."

"You've been fantasising about it, haven't you? When you're in bed at night, you imagine you're back there, laid out on my father's desk, completely at my mercy. You think about how my tongue felt against your sensitive pussy, how my fingers stretched you open. How I found that spot inside you that makes you beg like a little whore. And when you finally make yourself come with that image in your head, you call out my name, don't you?"

Her skin is covered in goosebumps as I brush my lips over her throat as I speak, closing the space between us and pinning her against the lift wall with my body.

"Tell me, Vixen. Tell me you get yourself off with me in your head and my name on your lips."

"Yes," she whispers. It's so quiet, so faint, that if it weren't for the silence around us, I might have missed it.

"Good. Because so do I. Every fucking night, I wrap my hand around my dick and think of you on your knees for me as I get myself off. There's just one problem, though." I pull back to look into her eyes. "I don't know your name, thief."

Her lips pop open, but if she was about to confess the details I've been dying for, then they're cut off by the ding of the lift and the doors opening on the floor I directed us to.

"Huh, saved by the bell. Again. You're getting a little too lucky tonight for my liking," I tease.

Taking her hand, I tug her out of the enclosed space and down the hallway to the room I have for us.

"Y-you're bringing me to a hotel room?" She baulks, looking around the second I bring her to a stop in the middle of it.

She blinks as confusion wars behind her eyes.

"Yep, and I'm locking the door so you can't escape this time."

Obviously, I can't actually lock us in, but she's drunk enough to startle when I make a show of flicking the lock.

"I-I—" she stutters as I close the space between us.

"What's wrong, Vixen? Worried I can't afford the whole night with you?" I taunt.

"I'm not a whore," she hisses, heat rising on her cheeks.

"Good, because I'm not paying you in anything but orgasms this time," I confess.

Reaching out, I cup her cheeks in my hands and finally, I slam my lips down on hers.

She doesn't react to start with, her entire body like a statue, but then I tease the seam of her lips with my tongue, and her resolve shatters.

Her arms lift, resting over my shoulders as she stretches up and twists her tongue with mine.

Her taste explodes in my mouth and I fucking drown in it.

My fingers thread into her hair, holding her captive, afraid that if I let go, she might disappear into the night like the previous two times I've had her.

Dropping one hand, I trace the curves of her body, the fullness of her breast, the dip of her waist and the roundness of her hip.

My cock strains painfully behind my jeans as I grind it against her stomach, giving her little choice but to feel how deeply she affects me.

"I swear to God," I pant after finally breaking our kiss to suck in some air. "If you run from me this time, all gloves are off. I'll hunt you the fuck down and lock you somewhere no one else will ever find you."

All the air rushes from her lungs at my threat as I hold her eyes, letting her see just how fucking serious I am.

"Oh," I say a little softer, dragging my fingertip over her cheek until I find the fullness of her bottom lip. "I thought you already knew who I was." She swallows nervously. "You've got into bed with the devil, Vixen. Now you need to suffer the consequences."

"Alex," she cries when I tug the bow that's sitting at the nape of her neck, allowing the two strips of fabric covering her tits to fall around her waist.

"Better. But not enough."

Tucking my fingers beneath the waistband of her playsuit, I shove it over her hips, allowing it to pool at her feet.

"Hell yes," I grunt, pressing my palm between her breasts, giving her a sharp shove.

She falls back, bouncing on the bed, allowing me to pull her trainers from her feet and free the fabric from her ankles, leaving her in just her thong.

"I thought my imagination was pretty good," I confess, staring down at her laid out for me like a sacrifice. "But it pales in comparison to this."

She watches me, her eyes blown with lust and glassy with alcohol.

I should be a gentleman and not take advantage, but I'm not a fucking gentleman.

I'm Alex fucking Deimos, and I need my little vixen almost as much as I need my next breath.

I pounce, making her scream.

"That's it," I praise as I find her wrists and pin them above her head. "But next time, I want my name tumbling from your lips."

Without giving her a chance to respond, I crash my

mouth back to hers, already missing having her lips on mine.

I kiss her until my head spins and my lungs burn for oxygen.

"Who are you, little thief?" I whisper roughly in her ear as we both fight to catch our breath.

"No one," she breathes, sounding a little too resolved by that confession.

"Never. You're way more than that, or I wouldn't have spent the past few months trying to find you," I confess, unable to catch the words before they tumble free.

Praying she didn't catch that slip in my armour, I latch my lips onto her neck and suck on her skin until I'm confident she'll have a reminder of me there for a few days to match the one on the other side I gave her in The Avenue.

Her back arches off the bed, and unable to resist the lure of her naked body, I crawl lower, kissing over her collarbone and then to the swell of her breast.

"Do you know how many men imagined doing this tonight?" I ask, brushing her hard peak with the tip of my nose.

"Please," she whimpers, shamelessly offering herself up to me.

"With fucking pleasure, Vixen," I groan before sucking her nipple into my mouth, teasing it gently with my tongue before biting her until she screams for me.

"Alexander," she cries when I switch to the other side, making me still for a moment. It's not very often anyone calls me by my full name. And never during sex.

It's... weird. But from her, I kinda like it.

"Time we picked up where we left off, huh?" Continuing to shimmy down the bed, I tuck my fingers under the sides of her knickers and rip them from her body. Pressing my palms to the inside of her thighs, I stare down at her. "The thing my dreams are made of. I hope you're not tired, because I have every intention of eating this all fucking night."

16

———

EVIE

I'm floating. Flying so high that the only thing I can focus on is the pleasure flooding my body and the disturbing man between my thighs.

There have been so many red flags. So many things that should have made me run in the other direction as fast as I could. But just like everything since the first night I met Alexander Deimos, my body has betrayed my own thoughts by doing the very opposite of what I should.

"Alex," I scream, my hand moving from where he left them above my head in favour of twisting in his hair, holding him against me, ensuring he's not about to disappear on me.

I can't do that. Not again.

I've spent weeks craving that lost orgasm. Tonight, no matter what, he's finishing the job he started when he pushed me to my knees.

It's been months since that night, and this has been building ever since.

"Yes," I cry when he spears me with two fingers, curling them almost immediately to find my G-spot.

I've never been with any other guy, but I'm not naïve to think they all find that spot quite so quickly.

That thought adds another red flag as to why I shouldn't be doing this right now to all the others I'm ignoring.

Just how much experience does he have with a woman's body to play me quite so easily?

It took me weeks, maybe even months, to discover what I liked, what pushed me over the edge into oblivion. Yet he seems to have a fucking road map. A map no one bothered giving me.

My entire body tingles with my impending release as he continues to do exactly as he promised.

It takes every bit of energy I have to lift my head, but I do it because the sensation alone isn't enough.

I need to see it.

My breath catches when my blurry vision clears enough to take him in.

His silver eyes are almost black as he stares up my body at me.

"You like seeing me eating you, Vixen?" he asks, not moving his lips from my core, sending delicious vibrations through my body.

"Don't stop," I breathe, making him chuckle darkly.

"Come on my face, thief. I want it all right fucking now."

He sucks on me harder than he has before as his fingers pick up pace inside me, and in only seconds, my entire body quakes in a way I've never experienced before, and I free-fall into the most incredible release. I didn't even know it was possible for it to hit so hard.

My eyes slam closed as I convulse on the bed, forgetting that every single thing exists outside of this room. Outside of him.

"So fucking beautiful. Totally worth the wait. But it's not enough. This cunt is mine, Vixen. You got that?"

I nod, barely able to register his words and agree to anything. I was already pretty wasted; add his drugging kisses and an orgasm with that intensity to it and I'm done. Totally fucking done.

Shifting between my thighs forces my eyes open, and I'm instantly disappointed when I find him still fully dressed.

I'm lying here with my legs spread, everything on display, and he's hiding from me.

"Alexander." His name is nothing more than a slur rolling off my tongue.

I don't even know what I'm asking for; I just know I need something.

He wipes his mouth with the back of his hand, a smirk firmly in place on his sinful lips.

I want to chastise him for being such an arrogant fuck, but honestly, what he just did to my body... yeah, I'll let him have it.

Then, his hands drop to his waistband and my breath catches in my throat.

With his eyes locked on my body, he shoves his jeans and boxers down over his arse, exposing his thick, hard cock to me.

The tip glistens with precum and it makes me lick my lips with my need to taste him again.

That night was such an eye-opener for me, and I can't help wanting to do it again. I won't be so shocked by everything the second time. Although, as he wraps his hand around himself, I can't say I'm unfazed by the reminder of just how big he is.

A groan rips from his throat as he strokes himself once, twice.

"Oh fuck," I cry, when he rubs the head of his dick through my folds, coating himself with the evidence of my orgasm. "Alex, no. I haven't—"

"Don't worry, my little thief. When I push inside you for the first time, you will be fully sober and aware of what's happening. I'm not risking you forgetting a second of me owning you."

He teases my clit, awakening the beginnings of another release.

I've managed multiples before, but only with the help of my vibrating friend.

Could it be that... that he's even better than battery-operated assistance?

His throat ripples as he swallows harshly, his hooded eyes lifting to find mine as he continues teasing both of us.

"I don't know who you are, or where you come from, but I want to keep you," he says so quietly I'd think I was imagining it if I didn't see his lips move.

His words, along with the feeling of him rubbing against my clit is enough to send me crashing into another powerful release.

"Vixen," he yells, his deep voice echoing around the room.

I just manage to open my eyes in time to watch him throw his head back as he rides out his release, his cock jerking against my core, the heat of his seed coating my overly sensitive skin.

His entire body pulls tight, intensifying his already defined muscles that remain hidden behind his shirt.

"Fuck, Vixen. That was..."

His words trail off as his eyes return to my barely open ones.

My chest continues to heave as I come down from my high, but my body is giving out faster than I can control.

Each of my blinks gets longer than the one before, and soon I can't keep my eyes open at all. Long before I'm ready, I fall into the darkness, my body still tingling in bliss.

17

———

ALEX

My shoulders slump and I sit back harder on my heels as she passes out before me.

Her dark hair is a mess. The pretty updo she left Paradise with has been long destroyed by my hands. My chest puffs out a little in pride that I've messed her up quite so much.

She looked stunning tonight, both in that cage and dancing with her friends. But she's never looked better than she does right now.

Her skin is glistening from the exertion of two releases, her nipples are still hard, her breasts covered in my bite marks, and her pussy... Fuck.

I shift back a little, taking in the sight of her cunt covered in my cum.

Best fucking sight in the world.

Well... maybe not. Watching it run out of her would be better. But I'll take what I can get right now.

Looming over her, I brush a loose strand of her hair from her face, gently tucking it behind her ear.

"Who are you?" I whisper again, desperate to know everything there is to know about my dancing cam girl.

A fierce wave of possessiveness washes through me as I think about others seeing her like this. Getting to watch the blush that spread from her cheeks down over her chest as she raced toward orgasm, and the way her eyes rolled back when pleasure slammed into her.

Pleasure that I delivered.

I guess that's something none of those motherfuckers on the other end of her cam call can claim.

I wonder if she's been thinking about me while doing whatever she does with them...

Dipping lower, I shamelessly brush my lips over hers, unable to deny my need to taste her.

"Sleep tight, little thief," I breathe before sitting up again.

I know I shouldn't, but I pull my phone from my pocket and snap a few pictures of her laid out before me. Then, I climb from the bed and tuck myself away.

Despite telling myself that she willingly puts her body on display for others to enjoy, guilt still niggles at me for stealing those images when she's sleeping.

It isn't enough to make me delete them, mind you. I'll just make sure she knows they exist so I'm not hiding more than I have to.

I spin toward the bathroom, but an idea hits me. I'm reaching behind my head and pulling my shirt off before I've realised I've made a decision.

In only seconds, I'm tucked up tightly behind my little thief's body before wrapping the duvet over her, covering up her delicious nakedness.

Pulling my phone back out, I open the camera and then position myself and snap a few photos from different angles.

In minutes, I'm back on my feet with my shirt on and padding to the bathroom. The temptation to stay exactly where I was, surrounded by her scent with the heat of her body burning into mine, was too strong. It would be so easy to close my eyes and fall fast asleep beside her.

But I can't. I can't do that to either of us.

I'm already too addicted. Spending the night would only fuel my obsession with this mystery woman.

I unroll one of the washcloths and run the hot tap until the water warms, and then I go back and clean her up.

She might think I'm the devil, but she's got a lot to learn about me.

Not that she's going to get the chance to.

As much as that final promise to her might be true. I know it can't be.

I refuse to entangle someone in my life. Even if she might understand.

No one is worth hurting like that.

Not even a sexy little thief like my vixen.

"Such a shame to cover up this sinful body," I murmur, pulling the cloth from her pussy and dropping it to the floor. "But we don't want you to get cold. I just wish I could stay and be your blanket."

She whimpers as I tuck her in.

Unable to step away, I run my knuckles lightly down her cheek.

"Alex," she moans, making my dick jerk in my pants.

"Fucking hell, Vixen."

Forcing myself to step back, I trip over her bag that I just about remembered to grab for her on the way out of the club.

With it in hand, I fall onto the chair that sits overlooking the bed and finally get the answers I've been craving for the past few months.

I go for her purse first and pull out a bank card.

"Evie Moore," I breathe, my eyes lifting from the card to the woman in question still sleeping soundly before me. "Suits you." My eyes find her address and my chest tightens. "Lovell. Of course."

Tucking the card back in, I pause, staring at the photo she has in here.

It's her, a blonde woman and a younger boy. Siblings, maybe?

Pulling her phone from my pocket where I stashed it earlier, I light it up, finding another photo of her with the same two people.

"Give me all your secrets, Evie Moore," I mutter, swiping up, praying she doesn't have a lock code set up. "Fuck," I bark a little too loudly before pushing to my feet to see if her sleeping face will unlock it.

But it doesn't. Not with her eyes shut.

"Damn it," I mutter, dropping back into the chair and trying my luck with what little information I do have.

Her provisional driving licence gives me her date of birth.

Eighteen in a few weeks.

Not sure if she should be working at Paradise, or for Dad, if she's underage, but whatever. Being too young never stopped us from doing anything we wanted to do.

Nothing I try lets me in. In fact, I end up locking it up tighter with all my attempts.

It's fine. I know who she is now. And I have a way to find her. It's all I need.

I pull the little kit Theo gave me not so long ago from my pocket and get to work.

My little thief won't be giving me the slip again, no matter how hard she tries.

Once I'm done and confident my invasion of her privacy won't be detected—yet, anyway—I pack her belongings back into her bag and place it on the dresser beside me. Then I sit back, watching her sleep like a creep.

I sat there watching her until the sun started to emerge on the horizon, turning the air outside a burned orange.

Dawn has always been my favourite time of the day.

In those first few moments of light, anything feels possible.

The world is serene, all the horrors of the night running back into the darkness where they belong.

Hope. That's what those first few rays of sun give the world.

Okay, so it's usually soon squashed when you realise that your life is the same fucking shitshow as it was the day before and will continue being so for all the days which follow.

But in those few moments, it all just... disappears.

Leaving her was the hardest thing I've done in a while, but after brushing a kiss over her warm cheek, I forced my legs to move, pulled the door open and walked out of The Empire as if I didn't carry her inside here last night, possibly against her will.

Hell, I've done worse here. A hell of a lot worse.

And she loved every second of it.

I could have taken so much more from her, but I was a good boy.

Can't say that it'll be the same the next time I get my hands on her, but hey ho.

The Uber journey home was short, spent staring out the window at the sunrise, and the second I got into my flat, I stripped out of my clothes and fell front first into bed. I'm pretty sure I'm asleep before my cheek hits my pillow.

A bang somewhere in my flat jolts me awake after what feels like no more than thirty minutes of sleep and I groan, rolling over and dragging the spare pillow over my head.

But another bang follows, and then the deep rumble of voices, and then the scent of coffee.

That final one perks me up, but it's still not enough for me to make any attempt to get up.

Unsurprisingly, the voices get closer, the footsteps get louder, and before I know what's happening, cool air rushes over my naked body as the duvet is ripped away from me.

"Wakey, wakey rise and shine, lover boy," Seb announces loudly.

"Fuck. Off," I grunt, not moving from my hiding spot under the pillow.

"Ha, yeah, because that's going to work," he deadpans.

"Get your arse up, soldier," Theo demands. "You've got some explaining to do."

"I haven't done anything," I groan, aware that it's a total lie. I've done plenty of fucking things, most of which he probably knows about, because that motherfucker somehow knows everything.

"Not what your Instagram says," Seb adds.

"Then maybe you should stop looking at it."

"What's the fun in that? You want the world to know your name? Well, we're watching, so suck it up."

With a groan, I flip onto my back, gifting them both an unrestricted view of my semi.

"For fuck's sake, Deimos. Put that away. It's almost offensive, being so small," Seb taunts.

"Fuck you. We all know you'd give anything to have one this big. Honestly, I'm surprised Stella hasn't got bored and come begging yet."

The pillow I'd lifted to ensure he'd hear my words clearly is quickly pressed back against my face, smothering me and cutting off my air.

"My girl needs a man, not a boy, Alexander. You'd never satisfy her," he barks.

"Jesus Christ," Theo scoffs. "I'll go finish the coffee."

"You're just smug because we all know that yours is bigger than Seb's too," I bellow when he lets up a little.

"You fucking cunt," Seb seethes, returning to putting his whole weight on the pillow in his attempt to end me.

I give him ten seconds. Then, I fight back.

He grunts as my leg collides with his ribs, knocking him from the bed and sending him flying to the floor with a thud.

Suddenly feeling awake, I jump down, wrestling him.

"I don't care how small your dick is. I don't want it rubbing all over me," he shouts as we roll across the floor.

"Shut up, you fucking love it. If you had the chance, you'd be on your knees sucking it."

"Sorry to fuck over your fantasies, but that's never happening, bro. Stella's pussy is it for me."

"She'd suck it."

Crack.

I fall back on my bare arse and rub my sore cheek.

"What the fuck?" I ask as Seb shakes out his fist and gets to his feet.

He shrugs, not giving a shit about the bruise I'm going to be sporting in a few hours thanks to his right hook.

"Talk about my girl sucking your teeny weeny again and see what happens."

My lips part to respond but Theo beats me to it.

"Coffee. Unless you want me to leave so you can fuck it out."

"Fucking arsehole," Seb mutters, stalking toward the door. "Cover your arse up. You're yet to find a woman who wants to look at it. We certainly don't."

"Cunt," I bark as he disappears from my sight.

With a sigh, I push to my feet and pad through to my bathroom to take a piss and brush my teeth.

When I walk back into my bedroom, I discover I was right. I've barely been asleep for four hours.

Knowing better than to fall back into my bed for more sleep with those two pricks out in my living room, I pull on a clean pair of boxers and some shorts and head out to find out what they've got to say that's so important they had to drag me out of bed this fucking early.

The second I'm in my living room, I reach for the mug on the coffee table and take a sip.

"Why the fuck are you here so early? Shouldn't you be in bed with hangovers after last night?"

"We were good," Seb shrugs, trying to look innocent.

"And we're not here to talk about our night. We want to know about yours." Smirks cover both of their faces as they wait for me to spill the beans.

When I keep my mouth shut, Seb pulls his phone from his pocket, taps on the screen and then turns it around to me.

"Care to explain?"

18

———

EVIE

My phone vibrating again drags me from the final clutches of sleep. Stretching out my legs, I frown at the softness of the sheets.

They don't feel like—

My eyes pop open, last night's caked-on mascara threatening to rip my lashes out in the process.

But I quickly discover that's the least of my worries when I take in the room around me.

"Oh shit," I whisper as memories from the night before come back to me in vivid, colourful detail.

I sink further into the sheets, wishing I could hide from everything and let the darkness swallow me whole once more.

My head pounds, my mouth is gross, my tongue thick and furry.

Too much champagne.

The room falls silent once more and I breathe a sigh of relief, praying for sleep.

But I'm not that lucky, because not three seconds later does the vibrating start up again.

"Ugh," I groan, flipping the covers back and opening my eyes just enough to scan the room for my bag.

Crawling over, my skin erupts in goosebumps as the cool air points out the fact that I'm naked.

My cheeks burn despite the cold.

As fast as I can, I dig about in my bag until my fingers wrap around my phone and pull it free.

I'm hardly surprised to see my sister's name lighting up my screen, but a groan of frustration still rumbles in my chest.

Swiping to accept the call, I lift it to my ear.

"Evie, shit. Are you there? Are you okay?"

"Y-y—" I have to cough to clear my throat, but even still, when I speak again my voice is still deep and raspy. "Yes, I'm here."

"And you sound like you've had a good night," Blakely laughs in my ear.

I fall back onto the bed and close my eyes once more.

When Blakely speaks again, her voice is quieter.

"Is he still there?"

I frown. "H-he? W-what are you—"

"Evie," she teases. "I know you spent the night with Alex. It's a little late to play shy with me. I know all about what goes down when you're together."

I can practically see her eyebrows wiggling and a smirk playing on her lips as she says those words.

"So... is he still there?"

My eyes pop open to scan the room again, but it's pointless. I already know the answer. I felt it when I first woke, his absence. The coldness of the room without his overwhelming presence.

"No," I whisper, hating that my eyes burn with tears at my admission. "He's gone."

"Oh. Gone as in he gave you a knee-weakening kiss and let you sleep off your night, or—"

"He snuck out when I was sleeping."

"Wanker," Blakely hisses.

My chest tightens as a lump grows in my throat.

"It's fine. It's for the best. Last night was—" I cut myself off, swallowing hard in the hope of banishing the emotion.

"Mind-blowing? Incredible? Life-changing?" she offers.

"A mistake," I confess. "I-I don't even... he found me at The Avenue with the girls. How did he even know I was there?"

"Luck, I guess. It's a pretty popular place," she assures me.

I shake my head, keeping my mouth shut about the fact he was at Paradise first. He obviously followed me.

But why? So he could get me back here just to sneak out again the moment I fell asleep?

"Have you checked his Insta this morning?"

I cringe, hating that she knows about my obsession.

"You woke me, Blake."

"Okay, well, put me on speaker and check. You need to see what he's posted."

Tucking the duvet around me tighter, I pull my phone from my ear and follow her demands.

I open Insta and hit the little magnifying glass. Unsurprisingly, Alex is the first person in my search history. Didn't see that coming. I tap his name and wait for his feed to load.

The second it does, my heart drops into my stomach.

"Oh my God. That's me," I gasp, my hand trembling as I stare at the image.

"Uh-huh. He totally likes you."

"No. He doesn't. He just—"

My eyes drop to the caption beneath the photograph of us in bed together, him with his lips on me, looking entirely too content and comfortable.

TheOneAndOnlyAlexD: Steal dreams and always leave them wanting more.

"Oh my God," I repeat, struggling to come up with anything else to say.

"He's never posted a picture of a girl on his account before, Evie. You are the only one. He's telling the world, or his thousands of followers, at least, that you're in his life. That you are important."

"I'm not, though. I'm the girl he's punishing for stealing his watches."

"You weren't stealing his watches," she argues, sticking up for me without question.

"We know that, but he doesn't. He just sees a desperate girl doing anything to make a quick buck," I say, hating the bitterness that floods my voice.

"He does not think that, Evie," Blakely warns.

A pained sigh falls from my lips before silence falls down the line.

"So," Blakely pipes up, forcing some cheer into her voice. "Where are you?"

Her question makes me pause. and I drag myself from my memories of a boy I shouldn't be thinking about to look around the room once more.

It's nice. Really nice, and way swankier than any place I've ever stayed before. Hell, I've barely ever stayed anywhere but our flat.

Three walls are a warm caramel colour. The one behind me with a giant headboard attached is covered in gold floral wallpaper. The bedding and curtains match and all the ornaments and trinkets are in keeping. The furniture is chunky dark wood. Walnut maybe, I've no idea really. But one thing is more than obvious. It's expensive. All of it.

"Uh... a hotel, I guess."

"You guess."

"I... um... I was drunk and..."

"And?" Blakely asks, concern edging into her tone.

"My memory is patchy," I confess, hating that I allowed myself to be so vulnerable with him.

"But you remember it, right? It's not all a blur?"

I lick my dry lips as I think about what happened in this room last night.

The image of him stripping my clothes off me appears in my mind. Him looming over my naked body, peppering kisses across my heated skin, working his way down until his head was back between my—

"I remember what happened back here," I confess, my body burning up from the memories alone.

"Okay, that's good. Did you..." She pauses, I think waiting for me to finish her sentence, but I slam my lips shut, waiting for the inevitable question. "Did you sleep with him?"

The memory of him coming all over my pussy slams into me, making my breath catch.

"No," I whisper. "We... it didn't go that far."

"Right," she mutters, allowing me to hear the doubt in her voice.

"What? Don't you believe me?" I snap.

"No, of course I believe you. I just... we know what guys like him are like, Evie. You can't blame me for being suspicious of his intentions taking an obviously drunk girl to a hotel room. A girl he has a history with."

Closing my eyes, I hang my head. "He... he didn't even ask to—"

"But you messed about, right? In that photo, you're topless at least."

"Yeah, he..."

"Tell me he finished what I interrupted?"

"You are way too invested in him making me come, Blake."

"You deserve it. No one likes being dropped cold turkey."

Sliding to the edge of the bed, I swing my legs over and look at the items on the unit on the opposite side of the room.

"The Empire," I blurt, praying it's enough to put an end to the previous line of questioning.

"Wow," she breathes. "Make use of that flashy room. I'll be thirty minutes. Message me with your room number."

"What?" I blurt in shock.

"Babe, that boy has booked you a room in one of the nicest hotels this side of the city, and he'll be paying for it. So we're going to make the most of it."

"No, Blake. I can't."

"We're not going to take the piss. Just breakfast. Maybe dip our toes in the jacuzzi and sauna."

I suck in a breath, preparing to go toe to toe with her over this. But then she speaks again and all my fight vanishes.

"He snuck out when you were sleeping, Evie. He wasn't man enough to stick around and do the morning after thing. He deserves to pay for that."

"Yeah, okay," I concede. I might not agree with taking his money, but she's right. He should have had the balls to face me this morning. He went to all that effort to follow me last night and then he just... ran.

I shake my head.

Blake's right. And I'm going to prove it by having the most expensive and extravagant breakfast on the menu.

"I'll message you the number. Just—"

"I'll pack everything you need. Order yourself a fancy room service coffee and sober yourself up, yeah?"

"I'll see what I can do."

After hanging up, I force myself to abandon my phone to get out of bed.

Every inch of me hurts, but nothing has anything on my head.

I've experienced a couple of hangovers in the past, but this... shit. Literally feels like someone is going at my skull with a pickaxe.

I pad through to the bathroom, my eyes wide as I take in the luxury surrounding me.

There's a massive jacuzzi bath and a walk-in shower with jets everywhere. A double basin and more mirrors and bright spotlights than I can cope with.

I beeline for the toilet before stopping in front of one of the basins. I've seen myself moving around in the mirror, but I've purposely not focused on my reflection. That needs to end, though.

Curling my fingers around the marble counter, I suck in a deep breath and reluctantly look up.

All the air is punched from my lungs as I take in the state of me.

Lifting my hair from my neck, my eyes move from mark to mark until I find the ones on my breasts.

Holy shit, I'm a dot to dot.

Lifting my hand, I press one fingertip to the brightest mark on my neck. My body stirs to life as I remember the feeling of him sucking on my skin until it hurt.

I should have hated it. But that was far from how I felt while he played my body like it was his personal instrument.

I close my eyes as memories swirl around, my body reacting to each one. I should regret last night. I should be standing here now, writing it off as a drunken mistake.

Reaching for the toothbrush and courtesy tube of toothpaste sitting on the side, I attempt to fix the state of my mouth.

I hold my eyes in the mirror the entire time, watching as question after question about what happened last night rolls through them.

Once I'm done, I move to the shower and figure out how to get it working.

But no matter how much I scrub my body, the marks never reduce, and the memories never leave my head.

Aware that I've probably been in there trying to make the most of the incredible jets pounding against my tense muscles too long, I finally turn it off and step out.

I find a thick white fluffy robe hanging on the back of the door, and I wrap myself in it before going to find out the room number to let Blakely know.

I shouldn't allow her to exploit this situation like she is.

But I figure that I'll just add it to my already long list of regrets I have when it comes to Alexander Deimos and crack on.

Hell knows I need a moment after last night.

I grab my phone from the bed as I walk toward the huge windows to look at the city before me.

I could tell from a distance that we're high up, but I didn't appreciate how high until I look down and find what appears to be ants walking along the pavements beneath me.

I shoot off a message with my room number to Blakely, who's already sent me a gif with a man staring at his watch.

Rolling my eyes at her impatience, I close our chat down. My thumb hovers over the Instagram app.

Don't open it, Evie. Do not obsess over that photo and how he looks kissing your skin.

But as with everything that has to do with him, I don't listen to reason, and before I know it, I have his profile open in front of me and I'm scrolling through the comments.

Most of them are some variation of 'lucky lady'. Some are more explicit than others, which makes me blush. Then there are the trolls that I've seen popping up in his comments often who like to remind him what a manwhore he is, and asking why any self-respecting woman would willingly get into bed with him.

They're disgusting and make my stomach knot up painfully. I might not know him all that well, but he's not a bad person. I don't think.

I chew on my bottom lip as uncertainty trickles through my veins.

I know who he is, who he is connected to, who he works for. Of course, he's bad.

He's the fucking mafia. They're the epitome of bad.

But when you've grown up in the pits of hell with dealers, prostitutes and gang members on every corner, I guess things get a little skewed, because he doesn't scare me. Well... not in the way I'm sure he should.

The most terrifying thing about Alexander is how I feel when I'm with him. Hell, even when I think about him.

A knock on my door drags me from my thoughts and I pad over on the thick, spongy carpet.

My hand trembles as I lift my palm to the door and lean closer to the peephole. There's a big part of me that wants it to be him. To discover that he didn't just up and leave, but that he had a legitimate reason to slip out and that he's come back to—

I shake my head as my sister's blonde hair fills my vision.

With a sigh, I pull the door open.

"Well, you could look at least a little excited to see me," she says teasingly.

But as she steps into the room, something inside me snaps and a sob rips from my throat.

"Evie," she sighs, pulling me into her arms and holding tight.

The click of the door closing behind her hits my ears, and I fall even deeper, trusting her to hold me up.

19

ALEX

"Dude, that was fucking dirty," I bark, rolling onto my back and staring up at the clear sky above me.

The sun beats down on my sweat-slicked skin as my chest heaves with exertion.

I didn't stand a fucking chance of getting out of this. Especially when I refused to answer the million and one questions Theo and Seb fired at me about the first girl I've ever posted on my Instagram.

I regretted it the second I remembered posting it on the way out of the hotel room this morning. But it's too fucking late to take it down now. It's got thousands of likes and hundreds of comments.

Plus, there's a part of me that doesn't want to delete her. My feed is my life, or at least the parts of it I can post, and right now, she's a part of that.

I've no idea quite how she wiggled her way in, but she has.

Dragging my hand down my face, I wipe away the blades of grass that covered me after Seb's bookable tackle.

If we were playing properly, he'd be carded for that and banished to the bench. Sadly, the smug fuck knows that as well as I do, and instead of getting a roasting from our coach, he just climbs to his feet and stares down at me.

"Might have gone easier on you if you'd given us all the details, Deimos."

"Fuck you. We don't all kiss and tell like you and Stella," I grunt, pushing myself to sit up.

"Fuck that. We just do it in front of you."

I roll my eyes at him and push my sweaty hair back from my brow.

"Don't we fucking know it?"

"Gonna get off the fucking grass anytime soon, Deimos?" Nico shouts, getting impatient with me.

We met both him and Toby on our way out of the building so we could come and play a five-aside game with some other guys from our school team.

"Fuck you, Cirillo. At least I'm not rolling around clutching my leg like a pussy," I tease.

"It fucking hurt."

"You really have handed Brianna your balls, huh?"

"You should know all about that with your new mystery woman."

Flipping them all off, I get to my feet and straighten my shorts.

Coming out and getting covered in sweat and fucking grass stains after barely any sleep wasn't all that high up on my to-do list today. But I didn't have a fucking lot of choice, seeing as the guys keep reminding me that I was actually the one to organise this game. Pricks.

"Twenty minutes left," Theo barks, always the fucking boss.

"Yes, master." I salute him and get into position.

"Does he ever have a day off?" Greg, one of our best strikers—after me, obviously—says, watching the man who's happily embracing his captain role.

"Do I really need to answer that?" I ask. He's been on the Knight's Ridge team with us for years. He's more than aware of Theo's control freak ways.

Theo blows his whistle violently, and Toby barks my name, dragging me back into the game.

We won. Obviously. Theo wouldn't have had it any other way. I mean, we are better than them, so it was always going to be the outcome.

"Come on, I'm fucking starving," Nico says, throwing his arms around mine and Seb's shoulders as we stand on the sideline drinking from our bottles.

"Same," Seb agrees. "But I don't need your sweaty pits anywhere fucking near me." He ducks from under Nico's arm, shooting him a glare.

"Wouldn't put my girl off," Nico teases.

"That's because Brianna's a dirty whore," Toby offers up, coming to join us.

Nico's face twists in disbelief and then anger at someone talking about his girl like that. But before punching his best friend, a wide smile spreads across his face.

"Fuck yeah, she is. And I fucking love it. We need to go to Hades again soon. Been too long, man."

Nico trails after Toby as they head toward the car park.

Ideas begin popping up in my head at the mention of our sex club. Ideas that make my dick jerk in my shorts.

"What's that look for?" Seb asks.

"N-nothing," I stutter, although the more I think about it, it's not nothing. It's actually fucking perfect.

"Looks like his girl's a freak too," Theo supplies.

"She'd fucking have to be to capture this dirty dog's attention," Seb jokes. "Anyone too vanilla will be out on their arse faster than they thought possible."

"What are you trying to say, Papatonis?" I growl.

"You know exactly what I'm saying, *motherfucker*."

"Fuck you. I need food."

Leaving them behind to laugh at my expense, I trail behind Nico and Toby, more than ready for the next part of our morning before I can go home and pass out. My stomach growls just thinking of the fry-up I'm about to devour.

Thankfully, the conversation changes by the time Theo and Seb pile into Nico's car beside me, and instead of grilling me about Evie, they focus on their plans for our week off school.

Pretty sure we're all meant to be studying for our final few exams, but that seems to be the last thing on everyone's mind.

It's only a short drive to our usual breakfast café, and before I know it, the server is lowering a plate full of delicious fried food before me. It's exactly what I need to fill my belly before heading home to sleep the night away.

"Plans for tonight?" I ask, figuring that there has to be a party or something happening somewhere.

The second all their eyes turn on me, I know exactly what the boring fuckers are about to say.

"Night in," Theo says, while the others all nod.

"Whipped motherfuckers," I mutter around a mouthful of sausage.

"Didn't stop you last night, did it? Where did you all fuck off to, anyway?" Seb asks. "One minute you were there and the next—"

"Nice of you to all notice. We went to Paradise."

"Paradise? Seriously?" Toby asks.

"Yeah, why not? The dancers are hot. In fact, we need to get someone down there to poach a few, because damn." I wiggle my brows just in case they're not following.

"I'll speak to Galen," Seb agrees. "We have the best girls in the city, not the fucking Italians."

"Do we need to start a war with Matteo quite so soon?" Nico asks with a frown.

"We can do it discreetly," Seb assures him.

"When the fuck have you ever been discreet with anything?"

Seb's lips part, but no words come out. "Fuck off. It's not like you lot are any better."

"Speak for yourselves. I'm discreet as fuck, and you all know it."

They roll their eyes at me.

"And those who have fallen for it sure fucking know about it," Theo teases.

"Get the job done, don't I?"

"Don't know how you do it, man," Toby says.

I shrug. "It's my job. We've all got our skills. Do you hear me going off on yours?"

"Not exactly the same, though, are they?"

I grunt in response, wanting to talk about my job as much as I want to tell them everything about Evie.

She's my secret. And she'll remain that way for her own good.

As the others fall into conversation about fuck knows what, I pull my phone out to check the comments on my post. But before I get there, my messages catch my eye. And one specifically.

> Blakely Moore: What did you spike my
> sister's drink with last night?

Fury burns through my veins at her accusation. But it's more than that. What the fuck has Evie been telling her?

"**I**f you change your mind about being a bunch of whipped pussies tonight, message me, yeah?"

When all I get is a round of weak agreements, I know I'm going to be spending my evening alone unless I go out and find my own fun.

It's Saturday night, we're eighteen and about to embark on the best summer of our lives, and yet they're all spending it in their flats with their women.

If you had one waiting for you inside your flat, you'd happily spend your night inside her too...

I groan at the little voice in my head, because as much as I fight it and pretend otherwise, I know it's right. If I could have that, I'd lose myself in it in a heartbeat.

But I can't. I knew that the second I was forced to sign my body and soul to the devil.

I never thought it would be an issue. I didn't see a future where any of us found girls and settled down. But then Stella arrived, and it set off something of a domino effect through my friends. And now, here we are. All of them are living with girls. Theo is a husband. Nico is engaged. My brother is having a fucking baby. A fucking actual baby with Calli Cirillo.

The whole thing blows my mind.

Leaving Seb and Toby behind at their front doors, I keep walking to mine and press my hand to the scanner.

I'm sure my flat has never felt so cold and empty as the door closes behind me.

Kicking my trainers off, I dump my muddy football boots on the rack to stink out the hallway before marching through the living area and to my bedroom, stripping out of my dirty clothes as I go.

I'm about to put my phone on the counter in the bathroom so I can shower, but I stop at the last minute, the memory of the images hiding on my camera roll hitting me.

The second I see the thumbnails, my cock begins to swell.

My teeth grind and my grip on my phone tightens as I vividly remember how it felt rubbing myself against her soaked cunt last night.

She was so hot. So fucking tempting.

All I had to do was thrust forward just slightly and I'd have been inside her.

I wanted to. Fuck, did I want to.

I knew how tight she was the second I pushed my fingers inside while she was laid out on my dad's desk.

She would feel incredible wrapped around my cock. I've no doubt that she'd squeeze it so tight that I'd forget my own name.

But I also knew the second I did, I wouldn't want to give her up. And I have no right to have her, let alone keep her.

My cock aches, trying to convince me that we need her. And being nothing but a slave to my baser instincts, I wrap my hand around my length and allow myself to drown in memories of the girl I can't have.

Leaving my phone behind, I stumble forward, stepping

into my shower as I work myself hard and fast, punishing myself for being such a pussy.

Anyone else, I'd have just fucked them and walked away without a second thought.

What is it about her?

Is it her job? The fact I don't want to drag her any deeper into the life she's found herself in already?

Is it the innocence that pours from her eyes every time I look into them?

I want to rescue her. Show her that she doesn't have to choose to live that kind of life.

But as I stand with my palm against the cold tiles, hanging my head as my orgasm approaches, I figure that I might be pushing my own issues onto her. She might want that life. It might be what she's always wanted to do. There's no shame in that, if it is. Fair fucking play if she's living out the life she's always dreamed of.

But what if she's not...

What if she's been forced into it?

I know all too well how that feels.

To live a life that has been dictated by someone else.

Despite my depressing thoughts, my release still slams into me. Evie's name rolls off my tongue as I spill my seed into the dry shower tray at my feet.

The release might take the edge off, but it's nowhere near what I need. It's hollow without her.

Shoving those thoughts away, I turn the shower on and try to think about something else.

My exams.

They really should be my sole focus right now. But no matter what I do, my thoughts always drift back to her. It's been the same since I found her at Christmas.

I clean up, watching as the mud from our match swirls

down the drain before I step out and wrap a towel around my waist.

Unable to stop myself, I snatch up my phone once more and pad through to my bedroom, dripping water all over the floor.

I fall onto the end of my bed and pull up the App Store, searching for the camming app on the card Vincent gave me last night.

I tell myself that I'll just find her, follow her, because... why the fuck wouldn't I? and then focus on some revision.

I set myself up an account, giving myself what I hope is a generic enough name, and then I start my search.

Thankfully, it only takes seconds. Now I've had a taste of her, I've no interest in anyone else on this site.

I'm pretty sure I stop breathing when her profile appears before me.

*Miss Vixen, a young and innocent schoolgirl. She'll tease you in any way you please. All you need to do is ask nicely. *winky emoji**

Follow to get notifications of live streams, and always open to one-on-one calls.

"Jesus," I mutter, pushing my wet hair back from my brow.

My hand holding my phone trembles as I think about other men watching her... well, pretty much doing whatever they ask of her.

Acid swirls around in my stomach, threatening to make an appearance as different scenes play out in my head.

She might enjoy it. It might be her calling in life, a little voice says in my head. *She might get off on that more than she does with your hands on her body.*

Closing the app, I place my phone screen side down on the bed and blow out a calming breath.

She's just a girl, Alex. Just like all those you've been with before.

She's happy. She loves her life.

She doesn't need you swooping in to rescue her.

"FUCK," I bark, falling back on my bed, and making the mistake of closing my eyes.

I'm woken by my phone ringing beside me sometime later.

Glancing at the window as I reach for it, I realise that it's quite a long time later, because the sun is sinking in the sky.

"Brilliant," I mutter, lifting my phone in front of my face and groaning when I find my dad's name lighting it up.

"Dad," I groan into the phone, my voice rough with sleep.

"You okay, Son?" he asks, concern in his voice.

"Y-yeah. I was just... sleeping."

"Really?" he asks in disbelief. "Last night's party must have been something, huh?"

"Something like that. What's up?" I ask, already dreading the words that are going to roll off his tongue.

"Got a job for you."

My stomach sinks.

"Alex?" His deep voice rumbles down the line when I don't respond. "If you've got plans tonight, you're going to need to cancel them. This is too important."

Isn't it always?

"Sure. Give me the details."

"See, wasn't this the best idea ever?" Blakely asks from her lounger as she sips on a cocktail.

Honestly, other than the fact that I'm waiting for him to appear and accuse us of taking the piss out of his generosity, it was a pretty great idea.

Despite the hotel being busy, or at least the reception looked to be, the pool is pretty quiet.

There have been a couple of families making use of it for an hour, and there have been some couples who are blatantly away on dirty weekends molesting each other before disappearing into the sauna, which we made sure to avoid until they emerged red and sweaty.

But mostly, it's been just us and the waiter from the bar upstairs that Blakely manipulated to keep making regular cocktail deliveries.

Poor guy isn't very old, and I'm pretty sure he's a virgin. He could barely take his eyes off her almost-naked tits. There was no way he was going to refuse her request.

"Ah, look, here comes Dylan for a refresh." She downs

her Manhattan as he approaches, his eyes locked on her body.

"Ladies," he drawls, lowering our fresh drinks to the table between us. Alcoholic for Blake and a virgin for me. My hangover might have faded, but I'm nowhere near ready for alcohol again yet. Or ever. "Are you enjoying your afternoon?"

I fight a smile as I watch the blush on his cheeks from just asking an innocent question.

"Not bad, Dylan. It would be better if you could join us, obviously."

Blakely shifts on her lounger, arching her back and giving him a nice show.

The poor kid looks like he's about to blow his load just watching her.

"I-I-I don't get off for—"

"I'm sure we can rectify that," Blake offers, running her tongue along her bottom lip and her eyes down his body.

"Whore," I cough, not that Dylan notices. He's completely under my sister's spell.

"I'm sure the three of us could have some real fun."

His eyes widen, and his chin drops, his dirty thoughts following right along with Blake's wicked suggestions.

"The... the three of—"

"What time is your shift over?"

"Uh... um..." He looks over to the giant clock hanging on the wall. "Uh... s-six."

"Okay, well, if you're a good boy, maybe we'll see you after six, yeah?"

He nods eagerly and stumbles back, getting a little too close to the pool before he turns to run away.

"Hey, Dylan," Blake calls as she absently adjusts her bikini top.

"Yeah," he squeaks.

"You forgot our empties." She bites her lip and holds her glass out for him.

"Oh, I'm so sorry, Miss…"

"Blakely," she offers, her voice all deep and seductive. She's way too fucking good at wrapping men around her little finger. It doesn't matter if they're barely legal or heading for a bus pass and hardly able to stand. They all want what she has to offer. She exudes sex appeal in a way I can only dream of.

"B-Blakely," he repeats before taking our empties and practically running away.

"You're evil," I state, desperately trying to hold back my laughter as the door closes behind him.

"What? No. I just totally made his day. Do you think he brought a spare pair of pants to work today because he blatantly just jizzed in those? Might accidentally pop a nipple out the next time he comes."

"Don't you dare," I warn, although my amusement ensures it doesn't sound all that serious.

"One thing is for sure," she says, sipping her fresh drink.

"That he needs to stop supplying you with such strong drinks?" I ask.

"Nope. We need to be gone by six. I'm not having him down here drooling, hoping for a quickie."

"After the way you've tortured him, you owe him a blowie at least."

"Evie Moore, do you talk to your father with that mouth?" she teases.

"Sadly, yes."

Unfortunately for poor Dylan, when five-thirty rolled around, Blakely and I made our way out of the hotel and into an Uber.

I felt bad for the poor guy. Although not bad enough to hang around and fix the situation for him.

Without meaning to, a heavy sigh falls from my lips as we head through the city, leaving the lights and excitement behind in favour of the dark and dingy surroundings we're used to in Lovell.

"You're still thinking about him, aren't you?"

"Dylan? Of course, I feel sorry for him," I say, hoping she'll accept the fact that I'm clearly lying and let go of what she really means.

Sadly, she doesn't do that.

"I'm not talking about Dylan, Eve."

My eyes drop from the buildings passing by in favour of my lap, Blakely's stare burning into the back of my head as she waits for me to be honest.

I know she's worried. I totally understand that. It's been killing her all afternoon not to talk about it. When she first turned up and questioned me about how I was feeling, how much I remembered of the night before. I know she's concerned he drugged me. Hell, I thought he was doing exactly that when he made me drink that last glass of champagne. But when I questioned him on it and he told me he hadn't put anything in it, I believed him.

It might have been incredibly naïve of me. I might have stalked him incessantly on Instagram for weeks, but that doesn't mean I know him. And it really doesn't mean that I should trust anything that comes out of his mouth.

I told Blakely just as much, but I could see the doubt in her eyes. I hated it, but I could hardly blame her.

We know who Alexander Deimos is, and that is enough to have red flags flapping wildly.

He is capable of literally anything. A little GHB in a glass of champagne is nothing that would make him lose sleep, I'm sure.

"It doesn't matter if I'm thinking about him or not. It's —" I cut myself off, swallowing down my pain at the words I need to say. "It's nothing. A mistake. All of it. He just... he owed me. And I hope you feel guilty, because the only reason he owed me was because you ruined it all the first time."

"Nice," she jokes. "You get taken to a hotel room by a hot mafia soldier, and it's my fault."

Finally lifting my eyes, I glare at her on the other side of the back seat.

"Too soon?" she asks with a wince.

"Just forget it. All of it. That's what I'm going to do," I lie. It's what I should do, but I can practically hear my phone and his Instagram account calling to me.

Goddamn him and his hypnotising silver eyes, arrogant smirk and talented fingers.

I hate him.

Hate. Him.

The car pulls up at our first stop.

"Right, I'll go grab the rug rat," Blake says, pushing the back door open. "Won't be a tick."

She walks toward Zay's best friend's house, but before she gets anywhere near, the door opens and Zay comes rushing out with a massive smile on his face.

Some tension locking up my muscles abates the moment I see him so happy.

Josh's mum appears a few seconds later and she and

Blake share a few words before the two of them walk toward the car.

"Evie," Zay says happily when he sees me sitting here waiting for him. "Did you have a good night with your friend?" he asks innocently as he buckles himself in.

"My friend?" I ask, glaring at my sister over Zay's head.

"Yeah, Blake said you were having a sleepover with a friend after work."

Blake shrugs innocently.

"Yeah, it was good, bud."

"Did you have a midnight feast?" he asks, making Blakley snort unattractively.

"Yep," she agrees, quickly trying to cover up her reaction while I pray the car will just swallow me whole. "Plenty of eating going on."

Jesus Christ.

I shoot Blake a death glare and breathe a sigh of relief when she changes the subject by asking him what he's been up to.

He's getting older, and it's not going to be long until we're both going to have to confess a lot of things to him. There's no way I'm allowing him to start at Lovell and have other kids tell him what his older sisters really do for a living.

It's one of the reasons I almost didn't start camming. The thought of anyone ever showing Zay fills me with dread. But I also don't want to live my life in fear. And if it pays off, then we can move, Zay can attend a better school, and life can be totally different for all of us.

But why is it as I even think about moving away from the city, which isn't even within reach right now, that I feel a pang of hurt leaving *him* behind?

The second we get into our flat, Zay runs to his room so

he can start gaming online with the friend he only just left. I would tease him about his addiction, but I feel like a hypocrite when I'm harbouring one of my own.

Dad is nowhere to be seen. Nothing new there, and I'll be happy if it stays that way. From the smell in the flat, though, I'd hazard a guess that he's not too far away. Gross.

I throw the living room window open as I pass, moving toward the kitchen for a bottle of water.

I've barely twisted the cap when there's a knock at our front door.

One look from Blake and I know she's not going.

"Fine," I hiss.

"What? I haven't ordered anything," she argues.

"So that has to mean I have," I quip.

She shrugs as she grabs the TV remote and gets comfortable.

Pulling the door open, I find our usual delivery guy staring back at me.

"Hey, Dave. How's it going?" I ask. He's an older guy. Married with three kids. He's really quite sweet, always ensures our parcels are delivered and not left out for anyone to steal like other companies do.

"Not bad, not bad. Just the one today."

He passes me over a slim box before nodding his head and marching down the hallway toward the stairs.

"Have a good evening."

He waves at me over his shoulder before disappearing.

"What is it?" Blake asks before I've even had a chance to close the door.

"Seriously?" I hiss.

"What?" she argues.

"Does the box look invisible to you?"

"Jeez, you're no fun when you're hungover."

"I'm not hung— just shut up, yeah?"

Seeing as it's got my name on the label, I rip the box open as I walk back to my abandoned water bottle in the kitchen. My eyes almost pop out of my head when I pull the contents out.

"What is it?" Blake askes again.

"It's…" I turn it over, double-checking that I'm not seeing things. "It's a date rape testing kit. And…"

I pick up the scrap of paper that fell out with the smaller box. My chin drops in shock.

I told you that I didn't need drugs to get back between your legs. But just in case you need confirmation.

Yours,

Alexander

"Huh, weird," Blake says over my shoulder, letting me know she's come to be nosey.

Dragging my attention from his handwriting, I narrow my eyes at her suspiciously.

"What?" she asks, sounding guilty as fuck. "Okay, fine. I might have messaged him on Instagram."

"Blakely," I shriek.

"What? I was worried that he'd drugged you."

"I told you that he didn't."

She sighs. "No offence, Evie, but you couldn't have known. He might have given you a mild dose."

"Fucking hell. I can't believe you."

"You'd rather I just allow him to run around town acting like he's God, taking random women to hotel rooms and having his way with them?"

"He didn't… that's not… fuck, Blake," I state at her, completely outraged. "I thought you trusted me."

"Babe, I do. You know I do. The person I don't trust here is him. The first time you met him, he had you down on your knees because he thought you were stealing from him. The second time, I caught him eat—"

"Don't," I hiss, holding my hand up to stop her.

"And the third—"

"Yeah, okay. I get your point. But I'd also just like to point out that you're not my mother, and I can deal with this stuff without your meddling."

"Please, just do the test. Then we can all be sure what we're dealing with," she begs.

"What does it even matter? It's done. Over."

She stares at me, giving me the puppy dog eyes that she knows I can't refuse.

"Fine. But then we're never talking about any of this again. Okay?"

"Sure," she lies. "Whatever you want."

I flip her off as I walk toward our bedroom with the damn test in hand.

I quickly read the instructions before doing what I need to do. The fact it says that it needs to be done as soon as possible after suspected spiking doesn't fill me with confidence. This is going to be negative even if he had drugged me.

Despite knowing that, I do my thing then wash my hands and attempt to tidy up the mess that is my hair as I wait for the result.

"Finally," I mutter when it shows.

Taking the whole thing, cup of pee and all to the kitchen, I put it on the counter in front of Blake.

"Happy?" I bark.

She looks at it before snatching the instructions from me to look at the image of the two results it can show for confirmation.

"No, not really. But I'm glad to see it's negative."

I keep my mouth shut. No good can come of me pointing out just how unreliable that test was. If it's put her mind at rest, then I'm not going to mess it up.

"Just put it all in the bin," I say, shoving it all toward her, needing it out of sight. I already know I stand no chance of getting it out of my mind.

"You sure you don't want to keep this?" she asks, holding the note between us. "A reminder."

With one final glare, I spin on my heels and march toward our bedroom, slamming the door behind me like a petulant child.

I stomp around tidying my shit up, although there isn't much of it—as usual, it's all Blake's stuff lying around.

Before long, I've grabbed my tablet and I curl up on the bed with a blank page before me and memories of a certain boy filling my mind.

Before I can stop myself, I start drawing, quickly losing myself in my art. I've got an hour before I need to get ready to work, and I don't intend on spending that time arguing with Blake or staring at his Instagram.

Everything is calm until there's a loud bang out in the living area and a deep voice booms, "Evie."

My heart sinks into my stomach. Nothing good ever comes from Derek calling my name like that.

With a sigh, I put my tablet to sleep and place it and my pen on the bedside table.

After checking my reflection briefly, I pull the door open to face the man who seems to control a little too much of my life right now.

When I agreed to step up and take over Blakely's shifts while she was sick, I didn't realise it came with handing my puppet strings over to the man who likes us to call him uncle. Seriously gross.

"Ah, there she is, little miss vixen."

Double gross.

I swear to God, if I ever find out he's been watching any of my camming sessions, I will throw up on his feet right there and then. He might not actually be my uncle, but he's been in our lives... well, all our lives. It's wrong. So fucking wrong.

"What is it, Derek?" I ask coldly. "I need to get ready for work."

A weird sense of dread and excitement fills me at the thought of getting back in my cage at Paradise. Alex knows I work there now. Will he turn up again and watch me?

Or was his middle-of-the-night disappearing act evidence that he's had his fill of me?

He finished what he started, he made me come, stroked his ego, and now we're over.

That thought really shouldn't hurt as much as it does.

"Change of plans tonight," he says, making my steps falter as I try and escape back to our bedroom. "You're not at Paradise."

"Why?" I ask, hating that I'm actually disappointed.

What is wrong with me?

"I've got something else for you. I don't have the location confirmed yet but—"

"No, Derek. You can't send her to—"

"I can and I will. They'll love her. I would offer for you to join her, but we both know you're not up for it. Plus, I've got something else to offer you. We'll talk in a bit, yeah?"

"Where are you sending me?" I don't know why I'm even asking. I already know the answer. I've watched Blakely live this life long enough to know what it means when Derek doesn't have a location.

"A car will be here for you at nine-thirty. Be ready." He

throws a bag at me before sauntering down the hallway toward our father's bedroom. He turns back at the last minute and grins; it's nothing but malicious. "Do a good job and I'll pay you double. The rest of what I owe you is in that bag." With a nod, he disappears.

Opening the bag, I peer at the outfit inside before digging around for the roll of cash. Okay, so it could be worse, I guess.

"This wasn't the deal," Blakely fumes.

"It's just one night. They're probably short. I'm not sure he'd ask otherwise," I say, like there's even a chance of Derek actually caring about either of us past the money we bankroll for him. "He doesn't offer up double pay for nothing."

"He won't pay you double," Blakely sulks. "He always finds an excuse to get out of it."

She continues to fume as silence falls around us.

"I'm going to shower; then will you help me get ready?" I ask, hoping it'll help distract her.

"You know I will. And I'll order pizza. You're going to need sustenance for tonight."

I've got my fingers wrapped around the bathroom door handle before the question spinning around my head falls from my lips without permission.

"Do you think he'll be there?"

"Evie," she sighs.

"I know. I'm sorry."

I slip into the bathroom before she can say anything else that I don't want or need to hear.

I should stay well away. I know that. But this kind of feels like fate... no?

21

ALEX

Dad doesn't tell me anything other than to get ready and to meet him at his place.

It doesn't fill me with joy, but I don't have any choice but to follow orders like a good little soldier. It's what I've always been taught to do, and I won't stop now.

From the minute we were born, or not long after, we've been trained to live this life.

I'm sure our grandfather was monitoring us for our skills before we were even walking. And then he spent years coming up with his training regime that would either make us or break us. I'm not even sure at this point if I'm glad he never broke us or not.

If it were the latter, we could have left with Mum. Started new lives. Been... normal.

I can barely hold in the laugh that thought causes.

Normal.

There's nothing normal about us.

About any of us.

From almost as early as we can remember, we've all been trained.

Theo and Nico moulded into the leaders of the future. Toby encouraged to pursue his skills with IT to ensure the Family is on top of all the modern developments. Seb, although not trained by his father or grandfather like the rest of us, has been trained to lead, to one day be the capo his father used to be. Daemon, our resident devil, and his unique torturing methods to get blood out of a stone when needed. And me, the resident softie with the skills to seduce information out of our enemies. Hell, even our allies, when the need arises.

There was a time when I thought I'd definitely drawn the long straw where training was concerned. But as time passed, I realised I was wrong.

I might not have had the brutal treatment Daemon did when I was allowed to walk out of our grandfather's shed, but there's a very good chance his career choice for me is going to fuck my life up more than his.

He's found an incredible girl who can accept that he maims and kills for a living. She embraces his darker side and loves him because of it.

No woman will ever love and accept me with what I'm forced to do.

How could they?

Why would they?

With my mood darkening by the second, I put my phone to sleep without looking at Instagram or the tracking app. What good would it do?

I've got a job to do tonight. The last thing I need is her up in my head, making me wish I were elsewhere. Making me wish I were with her.

I dress on autopilot, pulling my suit on in the hope it'll turn me into the robot my grandfather forced me to be.

Shut down your feelings. All you need is actions and a

whole lot of manipulation and you can get everything you need.

A violent shudder rips down my spine as I hear his voice as if he's right behind me.

Fuck, I hated him back then. And if it's possible, I hate him even more now, despite him being worm food.

My reflection taunts me in the mirror as I get ready. I might not pull a wig on like Evie does before heading to work, but I'm not far behind her, changing myself so that I can hide who I really am the best I can.

By the time I pocket my phone and wallet, I've locked the real me inside the box I keep inside for nights like these, and I'm ready to do whatever is going to be asked of me.

The second I pull my front door open, I find two figures standing a little farther down the hallway about to step into their flat.

"Hey, man," Daemon calls, spotting me before I can hide. His eyes drop to my suit and understanding washes over his face. "You got a job tonight?"

Letting my door slam behind me, I walk toward them, smiling at Calli as I go.

"Yep, Dad called about half an hour ago. Any clue what it is?" I ask, already able to see in Daemon's eyes that he has a very good idea.

Fucker might think he can fool everyone, but I see more than the rest. I'm his other half, for fuck's sake. We shared a womb for... well, not quite nine months. There's not much he can get past me. Even if he doesn't know it.

Like Calli, for instance. He thought he had that secret locked up tight. Little did he know, I'd been watching him watch her for fucking years. It was so damn obvious to me. I also saw the changes in him when things started up between them. They were subtle. The others had no chance of seeing them. But I did.

"It's okay," Calli says. "I'll go in and you can talk."

She moves toward the door with her shoulders slumped. I'm more than aware of how much she hates being kept in the dark. But while things have changed recently, there are always going to be things she can't be party to.

"No, Angel," Daemon says, wrapping his fingers around her upper arm and hauling her back into his side. He drops a reassuring kiss on her temple before his eyes come back to mine.

A knot twists tightly in my stomach before he drops a bomb I was half expecting.

"We're working with the Riveras."

"Shit," I hiss.

"I don't know any more than that."

"I guess it was obvious when they turned up that they'd want something."

"Even more so when they did us a favour with Brad the Bellend."

"Which we repaid with Italian blood."

"That was never going to be enough though, was it?" Daemon states.

"Is what you're doing with them connected to what Brad was doing? The trafficking ring?" I ask.

"Possibly. The Riveras have their fingers in more pies than we do. It could be anything."

"Reassuring," Calli whispers absently.

"It's all good, baby C. You know we've got this."

She smiles up at me, but it's anything but reassuring.

Before I get to say anything, Daemon interrupts.

"Your girlfriend know you've got a job tonight?"

That question soon wipes the smile off Calli's face.

"Don't know what you're talking about," I mutter, walking around them, ready to escape.

"If you seriously think we haven't seen the post, then you're an even bigger idiot than I thought."

"You stalk me, little bro?" I ask teasingly.

"Gotta get some entertainment from somewhere. TV is shit these days."

I flip him off over my shoulder and continue walking away. It's only when Calli speaks that my steps falter.

"You don't have to do this. Not if she means something to you."

I fight to drag in the air I need, her words wrapping around my chest like a belt being tightened, crushing my ribs.

"Have a good night," I call before making a beeline for the lift and getting the hell out of there before Calli can say anything else to make me question everything.

I suck in a deep breath the second I'm alone in the small, enclosed space and focus on what I need to do, locking everything else out but my job.

By the time I let myself into Dad's house, the home I grew up in, I have my mask firmly in place and I'm ready to get this job done and over with.

I go straight for his office, knowing that it's most likely where he is.

The second I step into the room, my eyes zero in on his desk and I have to fight to keep the memories at bay.

"Son," he greets, forcing my eyes to where he's sitting in his office chair, studying me as if something has changed.

I guess I shouldn't be surprised that word has already spread about my phone call to Galen telling him to poach a certain dancer from the Italians so we can protect her.

"Give me the details that were too important to spill over the phone."

The fact he didn't just tell me has alarm bells ringing. I highly doubt our phones have been compromised, but when the stakes are high, things are just better done in person.

"I need you to clone a phone and laptop," he starts.

"Okay, easy. Whose?" I ask, lowering my ass to the chair and crossing my arms over my chest casually, desperately trying to hide the fact I'm already on edge over this whole thing.

"No one we've ever come across before. But it's his wife's birthday, and we've discovered she's got a kink he wants to give her as a surprise."

"A kink?" I ask, already dreading what's about to come out of my father's mouth.

"She wants him to watch her with—"

"Yeah, okay. I've got it," I say, cutting him off before he says any more. It's really not necessary. I heard those unspoken words loud and clear.

"They're expecting to meet you at Twenty-Five for drinks and then... well, you know. Do whatever you need to do to get your hands on what we need."

"Got it." This isn't my first rodeo, and something tells me that it'll be far from my last.

"Everything you need is there." He nods to a bag sitting on the other chair. "Get it back to me ASAP."

"You got it. What time are they expecting me?"

He glances at the clock. "Within the hour."

"I'd better get moving then."

Pushing to my feet, I reach for the bag and walk toward the door.

"Son," he calls, stopping me from escaping as quickly as I'd like.

Glancing back over my shoulder, I hold his eyes.

"Be careful. This couple is connected to some dangerous people. We're already more tied up in this than I want to be."

"You don't need to worry about me, old man. I know what I'm doing."

Without another word, I duck out of the room and march toward the front door, frowning when my eyes land on a vase full of dead flowers in the hallway I missed on my way in.

Looks like dear old dad has fucked and chucked another housekeeper.

I sit for a few minutes in my car a little down the street from the restaurant. Dread sits heavy in my gut as I stare at the sleek sign that sticks out from the building.

Nothing good happens here. This was where shit hit the fan with Nico and Bri. And I really don't want any kind of night that ends in a car crash like that. Literally or metaphorically.

Pulling my visor down, I stare at my reflection in the small mirror, hating what I see looking back at me.

The dread gets heavy, unease and disgust with myself trickling through my veins.

But what am I meant to do?

Refuse a job?

I shake my head at my own crazy thoughts.

That's not how this shit works. Dad or any of the other capos say jump, and we immediately ask how high.

One day, we'll be the ones making the demands. But until that time comes, we're soldiers that have to get our hands dirty and uncover the answers those above us need.

Slamming the visor back up with more force than necessary, a grunt of irritation spills from my lips.

I check my phone—anything to put off the inevitable. Opening Instagram, I find the conversation with the woman I assume is Evie's sister.

My latest message has been read, but she hasn't responded. I've no idea if that's a good thing or not.

She has to know that test needed to be taken first thing this morning if it was going to be any kind of reliable. I'm just hoping the fact that I acted on her message accusing me of taking advantage of her sister proved something. I mean, if I had actually drugged her, would I be offering up a test to prove I was guilty? Even if I knew it was unlikely to be reliable so many hours later?

Shutting the app down, I shove the phone back in my pocket.

The desire to shoot a snap of myself before a big date might be strong, but I can't. Not like this. This side of me doesn't get posted on social media. Ever.

With no other reason to put off going inside, I shove my door open, square my shoulders and march toward the restaurant.

The second I step inside, I know my couple.

They're sitting at the bar, her with an elaborate cocktail, him with a whisky, both of them smiling at each other as they lean in close and talk.

And if I didn't already know it was them, the smile that lights up her face the second she spots me moving closer is the confirmation I need.

Seeing her excitement, her husband turns to look in my direction.

This is the worst part. The people we target aren't often stand-up citizens who just want a hot and steamy night. They're purposefully chosen, the way we manage to slip into their lives to extract the information we need meticulously planned.

If either of them has any kind of suspicion of who I really am, it will all go to shit. It's one of the many reasons Dad roasts me any chance he gets about my online presence. Especially when it's not just my face he needs to worry about. If they've ever been unlucky enough to come across Daemon before, then my cover would be blown.

He's right. I know he is. But I also refuse to continue allowing every part of my life to be controlled by him and our dead grandfather. The person I am right now is just a part of my life; it isn't my whole existence. And I refuse to allow it to be.

I'll play the game now, but I refuse to do it for any longer than necessary.

Daemon might have fully embraced the dark and fucked-up side of him that our grandfather nurtured. He needs to spill blood, to cause pain. It's a kind of fucked-up therapy for him and everything that continues to haunt him.

Me, though? I don't fucking need this.

I can get laid perfectly fine on my own without having to seduce targets. One trip to Hades and I can live out any of my kinky fantasies without much effort.

I certainly don't need to be set up.

But here I fucking am.

Plastering on a fake-arse smile, I continue to close the

space between me and the couple, confident that neither of them are about to pull a gun on me for being Cirillo.

"Hi, I'm Aidan," I lie, reciting the shit on the profile Dad left in the bag now hanging over my shoulder, along with the tech I'll need tonight.

"Hi, Aidan. I'm Tessa. We're so excited that you could join us tonight."

Her smile literally lights up her face as she bounces on her barstool.

"This is my husband, Jude."

Ripping my eyes away from her glittering eyes, I turn to him and hold my hand out.

"Nice to meet you," I say politely, not missing the hesitation in both his eyes and his handshake.

No need to ask which one of them took the lead on this little birthday present.

"I guess I should buy the birthday girl a drink," I say, laying on all the charm as I smile back at Tessa once more.

They're younger than I expected. Neither of them can be older than their early thirties. And thankfully for me, they're an attractive couple.

There is nothing worse than turning up to these jobs and finding an old, haggard, desperate-for-attention singleton waiting for me to make their entire year.

It really isn't the highlight of the job.

In the past, I might have even enjoyed getting jiggy with this couple and making all of Tessa's dreams come true. Well, assuming Jude doesn't call time on it all before we even get started. He looks about ready to run for the exit already.

It makes me wonder what the hell he's done to require me to weasel my way into their life so I can clone his tech. Clearly, he's not always a scared little mouse.

Tessa orders herself a fresh cocktail and another whisky for her husband before she turns to me.

"Oh, um… just lemonade, please. I don't like to drink when…" I trail off, forcing my eyes to drop to check her out.

It's not a hardship. As I said, she's hot.

But she's not her.

As the image of Evie laid out before me last night plays out in my head, I almost change my mind and ask for neat vodka instead.

I can't. I need to be sober to do my job, even if it does make it that much harder to force myself through it.

You don't deserve her anyway.

She'd never want you.

It's a moot point.

Do your job.

And I do. I listen to my own advice as we take our seats and eat our dinner. I make bullshit small talk based on the information Dad gave me. Making up lies about what it's like to be a university student in such a big city. Blah, blah, blah. Each word is more boring than the last, and I'm soon wishing my lemonade was something much stronger again.

Even more so when Jude reluctantly asks for the bill.

My stomach knots up as Tessa squeals in excitement, the many cocktails and glasses of wine she's consumed ensuring that she's more than ready for her birthday present.

Just as we leave in favour of the Uber Jude calls for us, my phone buzzes in my pocket.

As discreetly as I can, I pull it free and glance down at the screen.

Fuck's sake.

I've been waiting for fucking ages for a fight, and they finally call one when I'm on a job.

Shoving my phone away with a huff of annoyance, I pray that I can get this over with as soon as possible and make it out to the location burning up my phone before it's all over.

Hell knows I'm going to need to pummel some cunt into the ground after what I'm about to endure.

22

EVIE

I know what to expect from tonight long before the car that was waiting outside our building as Derek promised pulls toward the old abandoned industrial park on the very outskirts of Lovell.

It's as close as they ever get to our part of town to host these events. Anyone would think the wealthy, egotistical members of the Cirillo and Mariano Families don't want to lower themselves by stepping any deeper into the ghetto.

I mean, I get it. But if they expect the Wolves to host this shit, then they should allow them to drag them into hell. We have to live here. I'm sure they could all cope with one night.

I shift on the back seat of the car as the driver pulls into the deserted land that surrounds the warehouses. The ground is uneven and full of potholes that we bounce in and out of. My driver complains about his suspension and paintwork with each one we hit, but I keep my mouth shut. What the hell could I say that would make any of this better?

I've watched my sister get dressed for one of these

events more times than I can count over the years. I've also watched her come home, tired, sweaty, and with more than a few horror stories about what happens at Circuit fight nights. And then there was the night last year she came home coughing her guts up from smoke inhalation and soot all over her skin. I'd never been more terrified.

They're bloody, brutal, no-holds-barred, violent shows of power.

The main players from this side of the city might put their differences aside for the events, or at least, they're meant to. I've heard stories that would suggest otherwise, but whatever.

It's not my place to judge or question what these criminals do. I've just got to show up, look pretty, hand out a few drinks, keep men entertained and hope that Derek comes through on his promise of double pay.

I'm bloody hoping he does, because I don't put myself in the position of being groped by some disgusting older man lightly.

Keep telling yourself that you're doing this for the money, Evie. You want to see him.

Thankfully, the car pulls to a stop in front of a set of rusted double doors, halting my internal argument.

My phone buzzes in my coat pocket and before I get out, I slip it free.

Blakely: Keep your eyes open tonight, and be safe. If all else fails, aim for the balls. It'll drop them to their knees every time.

I can't help but smile at her advice.

Blakely: And if he's there, please be smart.

Evie: Love you too. Give Zay a squeeze for me.

When I left, they were planning a movie night, seeing as Zay is allowed to stay up late on a Saturday. Sounded perfect to me. I yearned to snuggle up on the sofa with them and watch whatever they finally decided on. The debate was still going strong as I left the flat.

"You getting out, or what?" the driver barks, stealing my attention.

"Uh... yeah. Thanks."

"I'll be back later to collect you."

"Fantastic. I can hardly wait." Without waiting for a response, I push the door open and climb out.

The balmy early summer air rushes under my trench coat, reminding me of just how warm it was earlier.

I love spring and summer. They're by far my favourite times of the year. Feeling the sun warming my skin makes me think of long, hot days far, far away from Lovell and all the horrors that hide among these streets.

The image of a cabin somewhere in the woods where I could sunbathe naked and never fear anyone stumbling across me fills my head. I don't have expensive tastes; I don't need to leave the country. I just want peace and quiet. No pounding music, heated stares, and the constant fear that tonight will be the night where some drunk or high man will take things too far.

A shudder of fear races down my spine as I make my way to the doors.

It'll be fine. The men coming here tonight are coming for the violence, not the women.

Just like those I thought were going for the poker...

"Good evening," a well-dressed man that I've never met before says the second I slip through the doors. "Name?"

"Uh... E-Evie Moore. Derek sent—"

"All good, Miss Moore," he says, looking up from his clipboard. His eyes are cold and blank, making my stomach clench uncomfortably. And when his lips curl up in a smile I'm not sure is meant to be reassuring or threatening, the butterflies really start to take flight.

This was a mistake.

Even if he is here, it's not going to be worth it.

"Down the hallway, door on the left. You'll find the other girls." He checks his watch. "You've got twenty minutes, if you're lucky."

The door opens again and he dismisses me to find my way down to the others.

The second I push into the room, all eyes turn on me and I instantly regret my decision to be here. I should have argued, or at least tried. I could be at Paradise right now with friends. Or at least, after last night, I think Harper, Alyssa, and Naomi are my friends. Guilt twists up in my stomach. I just disappeared on them. And I'm not going to turn up to my shift tonight. Not exactly how you should treat friends.

Ignoring the stares of the unfamiliar girls, I pull my phone out and find Harper's contact.

My heart sinks when I find an unread message that I didn't see this morning and have now ignored all day.

> Evie: I'm so sorry, I didn't see this earlier. I'm not in tonight, last-minute change of plans. I hope you kill it. x

I hesitate to send it. She's probably spent all day

wondering if I'm okay. I know I would if she'd vanished like I did last night.

"Fuck it," I mutter to myself, hitting send and dropping it back into my pocket.

With the girls loitering around in here wearing very similar outfits to what I am under my coat, I let it fall from my shoulders and hang it from one of the hooks. Unlike Paradise, there aren't any lockers for our things. Blakely warned me, which is why the only thing I have with me is my phone. Thankfully, the ridiculous shorts are just about big enough to hide it inside.

"Hey, new girl," someone shouts, making my spine straighten.

Spinning around, I find everyone looking at me once again. The girl standing on an upturned crate lifts her chin, commanding both attention and respect.

Yeah, we'll see.

"Me?" I ask innocently, pointing at myself.

"Yeah, you," she snarls. "Are you sure you've got what it takes to work this fight? It's not some two-step barn dance, you know."

My brows lift at her audacity. Okay so I might not be Lovell's biggest bad-arse, but I'm hardly a delicate flower. Or at least, I like to think I'm not.

"I can handle it," I say, folding my arms in front of me, making my arguably small breasts pop up in the stupid cropped shirt thing I'm wearing.

Honestly, I can see where she got the barn dance idea from. We do all look a bit like slutty cowgirls. All we're missing is the boots and hats.

Her eyes run up and down the length of my body as if that will tell her all she needs to know about how I handle myself.

"We'll see." Her lips peel back as if just talking to me is insulting her.

Fine by me. I'm not here to make friends.

"I can handle myself," I say, feeling the need to defend myself again.

Tension crackles between us as she jumps down from her crate, landing on her stupid heels without so much as a wobble.

She closes the space between us, her eyes holding mine, her resting bitch face firmly in place.

"Don't say I didn't warn you."

A bell rings somewhere deeper in the warehouse and the group of girls surrounding their obvious ringleader all move toward the door and disappear.

"Ignore her. She's all bark and no bite," a soft voice says, emerging from a door I didn't see in the corner of the room.

"I dunno. I bet she could cause some damage with those talons."

The girl smiles.

"Maybe stay out of her way so you don't need to test that theory, huh?"

"I'll do my best."

"So, you're Blake's sister?"

"Uh..."

"It's okay. Blake and I did a few of these nights together. Had each other's backs. I've seen photos of you. Didn't think I'd ever see you here in person, though."

"Well, things don't always turn out how you're expecting," I mutter.

"How is she? I heard she was ill."

"Yeah, she's had a rough few months. She's almost there, though."

"Is she coming back?" she asks, sounding like she genuinely cares.

"She wants to. But her energy levels aren't where they used to be and—"

"That must be killing her. She lived to dance," she says, proving that she really does know Blake.

"She does. But she's restricted to doing it around our flat when she's feeling up to it right now."

She smiles softly before her eyes widen. "Shit. I'm Vickie, by the way. Sorry, I probably should have started with that."

"It's all good. It's nice to meet you."

A bell rings again, echoing through the steel walls surrounding us.

"Come on, we need to get out there. Our lives won't be worth living if Vincent finds us skiving."

"Vincent?"

"The guy at the entrance with the clipboard. Likes to think he's all important and shit."

"He isn't?" I ask.

"Oh, he totally is. He just likes everyone to know it." She pulls the door open and gestures for me to go first. "This is your first fight night, yes?"

"Is it that obvious?"

"You'll be fine. But there are a few things you need to know."

"Okay shoot. I need all the prep I can get."

"This isn't like working in a club. The place gets packed and you'll be expected to be right in the middle of it. Expect wandering hands, lewd suggestions, and more drunk men than you know what to do with."

"Sounds like my idea of hell."

"Security is tight. It has to be with events like this, and

they won't accept anyone overstepping. But that doesn't mean that people won't try."

My thoughts shoot straight to my first poker night when that letch grabbed me and forced me onto his lap.

My skin breaks out in goosebumps and my blood turns to ice.

There's a reason I agreed to be locked in a cage for all my shifts at the club.

"Try to stay to the edges of the crowd and keep one hand free, just in case."

I don't want to know what she means by 'just in case', so I keep my lips shut as we walk into the vast space of the warehouse.

There's a makeshift bar set up down one side, and in a line down the centre are three boxing rings.

The girls who were in the back room are all grabbing trays full of cans of beer and positioning themselves at what must be the main entrance. There are men littered around the room setting up, but I don't pay them any attention.

Not two seconds later, there's a bang so loud that it makes the ground beneath me vibrate and two massive roller doors are pulled open.

The rumble of male voices fills the air before they pour inside, taking drinks from the girls and racing for prime position at the rings.

The bell rings again, only it's so loud in here that a shriek rips from my lips.

"You need to lock that down. This lot will smell fear from a mile off," Vickie warns.

I take a step back as more and more men fill the huge space, my heart racing at the thought of getting in the middle of them all.

More and more enter, and I'm not sure why one catches

my attention. At first, I hope it's because it's Alex and that my body recognises him. But I soon realise that's not the case, because when my eyes find the ones that are staring at me and making the hairs rise on the back of my neck, it's not his silver ones I find, but a pair I never, ever wanted to look into again.

Grant. The guy from the poker game.

I've no idea if he recognises me with blonde hair and after so long. But I don't think it matters. The way he's looking at me makes me think he's already planning things he shouldn't be.

I stumble back a few steps, my heart racing and my palms sweating.

"Evie, are you okay?" Vickie asks, but it sounds like she's at the other end of a tunnel as my panic begins to take over.

"I-I can't do this," I whisper.

"You have to," she says, stepping closer, her fingers wrapping around my upper arms to shake me out of it. "You can't leave now you're here. Vincent wouldn't allow it."

The bell rings again and a roar of excitement rips through the vast space.

"The fights are starting. That'll distract almost everyone. You can do this, Evie. Breathe with me."

I focus on her instructions to breathe in and out, and after a few seconds, I begin to relax.

"Come on, we'll stick together and work the perimeter. You've got this."

But despite her assurances, I really don't think I do.

If she's right, and I can't leave, then the only other thing I need to focus on is staying the hell away from that man.

23

———

ALEX

Tessa's hand gripped mine so hard it almost hurt as she practically dragged me through their three-story townhouse in favour of hanging out in their bedroom.

She was eager to get the party started.

Her husband, though, wasn't quite as impatient.

As she pulls me along, I discreetly look into each room we pass, trying to find his office.

I've already seen him empty his pockets, including his phone, on the unit in the hallway, so that one is going to be easy.

The laptop though... in a house with this many rooms. Well, the thought of hunting it down doesn't fill me with joy.

I'm just hoping that Jude's jealousy will work in my favour.

He doesn't want this. And I have enough experience in these situations to know that if one partner is having doubts, then things usually come to a grinding halt fast.

It all seems like a good idea in theory. We can all

fantasise about the kinds of things that get us hot. But the reality of actually watching someone screw your wife, in your bed, right in front of you, is probably very different from your imagination.

Before I've spotted an office, Tessa is opening a door to the master bedroom.

It's immaculate. She's probably tidied it within an inch of her life, ready for this moment.

The door is kicked closed behind me, making my heart rate increase.

There have been plenty of times in the past that I've wanted to turn and run when we get to this point.

But my reasons for not wanting to go through with this tonight are very different from anything I've ever experienced before.

"Is this what you imagined, love?" Jude asks from behind me, the doubt in his voice making my teeth grind.

Tessa swallows. It's the first time tonight she's shown any kind of nerves over the situation. Being wasted probably helps.

But instead of listening to her doubts, she holds her head high and says, "Yes."

"Okay," Jude growls, walking deeper into the room and coming to stand beside us. "You're in charge here, love. It's your birthday. Tell us what you want."

Her eyes hold his for a beat before she jerks her head to the chair in the corner.

"Go sit down. I want your eyes on me while Aiden touches me."

Now it's my turn to swallow nervously.

Jude might not appear to be a threat, but I've learned over the years that just because they don't look dangerous, it doesn't mean they aren't. This room could be stacked out with weapons.

"Fine," he agrees, walking over and dropping his arse into the chair.

"So," Tessa purrs. "What are you waiting for?"

My phone continues buzzing in my pocket. It's been going crazy since the location of tonight's fight came through. I could easily use it as an excuse. Pretend that my father has had a really unfortunate accident and run out of this house without the intel we need.

It's so fucking tempting.

But I can't.

I was not trained to quit. I was trained to do the job no matter what.

So I lock everything else about my life down and focus on the task at hand.

I hate myself more than I ever have before, but I have no choice.

This is who I am.

What I was born for, trained for.

I'm a Cirillo soldier.

And my job comes first. Always.

Reaching out, I brush a lock of her almost-black hair from her shoulder. Swallowing down the bile that's threatening to rush up my throat, I lean forward and press my lips to her neck, refusing to go anywhere near her lips like I always do when I'm working.

She shudders beneath my simple touch, a quiet moan falling from her lips. But her reaction isn't the most obvious. That's the gasp from her husband and the way he jumps to the edge of the chair as if he's about to rip me from his wife.

By my guest, mate.

She's all yours if you want her.

"Yes," Tessa groans, her fingers twisting up in my hair. "Keep going."

Glancing up, I find her eyes locked on her husband.

If I gave a shit, I'd try to figure out the dynamic between them. But really, all I care about is getting what I need and walking straight out of this place.

"Tessa," Jude growls.

"Watch, Jude. Watch as Aiden gets me naked. You want it as much as I do. Look how hard you are already."

I squeeze my eyes closed, hoping that she's wrong.

Is his reluctance an act? Is this all some fucked-up kind of role-play that I've managed to get in the middle of?

Shooting a look over her shoulder, I watch as he rubs his cock through his trousers.

Fuck my life.

I'm torn between working slowly and hoping it gets too much for him, or her. Or going as fast as I can and getting it over with.

Focus and do the job, boy.

This is what you're good at.

This is what makes you an invaluable soldier.

With my grandfather's voice in my head, I set to work.

Before long, I have Tessa stripped bare before me.

Both her words and her body beg for more as I place careful kisses over her skin.

I know where to touch, how to drive women crazy. I focus on the innocent places, still holding out hope that this won't need to go all the way.

"I'm so wet," Tessa whispers, although loud enough for her husband to hear.

He's given up trying to pretend he's not into this and is sitting with his cock in his hand, his eyes locked on his wife's body.

Every time she cries out in pleasure, his hand moves faster.

"I want you to taste me, Aiden. Let my husband watch you eat me. You can tell him how sweet I taste."

Wrapping my hands around the back of her thighs, I throw her onto the bed and spread her thighs.

I look at her through hooded eyes, pretending to be more turned on than I ever have been in my life.

She's got a good body. She obviously works out. But it's not the one I want. And when I get to her cunt, that feeling of disappointment only hits harder.

It's not Evie's perfect, pretty little pussy from last night that I couldn't get enough of.

"Please," she moans, rolling her hips in invitation. Her husband works his cock almost violently. I can't help wondering if he's punishing himself—if she's punishing him —for something. People do all kinds of fucked-up things. I'm sure it barely scratches the surface of crazy where relationships are concerned.

Sucking in a deep breath, I begin sliding my palms down her trembling thighs.

I say all the right words, have her moaning for me despite the fact I'm barely touching her.

She begs and pleads for me to give her what she needs, but I hold out, keeping one eye on him.

Please, fucking break. Demand I stop.

Anything. Fucking anything to stop this.

But it doesn't happen, and I can only put off the inevitable for so long.

Dropping to my stomach, I hover my face right there, closing my eyes and imagining she's someone else. Forcing her smell out of my head and focusing on another.

I part my lips as her fingers tighten on my hair, dragging me closer.

I'm right there, about to connect with her, when everything comes crashing down around me.

Literally.

Pain explodes across my back before I'm shoved so hard to the side. I roll across the bed, my head colliding with the corner of the bedside table.

Lights flash behind my eyes as I fall to my arse, dropping my head into my hands as the pain only seems to get worse.

Wetness coats my fingers, and when I pull them from my face, I find blood dripping down them.

But before I can figure out what's going on while my head continues to spin, a loud moan rips through the air, forcing my eyes up.

On the bed, in the exact position I was just in is Jude, eating his wife out like the world depends on it.

I scramble back away from the bed, relief flooding my veins when neither of them seems to notice there's anyone other than them in the room.

"Jude, fuck. Yes. Right there. Fuck. I'm going to come all over your face."

"Not fucking yet you're not," he growls back. "Not until I remind you why the only man who should be eating this sweet pussy is me. This is mine, Tessa. Mine. Do you understand that?"

I get to my feet and silently move out of the room before I can hear her reply.

If she defies him and calls for me, then it's too fucking late.

All I can hope now is that they keep each other

distracted for long enough for me to do my job and get the fuck out of their house.

Throwing my bag over my shoulder, I pull out a pair of gloves before restarting my search for that laptop.

Thankfully, I find it sitting on a desk in the middle of an office on the ground floor.

But despite there being a floor between me and the master bedroom, Tessa's cries continue to hit my ears.

I mentally spur Jude on, willing him to drive his woman to the edge of sanity to give me the time I need.

The second I've cloned both the laptop and his phone, I let myself out of their house and walk calmly down the street and around the corner before calling for an Uber.

I've got somewhere else I need to be right now.

Somewhere that will help release the tension pulling at every muscle in my body.

I shoot Dad a message to tell him it's done, and the second my Uber turns up, I get in and get the hell out of dodge.

If I never have to see either of them again, it will be too soon.

"Holy shit, man. Are you okay?" the Uber driver says, reminding me that everything isn't hunky dory in my world right now.

"Oh, this?" I ask, gently pressing my fingertips to my temple. "Yeah. Just an accident. We're all good."

"Are you sure I shouldn't be taking you to the hospital?"

"I'm sure. Just drive, man. I've got places I need to be."

He agrees, although he doesn't seem very happy about it. Not that I care.

Getting in that ring and getting some cunt on the ground is all I can think about.

Finally, I open the group chat that's been blowing up

since the location landed, and I scroll through their conversation.

Daemon helpfully tells them that I'm on a job when they start tagging me over and over, asking if I'm too busy doing a whole host of things, although most involved having some part of my body inside my mystery girl. Fucking chance would be a fine thing.

By the time the car pulls up down the street from the old industrial estate where tonight's fight is being held, my knee is bouncing in anticipation and my fingers are curled into fists.

I've messaged Mickey demanding a spot. Probably not the best idea, seeing as I've already got dried blood down the side of my face.

But I need it.

I need it more than I think I ever have before.

I need tonight gone. It's either fight or fuck. And seeing as the one person I want to fuck needs to stay as far away from me as possible, it only leaves one option.

"Cheers, man. Have a good one," I say, climbing from the car.

He wants to be a good citizen and force me to go get checked out, I can see it in his eyes. But he knows better than to argue.

I march around the first derelict warehouse, dodging the potholes which are somehow full of water despite the fact it hasn't rained in... fuck knows how long.

The second I turn the corner, I make a beeline for the man guarding the door.

I recognise him instantly as one of us. He nods in greeting as I close the space between us.

"Mickey is waiting for you in the back room."

"Thanks, man."

"Good luck out there," he calls as I make my way to the man I want to see.

Noise echoes around the old building, the excitement from the main room and the fights happening right now filling the space. For the first time tonight, excitement shoots through my veins.

"Alexander Deimos," Mickey greets. "It's been too long, man."

I give him a one-armed man hug, slamming my fist against his back.

Pushing me back with hands on my shoulders, he studies my face, or more so, the blood.

"Are you sure you're good for this?"

"Yeah, man. I'm good. More than fucking good."

There are other guys in here. Some are getting ready to fight, and others have clearly lost already, nursing injuries that probably need medical attention.

Dumping my bag on an old chair, I start stripping out of my clothes. I throw them on the floor, wishing I could light them up and banish them from my life right along with the memories from tonight.

"Here," Mickey says, holding out a pair of shorts and trainers for me.

"You're the man, Mick."

I pull them on, adrenaline filling me so fast it makes my head spin.

Jumping up and down anxiously, I stretch out my muscles, my need to get out there and cause some pain getting the better of me.

It's been so fucking long since we've been able to do this. Everyone from our part of the city coming together to indulge in some friendly violence and gambling.

I've fucking missed it.

Getting in the ring is better than any other high out there.

Other than her.

"You got Xander tonight," Mickey tells me when we're almost at the door.

"Don't go easy on me, will you, Mick," I scoff.

"When the fuck have you ever wanted easy?"

24

EVIE

After my initial panic subsided, things improved.

Not long after the main doors slid closed, fighters emerged from a door at the back of the room and everyone's attention turned toward the rings.

I passed out trays of complimentary beer. I've no idea how one gets invited to these things, but from the money that seems to be being drunk in free alcohol, I suspect it comes at a high price.

Living in the middle of Lovell, it's hard to miss the fact that there's a dark underworld hiding just beneath the surface of normal life. But since dipping my toe into Blakely's world, it's never been more obvious.

Shouts and screams of the spectators echo around me as they urge the fighters on. And every now and then, when the volume of the crowd dips, the sickening collision of skin and the crunch of bones fills the air.

Each time I hear it, my stomach twists, threatening to spill its contents.

Why anyone would get up there and willingly hurt themselves in the name of fun, I literally have no idea.

I get the joy of winning—we all like that rush of adrenaline—but even the winners are stumbling out of those rings in pain and covered in blood.

And the losers... Well, I've seen more than a few carried out. A couple of which I wasn't even confident if they were even breathing.

It's horrific, brutal. And not something I'm going to forget for a while.

"See, it's not so bad, is it?" Vickie says when we meet at the bar to get our trays refilled.

"It's not great."

"Could be worse." And with those ominous words, she takes her tray and disappears into the crowd. The time of her babysitting me on the periphery of the action is over. I'm on my own now.

"Thank you," I say to the guy who's loading up the trays before spinning around and heading back into the chaos.

Despite Vickie's warning, so far, everyone has been pretty well-behaved. Any contact with others has been accidental. Their attention is too heavily focused on the fighters than us, thankfully.

I hand out more drinks and collect up empties as the fights continue around me.

I'm back at the bar once more for a refill when an almighty roar goes up around the warehouse.

"Jesus, what's going on?"

"It's Xander," the barman says, his eyes locked on the ring behind me. "He's a bit of a legend."

"Sounds like it," I say, quickly shooting a look over my shoulder to see what all the fuss is about. But with the mass of people surrounding the ring, I can barely see anything.

"Things are probably about to get wild. Be prepared."

I nod, never feeling less prepared for anything in my life. But nonetheless, I head back out.

I'm in a sea of bodies when the next roar goes up before the chanting begins.

The volume makes my head spin, and while I might look up to find out what's happening, it's pointless. I'm surrounded by men who are all easily a foot taller than me, even in my heels. The few women who are here tonight seem to either have front row seats or are sitting on someone's shoulders to get a better view.

Deciding it's better to put my head down and keep working, I push forward. Barely anyone takes a fresh drink, everyone's attention solely on the ring before us.

My ears ring with the noise, and what I can hear, I block out.

Sweat runs down my spine as I move through the screaming crowd. The temperature in here is unbearable. I've no idea how many bodies are inside, but it's way too many.

I shake my head at my own goody-two-shoes opinions and keep moving.

I'm bumped and jostled from all angles. By some miracle, I manage to keep the remaining drinks on my tray. Although, that all goes to shit when someone collides with my right side, sending my tray flying, and covering the man in front of me with what now must be lukewarm beer.

The guy who bumped me stumbles off without a word, leaving me to bend down and pick up my tray.

I'm almost at full height again when a large hand wraps around my upper arm, gripping so hard I have to fight not to complain. But when I look up into the eyes of the man holding me, I'm unable to keep the noise in and a scream rips from my throat.

It does little to help my situation. The noise is swallowed up by the crowd a beat before his filthy hand covers my mouth.

He easily overpowers me with his huge frame, walking me backward through the mass of bodies until my back collides with the wall before my head ricochets off it.

Black spots dance in my vision as pain seems to erupt in every inch of me.

All the air rushes from my lungs as Grant stares down at me with wildly excited, dark eyes.

I swallow nervously, attempting to fight, but he's too strong.

My entire body trembles as he looms over me. His beer-scented breath washes over my face, making bile race up my throat.

"You're a tease, and I'm not going to let you escape this time, little mouse."

A sob erupts—not that anyone would hear with his hand still clamped down on my mouth.

"You should have been mine at Christmas, but that entitled little prick stole you from me," he taunts as I stare up at him, wide-eyed in fear. "Did you really think the trashy blonde wig would stop me from recognising you?"

Reaching up, he twists his fingers in my wig and tugs it from my head.

The clips that were holding it in place refuse to give, and I swear he rips half my own hair out at the same time.

The tears that were already filling my eyes finally spill over as the pain shoots down my neck.

"Fuck, you're even better when you cry for me. I can only imagine how pretty you'll look sobbing around my cock."

He drops my wig at my feet, freeing up his hand to

squeeze my breast so hard it hurts, immediately making me cry harder.

We're surrounded by hundreds of people; how the hell has no one—

Before I manage to finish that thought, Grant's crushing weight and tight grip are suddenly gone as what can only be described as a roar from a wild animal fills my ears.

I stand there, frozen to the spot for a few seconds before reality comes back to me.

The crowd who had their backs to us only moments ago have now all turned this way and are staring down at the ground where a shirtless guy is throwing punch after punch at Grant's body.

He's like a fucking monster, not giving the creep a second to retaliate or even attempt to get away from him.

Recognition flickers at the edges of my thoughts, but the fear coursing through my veins is still too strong to grasp them.

I stumble from the wall, my legs barely steady enough to hold me up.

My knees buckle and I shut my eyes, bracing myself to hit the disgusting concrete floor at my feet, but it never happens.

"Whoa," a soft female voice says as arms wrap around me, keeping me upright.

I'm pulled into a warm body, and the second I suck in a sweet breath full of ladies' perfume, I relax a little.

"We've got you, it's okay," another voice says before a hand rests between my shoulder blades.

"Are they going to fucking stop him or what?" the first one snaps.

"I'm sure they will when they're ready."

"Jesus, Christ. Do we have to do everything?"

I'm transferred to another set of arms, and when I look up, I watch a woman in a pair of denim shorts and a black t-shirt march straight into the chaos and haul the shirtless guy from Grant.

She shouts something at him before throwing her arm back to gesture to me.

He stills, his shoulders dropping as his fists finally uncurl.

The man at his feet doesn't move, and it makes panic shoot through me.

If he's killed him because of what he did to me, does that make me an accessory?

But then, the shirtless guy turns toward me, and everything I couldn't quite grasp slots into place.

"No," I breathe, stepping away from the arms that are currently protecting me in my need to get away from this whole situation.

But as I take a step, the world around me tilts and everything goes black.

25

ALEX

Xander was getting the better of me. That was blindingly clear only seconds after I stepped into the ring.

But I wasn't going to go down easily. Especially while the crowd was wild.

They were like a pack of wolves who'd found a dead animal after months of starvation.

I understood. As Xander's fist collided with my cheek and I embraced the pain I was so desperate for, I roared like a feral beast, coming back at him savagely.

I wasn't going to win. I knew that just as well as he did. And I hate to admit it, but he actually went a little easy on me.

The head injury I'd already suffered tonight made my movements a little sluggish. Plus there was the fact that I was out of practise.

We'd been too busy dealing with the Italians, Brianna's disappearance, and a whole host of other shit for me to put time into training. Something I was regretting.

But the second I spotted movement in my peripheral as

Xander and I took a second to gather ourselves, everything came crashing down around me.

My vixen.

Before my brain registered what was really happening, I'd taken off across the ring, launched myself over the ropes and straight into the crowd, which, thankfully, parted for me.

The energy I was running low on while going up against Xander surged through me, and the second I was in touching distance, I unleashed everything I had on the motherfucker who thought he had a right to touch what was mine.

The second I got a look at his face. Well... I'm not sure I've ever felt anger like it.

I had every intention of killing him.

He deserved it the first time he put his hands on my little thief, forcing me to try and rearrange his face before he was dragged out of Dad's house with his tail between his legs.

But to try it again? He deserved to fucking die.

All I could see was red.

And when a hand wraps around my upper arm, attempting to pull me back, I almost take a swing at them as well.

The world around me fell away, the only thing I could focus on was the cunt on the floor at my feet.

Even when he stopped fighting, I still continued.

My fists were wrecked as pink-tinged sweat rolled down my body, soaking the waistband of my shorts.

I blink, fighting to break through the haze, and when my vision clears, I've never been more grateful in my life for holding back a punch before Stella stands there glaring at me with one brow quirked.

She growls something angrily in my ear, but I barely hear her with my blood roaring and my anger blazing. But I don't need to, because the second her eyes dart over her shoulder, I find my girl tucked safely into Emmie's side, I remember why I did this.

Evie's eyes widen as recognition sparks in their depths.

Her lips part, but if she says anything, I can't hear it over the chaos surrounding us.

She stumbles away from Emmie as if she's going to try to escape, but before she gets any further, her knees buckle and she starts to go down.

Just like when I first saw her, my legs move faster than my brain can compute, and I have her in my arms long before she hits the floor.

"Vixen," I growl, clutching her tighter to my chest.

But I get nothing in return.

Someone steps closer, pushing a lock of hair from Evie's face, allowing me to see her closed eyes.

A gasp of shock makes me look up, and I find Emmie staring down at Evie in surprise.

My brows knit, but she doesn't explain.

"We need to get her out of here."

"We've got it," Stella says, marching up to us with Seb hot on her heels. "I'll drive you back. Let's go." Stella shoves me gently on the shoulder to get me moving.

I take two steps before remembering what I should be doing.

Spinning around, I catch Theo's concerned yet intrigued eyes. He's not the only one watching me, but I don't spare any of the others a second.

"There's a bag out in the back room. It needs to be with my dad tonight."

"You got it, man. Call if you need anything else."

With a nod, I spin around and follow Seb and Stella out of the warehouse, leaving everything else behind in favour of taking care of my little thief.

Seb holds the back door of his car open for me while Stella drops into the driver's seat.

The second we're in, I try to make her comfortable. Thankfully, with her face tucked into my neck, I can feel her breath tickling across my skin, reassuring me that she's still with us.

"Be quick," I instruct as Stella brings the engine to life.

Seb chuckles.

"You don't need to worry," Stella says, throwing the car into gear and flooring the accelerator.

Stones ping against the paintwork, making Seb wince as we fly out of the car park, but he's not brave enough to say anything, and there's no way in hell I'm going to suggest she takes it easy.

Silence fills the car as we leave Lovell behind in favour of our side of the city.

"How's she doing?" Stella asks.

"Still out of it. Did you see what he did to her?"

She shakes her head.

"Didn't see anything until you flew through the air like Spiderman on a mission."

"No one touches her like that," I growl, immediately regretting it when Stella's excited eyes collide with mine in the rear-view mirror. "Oh don't start."

"I didn't say anything," she argues.

"You don't need to, I can see it in your eyes. And just so you know, the next time I'm in the back of your car with her, I'm repaying you for everything you forced me to endure."

"So it's serious then?" Seb asks, twisting around in the seat to study me.

My lips part to respond, but then the words I just spoke out loud come back to me and I swallow it.

My nostrils flare as I rip my stare from his in favour of Evie.

"No, it's not," I say quietly, "but that doesn't mean I can't torture the two of you a little."

"Big of you to assume we won't make the most of the situation."

"One of you will be driving," I point out.

"Won't be our first rodeo," Stella confesses.

"Fucking hell," I groan.

As my adrenaline begins to evaporate, pain starts to engulf my body.

I shift Evie a little so I can stretch my arm, and she moans quietly.

"It's okay, Vixen. I'm right here. You're going to be okay."

Stella's stare burns into the top of my head, but I refuse to look up and find her eyes in the mirror again. It's better to pretend we're alone.

The longer I can forget about the inquisition that will come my way after all this is over, the better.

I trail behind Seb and Stella as they move through the building, opening doors for us. Each step I take gets harder than the last. But I can't give in to it. I refuse to. Not when my vixen needs me.

"Almost there," I whisper, although I'm unsure if the words are for me, or for her.

I stumble closer to my front door as Seb presses his hand to the scanner and opens it for me.

"Do you want us to stay? Do anything? Get you both anything?"

"No," I grunt, walking straight through my living room in favour of my bedroom so I can lay her down.

"Are you sure? We can—"

"No," I bark. I'm grateful for their help, but I really need them to fuck off and leave me alone now.

Feeling guilty for snapping when they've been nothing but supportive, I add, "Enjoy the rest of your night."

I don't look back, but I sense them hesitate. I don't hang around to argue; instead, I march into my bedroom and kick the door closed behind me.

My feet barely lift as I stumble toward the bed, my arms dead and my body screaming in pain.

But somehow, I manage to lower her down gently.

Bent over, I rest my head against her shoulder and suck in a steeling breath.

I remain hunched over her protectively for a few seconds before the pain gets too much and I push to stand.

I only get halfway up before I pause when I find a pair of blue eyes staring back up at me.

"Vixen," I breathe, cupping her face with my dirty, messed-up hand.

Her eyes hold mine, confusion warring in their depths.

"You passed out," I explain. "I brought you home."

The second a sharp gasp passes her lips, I'm aware that she can hear me, understand me.

She blinks up at me, looking more beautiful than ever with her wide eyes and smeared make-up.

What I wouldn't do to mess it up even more.

"Do you remember what happened?" I ask.

Pain fills her eyes and they quickly flood with tears. It's all the reaction I need.

"Did he hurt you?"

This time, it takes a little longer to get the truth out of her.

"M-my head," she rasps.

Lifting my hand, I push my fingers into her hair, almost immediately finding a bump.

"Shit, Vixen," I breathe as red-hot fury shoots through my veins. "I should go straight back and make sure that cunt is dead."

The second I suggest leaving, her hand lifts from the bed, her fingers wrapping around my forearm. Her nails dig in, just to make sure I get the message about how she feels about my threat.

"It's okay, I'm not going anywhere. Not while you're in my bed."

She sucks in a breath, realisation hitting her. She doesn't argue or actually say anything, but I swear her eyes darken with the knowledge.

"Painkillers, yeah?"

She nods, the smallest twitch of a smile curling at her lips.

"I need you to do something for me though, okay?" She nods slightly. "I need you to stay awake. If you've got a concussion then—"

"I'll try."

"Good girl," I praise, cupping her cheek once more and rubbing my thumb over her satin-like skin. "I'll be right back, okay?"

She nods, although it's so slight I wouldn't have known if I weren't touching her.

Reluctantly, I pull away and stand back to my full

height.

Her eyes hold mine for a beat, a frown pinching her brows before they take in the injuries to my face and then drop lower to my body.

Pain, fear, and anger all swell like a storm in her eyes. And fuck, there's a part of me that fucking loves that she cares so much.

"I'm okay," I assure her, although I'm pretty sure I'm lying. I'm crashing hard. All I want to do is crawl into bed beside her and pass out. But I can't; she's my priority right now. I've got to take care of her before I look after myself.

Stumbling back, I move toward the door once more, her eyes never leaving me.

"I'll be like two minutes, I promise."

I go before I find enough reasons not to leave her.

When I get to the kitchen, I find two glasses of water waiting for me along with every packet of pills I own.

Guilt gnaws at my insides that I sent them both away when they've been nothing but sweet.

Ripping open two packets of soluble paracetamol—the kind that has the added caffeine in for shits and giggles that Mum gave me for emergencies—I dump them into each glass and then return to my bedroom. I'll message them later to say thanks, but right now, nothing exists past my girl.

"Can you sit up?" I ask, placing both glasses on the bedside table.

She nods before shifting about but not really getting anywhere.

Tucking my hands under her arms, I heave her up and quickly rearrange my pillows to support her.

"I'm okay," she assures me in a quiet voice.

"Don't lie to me," I counter, passing her over a glass. "Tastes like shit, but it'll get into your system faster."

She nods. "Ready?" I ask, lifting my own glass. "On three." A smile twitches at her lips.

"Three," she says, pressing the glass to her lips and starting to drink.

"Huh," I mutter. "I think I might have underestimated you."

She smiles as she drinks.

I follow her lead, trying not to gag at the vile taste of the medication, which only gets stronger as I hit the bottom.

"Ugh, that's fucking gross."

Evie's eyes flash with mischief. "Had worse things in my mouth."

Her words shock the shit out of me, but fuck, they're everything, and the perfect balm to the panic that's still bubbling under the surface from catching her as she dropped.

"Not sure now is the time to discuss all your conquests, Vixen."

She shakes her head. "There isn't— I hadn't— You were—"

"Shit," I hiss, lowering my head in shame, but once again she pulls the rug from beneath me when she reaches out for my jaw and forces me to look up.

"It's okay. I... uh... kinda loved it."

"Jesus, you really must have hit your head hard. I was... I was rough and angry and—" Fuck me, my cock swells thinking about having her lips around it that night.

"I could take it."

"You did," I blurt. "You took it so fucking well."

Heat rises on her cheeks as her eyes drop from mine.

"Hey, don't do that. Don't hide from me."

Reaching out, I give her little choice but to look at me again.

The second our eyes connect, it's like someone takes a baseball bat to my chest, and all the air rushes out of my lungs.

I forget about the pain wracking my body and all the other bullshit surrounding us as I lean in. The only thing I can focus on is her full, kissable lips.

She sucks in a small gasp as I close the distance between us.

But the second my lips brush hers in the softest, sweetest kiss I think I've ever experienced, everything comes crashing down around me.

"Fuck. I'm sorry. I... I can't. Fuck."

Before I know what I'm doing, I'm off the bed and rushing into my bathroom with memories of Tessa and Jude, along with everyone else I've ever been forced to spend time with, running through my head, reminding me what an utter piece of shit I am. And exactly why I don't deserve to be kissing the incredible girl currently lying on my bed.

26

EVIE

ll the breath rushes out of my lungs as he runs away from me and disappears into what I assume is his bathroom.

I sit there in silence, utterly confused.

Everything that's happened in the past hour is a blur.

One minute I was happily—okay, maybe not entirely happily—handing out drinks, and the next I woke up in Alex's bed with him staring down at me like I'm the most precious thing in the world.

The state of his face, the blood, the bruises didn't shock me when I woke. A part of my subconscious obviously remembered what happened despite my memory being hazy as hell.

It was something else about his appearance that rocked my foundations.

A loud crash followed by what I can only describe as a roar floods the room, making my heart jump into my throat.

Sitting forward, a sharp pain shoots down my neck. When I lift my hand, I find a nice bump on the back of my head courtesy of that dickhead.

I shouldn't, it's wrong, but there's a part of me that does hope Alex killed him. He's nothing but a letch and a predator.

Jail would probably be a better opinion, a little voice pipes up.

"Jesus," I mutter, dropping my head into my hands.

I've never wished anyone dead before. Even our waste-of-space father... okay, maybe once or twice over the years. But never anyone else.

It makes me wonder just how easy it is to get swallowed up in this underworld that most of the city has no idea exists.

A series of crashes come from the bathroom, and I move without thought.

He's in pain. He's suffering, and the least I can do right now is look after him like he did me.

Pulling my phone from my shorts, I abandon it on the dresser as I make my way for the door.

"Alex?" I ask quietly as I press my hand to the ajar door and push it open.

I take the fact he didn't shut it properly as some kind of invitation and step over the threshold.

Utter devastation greets me.

Bottles, spray cans, and smashed somethings scatter the floor. Blood splatters cover the white tiles to my left. But that's nothing compared to the harrowing sight of the man who's hunched over the basin with bruises and dried blood covering almost every inch of his skin.

"Alex?" I whisper, terrified of startling him if he's lost in his own head.

I take a step forward, ignoring the shards of ceramic scattered across the floor seeing as I'm somehow still wearing my god-awful stripper heels.

The muscles in his back ripple and flex as he grips the basin.

"Don't," he growls, his voice weak and resigned.

Swallowing down my apprehension, I stand still.

"I'm not leaving."

I've no idea where I dig the confidence from that spills free with my voice. I barely know this guy, and what I do know isn't all that good. But there's something between us. Some kind of magnetic force that always seems to be trying to pull me closer to him. And it's even stronger right now as he crumbles.

"You should," he says quietly, still not moving other than the heavy rise and fall of his back as he breathes.

"We all do a lot of things we shouldn't." Hell knows I have since meeting you.

I keep that final thought to myself, though. I don't think he needs to hear that right now.

A bitter laugh falls from his lips.

"You've no idea what I've done."

I shrug, quickly realising that he can't actually see me.

"You saved me. You looked after me," I say, moving deeper into the room. "The rest doesn't matter right now. Just... let me return the favour."

"You should be resting," he argues.

"I had a bump to the head. I'm not bleeding, unlike someone else."

"It's nothing new," he says quietly.

He flinches when I step right up behind him and press my palm to his back.

"Don't," he breathes, twisting away from me. "I don't deserve for you to look after me right now. Just... go back to bed and let me sort myself out."

This way his voice cracks with emotion as he says the words slices straight through my chest.

Sucking in some strength, I wrap my hand around his upper arm and force him to turn around.

Surprisingly, he allows it. We both know he's strong enough to overpower me, to stop me from forcing him to do anything.

The sight of his cut abs and deep V lines do something to me, but I'm quickly distracted by the blood.

This was not how I imagined seeing him half-naked for the first time.

It hasn't escaped my attention that while he's had me laid out before him completely bare, the only usually hidden part of him I've seen is his dick. And quite honestly, that was in my mouth most of the time, so I didn't really get a good look.

But while he might have turned for me, he doesn't lift his head or rip his gaze from the tiles beneath us.

Reaching out, I cup his rough jaw and force him to move.

He fights it, but not as hard as he probably could.

I can't help but gasp when his eyes finally meet mine. Despite the colour I'm not used to, the pain in them, the self-loathing. It's... it's a lot to take.

I want to ask, the question burning on the tip of my tongue.

And as the seconds pass, I can't keep it in. I miss the silver. Those sparkling eyes are just one of many things I obsess about daily.

"What's with the green eyes?"

His lids lower, and he fights to look away from me.

"Shit," he hiss, breaking our connection once more so that he can take them out.

I stand there with my chest heaving, watching him drop the contact lenses into the basin.

"Why?" I ask, curiosity burning through me.

"Vixen," he groans. "I just told you that—"

"It's okay," I assure him, ducking into the space between him and the basin to stop him hiding from me. "Nothing matters but this moment. I don't care what you did yesterday or earlier this evening." His eyes shutter, letting me know that I hit the nail on the head. "It's about right now, okay?"

He blows out a long breath which tickles across my face and down to my mostly exposed chest, reminding me that I'm still wearing this stupid, not-quite-cowgirl outfit.

My skin erupts in goosebumps and my nipples harden, pressing against the thin fabric of my pathetic excuse for a shirt.

We stand there holding each other's eyes as the seconds and then minutes tick by.

Nothing is said, but nothing needs to be.

It's both everything and nothing at the same time.

"Let me look after you, yeah?" I finally whisper. "I owe you."

He scoffs, his lips parting to argue.

"If you knew—" Reaching up, I press my fingers to his lips.

"Stop."

Taking his other hand, I drag him over to the toilet and flick the lid closed.

"Sit."

He follows my orders and lowers his arse down, his shoulders still slumped in defeat.

I'm about to step away when a thought hits me.

"If it makes you feel better, you can do me another favour."

His eyes brighten a little at that.

Lifting one foot from the floor, I place it on his thigh.

"Undo these for me. They hurt like a bitch."

He swallows thickly before running his eyes down the length of my exposed leg.

His fingers make quick work of the buckle, and I'm about to lower my foot to replace it with the other, but before I can, he grabs it.

"Oh shit," I moan when he presses his thumb into my arch.

Wobbling on one foot, I grab his shoulders.

He grunts in pain, but when his eyes meet mine once more, I read his unspoken warning loud and clear.

"Do not let go."

Our eye contact holds and our breaths mingle as he continues to massage my sore foot.

Little moans and whimpers spill from my lips, I'm powerless to stop them. What he's doing feels so freaking good.

"Switch," he finally says.

I reluctantly pull my foot away from his hand, placing it carefully on a clear bit of floor before lifting the other.

The moan that spills from me when he presses his thumbs against the ball of my foot this time is nothing but obscene.

"Jesus, Vixen," he groans, shifting his hips. His movement forces my eyes to drop to his waist. I regret it the second I find his erection pressing against the fabric of his shorts.

I have to clear my throat before I can speak again. "I'm meant to be cleaning you up."

"I think it's obvious to both of us that I prefer things dirty."

"I'm serious, Alex. Your knuckles—"

"Have been worse."

"Not the point."

Tugging my foot away from his grasp, I stand on two feet once more.

"Don't you dare move," I warn, pointing right at his face.

His eyes hold mine for a beat before dropping down my body.

"Sure. I can be a good boy... sometimes."

I roll my eyes before spinning around and bending over.

I can't help but smile when his groan bounces off the tiled walls around us.

I begin picking up the bottles, placing them back on the empty shelf I assume he dragged them off.

"You don't need—"

"Are you enjoying the view?" I interrupt.

"Yes. Fuck yes. But... your head."

"It's fine," I lie. Honestly, it's pounding like a fucking bass drum. But I either make myself useful, or I lie in bed listening to it beat in time with my heart. "You're going to need a new... one of whatever this was."

I pick up the big piece of ceramic something before shoving the smaller shards into the corner to sweep up later.

"Where's your first aid kit?"

"Seriously, Evie. It's fine."

I still the second my name rolls off his tongue.

"What?" he asks when I spin around to look at him.

"Say that again," I demand.

"Uh... It's fine?"

"No, the other bit."

His brows pinch in confusion as he replays what he said for a second before his eyes flash with understanding.

"Evie," he growls.

Flutters fill my belly at hearing him say my name. It's pathetic, but he's never called me it before and it does all kinds of crazy things below my waist.

A smirk curls at his lips, able to read my silent reaction.

"Under the basin, if you want an actual answer," he finally says, breaking the heated silence that had fallen between us.

With a nod, I head in that direction and bend over again.

"Those shorts should be fucking illegal. Do you even have knickers beneath them?"

"I do," I confirm, locating what I'm searching for and dragging it out.

I spin around and hold his eyes as I walk back toward him, hips swaying seductively.

His eyes track my every movement, his Adam's apple bobbing as he swallows, and the tenting of his shorts worse than ever.

I really shouldn't feel this good about the amount of power I hold over him.

Sure, I get plenty of attention when I'm dancing at the club or camming. But it's never like this.

The intensity between us, the chemistry... it's indescribable.

"They're just really, really tiny."

He groans again, his fingers curling into fists where they rest on his thighs.

"You're making this really, really hard, you know that?"

Biting down on my bottom lip, I lower myself to my knees before him. My heart beats so hard that I'm sure I might be about to pass out again.

This kind of excitement is probably not ideal when you have a head injury, Evie.

"So I see," I whisper, not risking looking up. Instead, I open the first aid box and grab what I need to clean up his cuts. "You need to relax," I say, gently prying his clenched fists open.

"Easier said than done. Have you looked in a mirror tonight?"

"I'm a mess."

"Look pretty fucking perfect to me." He hisses in a breath when I press the wipe to his knuckles.

"Baby," I tease. "I thought you'd be used to this by now."

"What are you trying to say?" he asks, trying to sound offended but failing miserably.

"You were fighting at an underground fight night. Are you trying to tell me that was your first time?"

He laughs. "I guess you've got me there. I should probably be thanking you, though."

"Oh yeah?" I ask, continuing to tend to his wounds.

Once I'm happy I've got any dirt out of his knuckles, I stand to my feet once more and start on his face.

It's harder to stay focused with his eyes locked on mine and his breath tickling over my already hyper-sensitive skin.

"Y-yeah," he agrees after a few seconds, reminding me that we were in the middle of a conversation.

I yelp when he wraps his hands around my waist and lifts me onto his lap, forcing me to straddle him.

I swallow and take a calming breath as his erection presses against the seam of my shorts.

"I was losing," he confesses. "The other guy, he's a legend."

"Wow," I say lightly. "Didn't have you down as the kind of man who would confess to losing easily."

"The second I saw you... saw his hands on you... I forfeited the fight. Fuck winning. Not when—"

My hand falls away from his split lip, our eyes lock, and I barely even notice that he stopped talking mid-sentence.

My chest heaves, my breasts suddenly too small for my shirt, my blood too hot in my veins.

But I don't move, and neither does he.

It's the most incredible yet frustrating moment of my life.

27

___

ALEX

I *really want to fucking kiss you.*

"So, what are you waiting for?"

I startle when she responds to a thought I wasn't aware I said out loud.

"Fuck it," I breathe, gripping the nape of her neck and crashing our lips together.

The bitterness of the antiseptic wipe she just used on me fills my mouth a beat before it morphs into her unique taste.

My fingers massage her neck as I tilt my head, deepening the kiss. My other hand presses against the small of her back, sliding her higher up my thighs.

My cock aches against her pussy. So close yet so fucking far with our shorts and her apparently tiny knickers between us.

I swallow her whimpers happily as the coppery taste of my blood spills into our kiss.

I loosen my hold on her, expecting her to break away, but she surprises me. Instead of being grossed out like I'm sure most girls would be—those aside from the fruitcakes my friends have found—it seems to make her hungrier, even more desperate for me.

Her fingers twist painfully in my hair, but it's nothing compared to the injuries covering the rest of my body.

"Fuck, Evie. I need you," I groan into our kiss.

It might be the truth, but that doesn't mean I'm going to do anything about it. Especially when she could be suffering a concussion.

Pulling back from the kiss, she rests her hands on my shoulders.

Her heated cheeks make my heart ache in the best kind of way, but it's the sight of my blood on her lips that really fucks me up.

"You trust me?" I ask, the question coming out of nowhere.

She smiles at me. It's the most breathtaking smile I think I've ever fucking seen.

"I shouldn't," she confesses.

"We all do a lot of things we shouldn't," I say, repeating the words she said to me not so long ago.

She nods. "Yes."

"Okay, good. Here's what I'm going to do."

Dropping my lips to hers once more, I kiss her until my head spins before dragging my lips along the line of her jaw until I hit her ear.

"I'm going to strip you out of this sinful outfit and find out just how small your knickers are. Then, I'm going to drag those down your legs as well."

"Alex," she whimpers, making my cock weep in my shorts.

"Then I'm going to carry you to the shower and wash every inch of tonight off both of us."

"How about I wash tonight off you?" she suggests.

"Fuck, you make me want everything I don't deserve."

"That's only your opinion. What about what I think you deserve?"

"You don't know everyth—"

"I'm not asking to be your wife here. I'm just offering to help turn a shitty night around. I've no idea what you've done tonight or in the past, and right now, I don't care. Just... let it go, yeah?"

My regrets, my self-loathing for the shit I might have had to do tonight with Tessa to complete my job, for all the things I've been made to do in the past... it all falls away as she leans in to kiss me again.

Ripping my lips from hers long before I'm ready, I push her back slightly.

"Stand," I demand, giving her little choice but to follow my orders.

She shuffles off my lap, making my cock instantly sad from losing contact.

"What are you—"

She cuts herself off when I stand too. There's barely an inch between us, just enough space for me to lift my hands and pop open the small buttons on her shirt.

The second the final one is undone, the fabric parts, revealing her bare breasts beneath.

"Fuck, Vixen," I groan, the sight of her hard nipples making my mouth water.

I wince as I skim my busted knuckles down her stomach. I expect her to chastise me, but it seems she's too lost to what I'm doing.

I unfasten her belt before making quick work of her denim shorts and shoving them down her thighs, leaving her in what has to be the smallest g-string I've ever seen.

"Fuck me, you weren't wrong," I mutter, running my fingertip along the thin strip of fabric that's almost around her hips it's so low. "Was there any point in wearing any?"

"So you could take them off?"

"Fuck. You're perfect."

Tucking my fingers under the sides of her knickers, I drag them down, letting them drop around her ankles with her shorts.

"You're so fucking beautiful, Evie. It's no wonder every man wants you wherever you go."

"Shut up, they don't," she argues naïvely.

It's endearing how she really has no clue how breathtaking she is.

"You should meet my sister. She's the one who has men drooling at her feet."

"Nope. Not interested in anyone but the girl standing naked in my bathroom."

Tucking my thumbs into my waistband, I shove my own shorts down, letting them join her clothes on my tiled floor.

She sucks in a sharp breath, staring down at me as my cock springs free, poking her in the hip. You know, just in case she needed any more evidence that my previous words are more than true.

Taking her hand in mine, I tug her toward my walk-in shower.

"Alex," she squeals when I turn it on, allowing us to get blasted with ice-cold water from every angle.

"Come here, Vixen. I'll warm you up."

I pull her into my body and wrap my arms around her as the water begins to warm.

Reaching for my shower gel, I squeeze a huge blob onto a puff and set about cleaning her up.

There's not an inch of her body that I don't scrub, and

as I sit on my knees at her feet, rubbing soothing circles into her thighs, all I can think about is throwing her leg over my shoulder and eating her until she's screaming.

But I don't.

Instead, I push to my feet and offer her the bubble-filled puff. Although, really, I want her hands all over my body.

Apparently able to read my mind, she drops the puff at our feet like it just burned her and reaches for my bottle of shower gel, squeezing some into her palm.

"You're bad," I groan when she presses her palms against my pecs.

"You make me bad," she counters, holding my eyes.

"I've never been a very good influence on people, I must be honest."

"Well," she says, moving down to my abs, making my dick jerk in excitement. "I guess I should do my worst then."

As the bubbles slip down my skin, she follows them with kisses, ensuring she's extra gentle where my bruises from tonight are already darkening my skin.

"Evie, no," I start when she drops to her knees.

"No?" she asks, running her hands down my legs. "You saved me tonight, Alex. If you hadn't done... who knows what might have happened." She bites down on her bottom lip and looks up at me innocently. If that's even possible with my rock-hard cock right in front of her lips. "So let me thank you by doing something I haven't been able to stop thinking about since Christmas."

All the air rushes from my lungs.

"Y-you've thought about—"

"Daily," she confesses. It's the final thing either of us says before she sticks her tongue out and laps at the precum beading at my tip.

Groaning, I give in to what she wants as she sinks down on my length.

My fingers twist in her hair, but I'm so fucking gentle, terrified of hurting her worse than she already is.

My hips beg to thrust, but I fight it. I fight all my natural reactions and just let her indulge.

She sucks me so fucking good. It's almost painful watching her.

Too fucking perfect.

Her eyes roll up my body, finding mine as if she heard that thought.

"Perfect," I murmur as she hollows her cheeks and takes me deeper.

Without warning, my orgasm slams into me. I don't even get a chance to warn her. Instead, my cock jerks and I roar loudly, spilling my seed down her throat.

She takes it all, swallowing me down like she's been doing it all her life.

"Holy shit," I gasp, my knees threatening to buckle with the force of that release.

"Good?" she asks with a shy smile after she's wiped her mouth.

"So fucking good."

Tucking my hands up her arms, I haul her to her feet and slam my lips against her.

"You've just shattered my resolve, Vixen. I was going to do the right thing and let you rest. But you just raised the bar."

"Whoops," she says innocently, smiling into our kiss.

The need to slam her back against the wall and fuck her like a savage is almost as strong as my need to end that cunt's life tonight.

But I don't.

I hold myself together. For her.

"Pass me the bottle of shampoo," I instruct, nodding to the shelf in front of her once I've turned her around.

"B-but—"

A wide smile splits my mouth. She wants me. And I fucking love it.

I've made a career out of getting people to want me. I won't lie, I always get some kind of rush when they fall for my moves.

But this... this right here... It's so much fucking more than any of that.

Resting my arm over her shoulder, I hold my palm out.

"Squeeze."

She immediately does as she's told, flipping the lid open and pouring enough into my palm to wash her hair.

"I'll be gentle, I promise," I whisper in her ear before lifting my hands to her head, being careful of the lump I know is on the back.

Before long, she's moaning in delight as I massage her scalp and my cock is hard once again, pressing against her arse.

"That good, Vixen?" I ask, kissing up her neck.

"So good. You secretly a hairdresser?"

A sad laugh falls from my lips.

"If only."

"Well, you could if you fancy a career change. Women would pay good money for this."

"To be standing in a shower naked with me while I massage their heads and whisper filthy things in their ear?"

"I don't remember any whispering," she teases.

"You're wicked."

"You started it," she counters.

"Okay, you want to know what I'm planning?"

She nods.

"Once I've done this, I'm going to work my way around every inch of your body, making sure you're dry, and then I'm going to carry you to my bed, lay you down on the pillows and kiss you like it might be the last chance I get."

Her breathing increases with every word I say.

"I'm going to kiss you until you're breathless, and then start working my way down your body." Releasing her hair, I illustrate my plans with my fingers. I trace her collarbone and gently move down until I'm circling her hard nipple. "Might linger here a bit, tease you, make you beg for more by sucking your nipples into my mouth."

"Alex," she moans, letting her bubbly head rest back on my shoulder lightly.

"And when I'm ready, I'll continue down, kissing over your stomach until I can part your thighs. You've got such a pretty pussy, Evie."

I bite down on her earlobe and she moans like a whore.

It's fucking everything.

When I get to the juncture between her thighs, she doesn't hesitate to open her legs for me.

"Fucking hell," I groan, dropping my fingers lower, greedily sliding through her folds to discover how wet she is for me. "Do you have any idea what you do to me?"

"I have an idea," she confesses, rocking back against my length. "Then what?" she asks, getting me back on track.

"Then I'm going to bury my face down here, lick your clit, fuck you with my tongue until you're writhing and begging for mercy." She gasps. "And when I finally give it to you, you're going to fall screaming my name."

"Fuck, Alex. Where did you learn to talk like this?"

I cringe at her question.

"Just telling you what I want to do to you. It gets you hot, doesn't it?"

"Take me to your bed," she moans. "Make good on those promises."

"Oh, Vixen, there's no worries about that."

28

—

EVIE

The moment Alex finished washing my hair, he turned the shower off, reached for a towel, which was thankfully dark grey because he was still bleeding, and he set about delivering all those promises.

By the time he ate me to my second release of the night, my body was exhausted and I fell into a blissful sleep.

All the events of the night were forgotten, the only thing left to dream about the tingles he elicited in my body and the weight of his arm around my waist as he spooned me.

And when I woke up a little over ten minutes ago, he was still there, his body like a wall of warmth against my back, his breath tickling over my shoulder the ultimate tease of what he'd done with that sinful mouth the night before, and his morning wood poking me in the arse.

A rush of heat surges to my core just thinking about him dreaming of me and waking up ready to go.

It makes me want to give in.

For years, I've told myself that I'll wait. I've watched Blakely use her body, her sexuality to get whatever we've needed over the years. She's done things I know she's not proud of, things that have made her lock herself in the bathroom once she's returned home and sob for hours.

I promised myself the first time it happened and I fully understood what had caused her reaction that I would never, ever give a man the kind of power that would cause me to break like that.

She might not have fallen in love, or even found anyone worthy of that. But it didn't stop them from breaking her heart. And in turn, mine shattered right alongside hers. I was just stuck on the outside of the bathroom, unable to hold her and tell her that I loved her.

I promised myself from there on out, when I gave myself over to a man, that he would be worthy. That I wouldn't come running home with the desire to lock myself in the bathroom and forget it ever happened.

I want it to be special, and memorable.

I know that's probably totally unrealistic. The kind of thing that only exists in movies and in books. But still, I want it.

Since diving into Blake's life, I've been surrounded by letchy men who'd willingly pay whatever for a quick fuck. I'm sure that's great for them and gets them what they need. But I am not that person.

Maybe I think too highly of myself, but I don't think any amount of money is enough to give away something so precious, so sacred.

Jesus, what do I sound like?

I just... I want more than the shitty hand life dealt us, and I don't care if that's realistic. I'm going to hold out hope that I'm not surrounded by men who only want to earn a quick buck or score a quick fuck. I want to believe that there is some good in people, and that their intentions don't always have to be sinful and twisted.

"Stop it." A quiet whisper comes from behind me, banishing my thoughts in an instant.

"I'm not doing anything," I argue.

"You are, you're thinking. Stop it. We're relaxing." His voice is rough with sleep, and it makes tingles spread through my body like wildfire.

I chuckle. "You can't tell me not to think."

"Okay, fine. Stop thinking about whatever is making your shoulders tense up and think about me instead."

"About you?" I tease.

"Sure. Honestly, I'm surprised you're able to think about anything else after those orgasms I gave you last night."

I shrug the shoulder I'm not lying on.

"I mean, they were okay," I confess. "I've got a pretty good vibrator at home that will—" A shriek rips from my lips as I'm suddenly shoved to my back with an incredibly sexy yet bruised man staring down at me.

"You're going to compare this tongue to a vibrator? Shame on you, Evie Moore. Shame on you."

He pins me to the bed with my arms above my head and my thighs trapped beneath his.

"So... what are you going to do about it?"

A growl rumbles deep in his throat as he stares down at me with dark silver eyes that are full of hunger and need.

Need for me.

Me.

It's a heady feeling.

This powerful, brutal, sinfully beautiful man needs me.

He could have any girl out there. Hell, knowing who he is and how high his confidence levels are, he's probably had his fair share.

But right now, his sole attention is on me and my body.

"How's your head?" he asks, dipping low and pressing me into the mattress with his strong body.

"Perfect," I lie.

It hurts. But nowhere near as bad as last night. And certainly nowhere near enough to stop whatever is swirling around in his eyes right now.

"What about you?" I ask.

He doesn't look good. His right eye is swollen, his cheek is purple, and the split in his bottom lip looks sore as hell. And that's only his face. His ribs and back were darkening with bruises long before we got in the shower last night; I can only imagine how much they must hurt.

"You're naked in my bed. I'm perfect, Vixen. Fucking perfect."

He moves faster than I can compute, his lips pressing against mine, his tongue searching for entry.

But I hold firm, mumbling, "Morning breath," the best I can without giving him what he wants.

He laughs. "If you think that's going to put me off, then you really need to get to know me better."

His giant hand cups my bare breast, his fingers pinching my already peaked nipple.

Pleasure shoots through my body and my lips part on a gasp, giving him the access he craves.

I cringe, more than aware of how gross my mouth is, but if he can tell or cares, he doesn't show it. He kisses me just as deeply as if I'd just brushed my teeth.

It's... all-consuming, and I'm powerless but to let him sweep me away into a land where only the two of us and endless pleasure exists.

"Need you so fucking bad," he groans, kissing along my jaw before sucking on the sensitive skin beneath my ear.

"Alex," I cry. "Please." I've no idea what I'm asking for,

but as my body begins to climb toward another devastating release despite him barely touching me, I don't really care what it is.

I know he'll make it good for me. And I... *shit*. I trust him.

"Vixen," he groans, sucking one of my nipples into his mouth, making my back arch from the bed.

But before I can really get into it, he shifts between my thighs and sits upright, giving me a full view of his body.

His chest heaves, but it's the bruises that really capture my attention.

"Alex," I breathe, reaching out for him.

"I'm okay. Promise."

I swallow thickly, hating that he's lying to me but aware that I have more than once when he's asked about my head.

His hands grip my thighs, trying to make me believe his words before one of them releases me in favour of his cock that's happily jutting out between his legs, begging for attention.

Shamelessly, he wraps his hand around himself and starts stroking.

My mouth runs dry.

Even with the cuts, bruises and swelling, this man is a god. His body looks like it has been cut from stone. One thing is for sure—he spends a lot of time in a gym somewhere.

Heat surges south as I think about watching him work out, all sweaty and—

"What are you thinking about?" he asks, cutting off my little fantasy.

"Umm..."

"The blush on your cheeks just spread to your chest. I want to know what gets you so hot."

"I was just..." He quirks a brow. "Thinking about watching you work out."

"Work out, huh?" Biting on my bottom lip, I nod, watching him through hooded eyes as his hand continues its slow movement. "Would it get you as hot as I do watching you dance?"

"Depends how much you like watching me dance." I smirk.

"Vixen, I fucking love watching you do anything. Whenever you're close, I'm hard. You're an obsession I'm struggling to break."

My smile grows at his confession.

"I know how that feels."

"Do you know what I want to watch you doing right now?" he asks, the tone of his voice dropping as his eyes roll down my body, focusing on the aching part between my thighs.

I shake my head, unable to speak. Not that he can see me.

"I want to watch you play with yourself. I want to watch you come."

My breath catches.

I don't know why I'm so shocked or embarrassed at the thought of touching myself in front of him.

I've done it in front of more men than I want to admit to on screen.

But sitting here with him in person... it feels so much more... intense.

Guilt and, annoyingly, shame flood my body.

I'm not ashamed about what I do to help support my family. But I am ashamed that I've let things get this far with Alex and not told him about it.

"Not going shy on me now, are you, Vixen?" he asks teasingly, dragging me from my thoughts.

His eyes find mine again, and confidence surges through me.

He wants me. He's going to get off on watching me, and in turn, I get to watch him.

Not some random guy through a screen. A real life man who is here offering me things I probably shouldn't want as badly as I do. Making me think about a future I have no right even considering.

Lifting my hand from the bed, I spread my legs a little wider and press my fingers to my clit.

Simultaneous moans fall from our lips as we watch each other pleasure ourselves.

It's hands down the most erotic experience of my life.

"That's it, Vixen. Show me all your moves."

His hand picks up speed on his shaft as he jerks off before me, precum glistening at his tip, making my mouth water for a taste.

"Your legs are trembling already," he says in surprise.

"W-watching you. It... it gets me—"

"Hot?"

I nod, chasing my orgasm that's right in my clutches.

"And here I was thinking you were the one who liked to be watched."

My eyes widen in shock. He doesn't know about the camming, does he?

No. If he did, he'd certainly have something to say about it.

"You're so fucking beautiful when you're about to fall, Evie."

God. The way my name sounds on his lips.

I should have told him it sooner. That would have been

a nice little addition to the fantasies I've replayed over and over in my head.

"Come for me," he demands a second before he pushes two fingers deep inside me.

It's exactly what I need to crash over the edge and free-fall into the abyss.

"Fuck. You're so tight. I can't wait to feel you strangling my dick."

With his fingers working my G-spot, I fall straight into a second orgasm, which comes as much as a surprise to me as it does him.

"Magic fingers," he grunts, his own movements getting jerky as his release approaches.

"Fuck, Vixen. I can't get enough. I—"

A door slams somewhere in his flat and my heart jumps into my throat as Alex groans, but I don't think it's in pleasure.

"Yoo-hoo, lover boy. Time to confess all your sins," a female calls.

"Fuck. Fuck," Alex barks, his muscles locking up. "I'm sorry. I'm so sorry. Fuuuuck."

29

ALEX

I can't take my eyes off her pussy, glistening with my cum.

It's fucking mesmerising.

A thought slams into me, but before I can act on it, I have to ask. "Are you on birth control?"

Lifting my eyes, I take in Evie's horrified ones.

"Who was that?" she asks, completely ignoring my previous question.

"No one important. You don't need to worry about them."

"Alex, a woman just let herself into your flat and called you lover boy. You really expect me not to freak out when I'm lying here like... well, this," she says, gesturing to herself.

"She won't be bothered. You shouldn't be either."

My words really don't relax her at all. I, however, can't keep the smirk off my lips.

"Unbelievable," she huffs, fighting to get away from me.

"Where do you think you're going?" I ask, wrapping my hands around her waist to stop her.

"There's someone right out there."

"So? They can wait. Hell knows I've had to enough times."

She frowns, but any response she might have had is forgotten when I pull her so she's sitting before me and crash my lips to hers.

When we finally part, our guests have got bored waiting and are crashing around in my kitchen. Evie relaxes in my hold the second a rumble of a male voice fills the air.

"I promise you, the woman out there is not mine. I'm not that brave."

She narrows her eyes at me, staring deep into mine as if she'll be able to read everything I'm not saying.

"Come on, let's go clean up and you can meet them."

"After your previous comment, I'm not sure I want to," she murmurs.

"Technically, you met them last night, but something tells me you don't remember."

Her eyes darken as she casts her mind back. It's all the answer I need, and honestly, I'm relieved that she doesn't remember that cunt touching her.

"Up you go," I say, lifting her small frame from the bed, swatting her arse as she rights herself, making her squeal.

"Alexander Deimos, you are a dirty dog," echoes down the hall outside my room.

"Good job you love me anyway, huh, Hellcat?"

"Deimos."

I'm laughing as I follow Evie into the bathroom and find her a new toothbrush.

We stand shoulder to shoulder, our eyes locked in the mirror before us, and a weird sense of calm washes over me.

This is where she belongs. Right here by my side.

It's just a shame that I won't be able to keep her.

"Here," I say, handing her one of my shirts to cover up.

"Where are my knickers?"

"Vixen, they're so small there really is no point."

"*I* know I'm wearing them," she sulks. "And I don't want to meet your... friends?" she guesses, "without knickers on."

"That's unlucky for you, because you're going to have to."

Taking matters into my own hands, I tug my shirt over her head, and the second she has her arms in it, I take her hand and drag her from the bedroom, much to her annoyance.

"I don't like you very much right now," she mutters behind me as the scent of caffeine and freshly baked something hits my nose.

My stomach growls loudly as we round the corner.

Two sets of eyes look up the second we appear, both as curious and amused as each other.

"Hey, how nice of you to join us. Sorry to interrupt, but you know, we need gossip and shit."

"Emmie," I growl in annoyance as Evie tucks herself into my side.

"Oh, please." She waves me off. "Evie and I know each other, don't we?"

Evie tenses in my arms.

"You know each other?" I ask, but I immediately feel stupid, because it should have been obvious.

"We went to school together. But I'm not sure we can really say we know each other," Evie says quietly.

I can't help but stare down at this timid version of my vixen.

"Oh, shush. Us Lovell kids are bonded for life after putting up with that shithole for any length of time. We got coffee. Didn't know what you wanted so went with a latte. Everyone loves latte, right?"

"Unless you're lactose intolerant," I point out.

"Shit, you're not, are you?" Emmie asks.

"No, all good. I love lattes," Evie says, finally relaxing.

"Okay, so this is Theo, my... significant other," Emmie says with a wicked grin as she gestures to her husband, who's silently watching all of this play out.

He scoffs as I throw my head back, laughing at the expression on his face.

"Husband," he corrects. "She means husband and her better half."

"Nice to meet you. I heard a rumour you got married," Evie says, tucking herself into my side on the opposite sofa to Emmie and Theo.

"Well, we didn't actually get married, but we have all the correct paperwork. Isn't that right, darling?" Emmie gives Theo a sugar-sweet smile that even sets my teeth on edge.

"You're a pain in my arse, Ramsey," he mutters.

"You love it," she teases.

Evie leans closer just as Emmie asks something about him making her arse cheek glow with pain. "I'm starting to understand what you meant when you said they wouldn't be bothered about what we were up to."

"Vixen, you have no idea. This..." I jerk my head in Emmie and Theo's direction. "Is nothing. Wait until you meet the others." I regret the words the second they fall from my lips. I can't introduce her to everyone. If I do, it'll look like this can be a thing. That we can have a future outside of whatever this is.

"There are more of them like this?"

"Probably best not to try and imagine it." Unable to stop

myself, I drop a kiss on her temple before turning back to the gatecrashers. "You brought food too, right?"

"Do you think we'd be brave enough to come without it? On the counter." Emmie jerks her chin toward my kitchen and I spot a box with a name on I don't recognise.

Releasing Evie, I walk over to grab something.

"Where's Betties?"

"By Brianna's old place. The pastries are insane."

"The ones Nico uses to get out of the dog house?" I ask, opening the box and taking in the delights before me.

"Those are the exact ones," Theo says, but he's closer than I was expecting.

Not a second later, he reaches around me to snag a pastry and then hops up onto one of my kitchen stools.

Glancing over my shoulder, I find that Emmie has dragged Evie into a conversation.

"You get that shit to my dad?"

"Yeah, man. Went straight there after you left. Don't sweat it."

"Do you know if he got what he needed?"

"No fucking clue. He didn't say a word. Literally. I think he had company."

"Ugh. He was probably interviewing a new housekeeper."

"Another one?"

I shrug. I lost count of how many he's fucked his way through a long time ago.

"I guess it's easy to see where you get your skills from. Who'd you get that intel from last night, anyway?"

I shoot a panicked look over my shoulder.

"Chill, bro. They're not listening."

I shake my head, regret and guilt poisoning my veins.

"I can't keep doing this shit, T. It's fucking killing me."

His face softens. It's an expression that not many people ever get to see from our future leader.

"She that important, huh?" he asks, looking at Evie.

My fists curl, breaking my wounds open once more despite the fact there's no heat in his eyes as he studies her.

"She seems cool. Emmie said she was always pretty quiet at school. How she'd end up working fight nights?"

"I don't know her story." He lifts a brow at me. "What? If I ask hers, she'll want mine."

He nods in understanding.

"You'll figure it out," he says confidently.

"Yeah," I agree, but I don't feel any kind of hope of that happening.

The only thing I can do is forget everything I feel for her and set her free.

She doesn't need a fuck-up like me in her life, especially when she obviously has enough issues of her own.

The weight of that reality presses heavily on my shoulders.

"One day at a time. We're surrounded by the most unlikely of couples. There's no reason to think she's not everything you need and will completely understand and embrace your life."

He squeezes my shoulder in support before stealing two more pastries and heading back to his wife.

Spinning around, I rest my arse against that counter and just watch them chat for a while.

I've no idea what the topic is, but Evie looks totally relaxed and happy in their company.

It's another stab to my fragile heart that I didn't need.

Sensing my stare, she eventually turns to look at me.

"What happened to breakfast?" she asks, a teasing smile lighting up her face.

"Sorry," I mutter, grabbing the box and walking over to rejoin her.

"Oh my God, they look amazing. No wonder you were hogging them."

She dives straight for some kind of jammy crown thing and immediately takes a bite, getting sweet, sticky goodness all over her lips.

"Ohmygod," she moans, chewing.

My cock jerks, and I can't stop myself.

Eyes from the other sofa burn into me as I lean in and lick up the jam.

"So good," I murmur, holding her eyes, letting her see everything I'm feeling right in this moment.

It's dangerous, but I can't fucking stop.

I don't want to.

Thankfully, I was able to push those depressing thoughts away as I was dragged into the conversation.

Emmie and Evie regaled us with stories from Lovell Academy. Theo and I both know that the place is the pits of hell, but some of the stories... Well, I've never been more grateful for our education at Knight's Ridge.

Honestly, it's something of a miracle that Emmie and Evie are as normal as they are after suffering for years in that place.

"So what's the plan for September then?" Emmie asks Evie.

My hand stills on her thigh as I impatiently wait for her answer.

It's something I probably should have thought to ask.

Once I knew her name, it was easy enough for me to find out that she's about to finish her sentence at Lovell Academy. But that was as far as I got. I guess it was naïve of me to assume she might just become a full-time dancer, or cam girl, or whatever.

I wince at the thought of other men getting even more of her undivided attention. But I keep those thoughts to myself.

It's not until Evie looks over at me that I realise my grip on her thigh has tightened to the point it probably hurts.

"Sorry," I whisper.

"You okay?" she asks, looking up at me with wide, concerned eyes.

"Yeah, I'm good," I assure her.

She smiles before looking back at Emmie.

"Hopefully uni," Evie explains. "I've had an unconditional offer from UEL for illustration."

"Unconditional, wow," Theo says, echoing exactly what I'm thinking. "You must be good."

She shrugs, the tips of her ears growing hot with the attention.

"What kind of things do you draw?" Emmie asks, obviously more than interested, seeing as she wants to follow in her father's footsteps one day.

"Anything, really. But I love people. I love capturing expression, hopes, fears, and small details."

"That's awesome. UEL is a good place for it too."

Theo's brows lift in surprise.

"What?" Emmie barks.

"Nothing, I just didn't think you'd been looking at options yet."

"I wasn't. But then I got myself this stupidly wealthy

husband and I thought, why not make the most of that situation?" she counters with a smirk.

"Watch it, Hellcat," he warns, his eyes narrowing on her.

"Or what, Cirillo?"

"Where are you looking at?" he asks, genuinely interested.

We've all known that Theo has had his plan in place for years. And he's been like a dog with a bone trying to get the rest of us to make a decision about our futures and universities, so this is well up his street.

"Well, obviously the Royal College of—"

Theo's phone ringing cuts over Emmie's words.

"Shit, sorry, Hellcat. I need to get this."

Pulling his phone from his pocket as he stands, he doesn't even bother looking at the screen as he swipes and puts it to his ear.

"Boss," he greets, making Evie look up at me with pinched brows.

I smile down at her, my stomach already sinking. We're about to be called in, and our time is going to be cut short.

That thought is only confirmed a few seconds later when Theo hangs up and marches over.

"Get dressed, lover boy. Work calls."

"Great. Have I got time to take Evie home?"

I can read the answer on Theo's face, but apparently, so can Emmie.

"I've got her, don't worry. Just leave me your car keys, yeah?" Her eyes light up with excitement at the prospect of driving Theo's car.

"Why did I ever think that intensive course was a good idea?" he grumbles, reluctantly passing his keys over. "How long until the car I've ordered for you arrives?"

Emmie doesn't answer him. Well, not with words. She waits for him to sit back down before throwing her leg over his waist and kissing the shit out of him.

"I think that's our cue."

Taking Evie's hand, I pull her down to my bedroom with the intention of kissing her breathless before we're separated once more.

30

EVIE

I sit on the end of Alex's bed and watch him get dressed in a sinfully sexy black slim-fitting suit. I've never really been one to find a suited man irresistible, but as he smoothes down the lapels of his jacket and straightens his tie, I realise that I was wrong.

"You look..." My words trail off as my mouth dries out.

"Hot, right?"

"Jesus. I'm surprised you don't have extra wide doors to allow your head to fit through."

He walks over, his fresh-from-the-shower scent mixing with whatever he's sprayed himself with not helping my simmering desire for him at all.

"Just imagine what it's like without the busted face," he says, grabbing my hands and pulling me to my feet.

"Oh, I don't know."

"Into the bad boy look, huh?"

"More like the *you* look."

His eyes glitter with excitement at my confession.

"That's good, because I'm pretty addicted to

your *you* look too. Especially when that includes wearing nothing but my shirt."

Before things take a turn for the better, a door slams and Theo barks, "Bro, let's go."

"All right, all right," Alex mutters before stealing one more kiss.

"I know some of last night was a bit shit," he says, resting his brow against mine. "But it was also a lot good. So... thank you."

I can't help but smile as butterflies take flight in my belly.

"Can I see you again?" I ask, hating how vulnerable I sound, and I regret the question even more when something dark I don't like passes through his eyes.

"I can't make you any promises, Evie. My life is chaotic at best. But," he starts, giving me a little hope, "I don't want this to be it either."

Releasing me, he pulls his phone from his pocket.

"Stick your digits in," he demands after unlocking it and passing it over.

I do, and I save the contact as Your Vixen.

"Ever had phone sex, my little thief?"

I shake my head, my cheeks burning up at the half-lie. Could camming be considered phone sex?

I've no idea. But I'm sticking with no for now.

"Alex," Theo booms.

"Shit, I really need to go."

"Message me," I blurt like an idiot.

"You got it."

Before I come up with anything else to say, he's disappeared around the corner and vanished from my sight.

My knees almost give out, sending me crashing back to

the bed, but I'm distracted when Emmie walks around the corner with an armful of clothes.

"Figured you didn't want to put last night's outfit back on," she says with a knowing smirk.

"You were there?"

"Yeah, we all were."

I drop my head into my hands as embarrassment swamps me. That was not how I wanted to meet my... Alex's friends. I don't even remember.

"Hey, what's wrong?" she asks, moving closer.

"I... I was dressed like a slutty cowgirl."

"I was more thinking hot cowgirl. Whatever it was, Alex loved it. So does it really matter?"

I finally fall back into his bed and look around. And not for the first time since I woke this morning, I notice every single difference between his home and mine.

Hell, his life and mine.

"What am I even doing here?" I ask, my eyes locked on my bare feet.

"Don't do that," Emmie says, coming to sit next to me. "Everything you're feeling now... I get it. Trust me, I've been there. But if there's one thing you need to know about these guys, it's that if they want something, they won't stop at anything until they get it. Same goes for if they don't want something.

"If Alex didn't want you here, you wouldn't be.

"He doesn't care that you're from Lovell, or that you were working last night. He might not seem it at first look, but he's deeper than that. He's seen something in you, enough to hook him. I haven't seen anyone else achieve that since I crashed into their lives."

Silence falls between us as I try to force myself to believe her words and not let my insecurities rule.

Previously, it was easier to push reality aside. But now I've sat in his flat, met a couple of his friends. Seen him go to work in his fancy suit. The divide between us seems far too great.

"Enough dwelling. He asked me to do him a favour before I take you home."

"Oh?"

"Em, you still here?" another female voice shouts through the flat.

"And backup has just arrived. Yeah, down where all the magic happens," she calls back.

"Pfft, if you need a bed for the magic, you and Theo are losing your edge," she teases as a flash of platinum hair bounces into the room. "Hey," she says the second her eyes lock on me. "How are you feeling?"

"Uh..."

"This is Stella. She's the one who pulled Alex off that prick last night to stop him from killing him. He totally deserved death, though, by the way."

"Uh... Hi," I say somewhat awkwardly, lifting my hand in a pathetic kind of wave.

"So, what's the plan? Hit up the gym, burn off a few calories then put them all back on at the waffle place?" she asks in an obviously American accent as if this is all entirely normal.

"Sure, sounds good. While the boys are away..." Emmie wiggles her brows.

"Um... I could go for the waffles." Although it's probably not such a good idea after the pastries. "But the gym?"

"Alex asked me to teach you a few things just in case you ever get stuck with some cocksucker again," Emmie explains. "So I called in our resident bad-arse to help me."

I look between the two of them, both dressed in leggings, sports bras and zip-up hoodies as if it's some kind of uniform, and something akin to fear assaults me.

They look like they know what they're doing and how to handle themselves.

All I know how to do is draw and roll my hips temptingly. I haven't even figured out how to pole dance yet. Honestly, I'm a really shitty dancer. If it weren't for Blake, and Derek trying to be my pseudo-uncle for some fucked-up reason, I don't think I'd have ever got the job at Paradise.

"We'll go easy on you. Promise. Alex would kick our asses if we worked you too hard. Something tells me that he's the one who wants to make you really sweat."

"We haven't had sex," I blurt like a complete moron.

"Oh?" they ask simultaneously.

"N-no. We've done... other stuff but not that. Yet."

"Well, even more reason to ensure you're on top of your game. Gotta stay match fit," Stella teases.

"Go get dressed. We'll be in the living room when you're ready."

"Well, if I wasn't already aware that we lived in different worlds, then this confirms it. If our building even has a basement, then I'm pretty sure it's a crack den, not a fully kitted-out gym. I mean, it's even better than... well, any I've ever seen before."

"I know, they're flashy. Just remember I grew up a few streets from you with a mother who was probably hanging out in that crack den. Just because we were born in the ghetto, it doesn't mean we have to stay there."

"I can't believe you live here."

"In the penthouse and everything," she says with a wink.

"Right, stop gossiping. We're gonna warm up and then we're going to show Evie how to take down a handsy asshole. First with our fists. Then, we can work up to a knife," Stella announces.

"A knife?" I ask nervously.

"Tell me you don't walk about that place unarmed?" she gasps.

"Um... yeah, actually, I do."

"Okay, I'll talk to Alex about fixing you up. You need to be safe, even more so now you're hooking up with a Cirillo."

"I'm not... we're not..."

"Did you or did you not get rescued by Alex Deimos last night and sleep in his bed? And did he or did he not get you off better than anyone ever has in your entire life?"

My cheeks burn red hot.

"There you go. Hooking up with a Cirillo, ladies and gentlemen," she says with a smirk, holding her arms out to accept praise from our non-existent crowd. "Emmie, music. And make it decent. Not that emo shit you love."

"Watch your mouth, Doukas. You know I can take you down."

"I'll teach you how to fight properly. Emmie will show you how to do it dirty."

"Lovell style. Archer Wolf taught me almost everything I know."

"You're in with the Wolves too?" I blurt. I mean, I know she used to hang out with them, but I didn't know that there was anything more to it.

"Girl, stick with me and you'll be Lovell royalty before you know it."

I stare at the two of them, wondering if it's possible that their egos are as big as Alex's. Maybe it's something they put in the fancy air con that's pumping around this building.

Suddenly, an upbeat song pumps through the speakers.

"Good enough for you, Princess?" Emmie taunts.

"You're going down, Ramsey."

The next four hours are the most exhausting of my life. If I thought that dancing was good exercise before this, then I was wrong. Oh so very wrong.

These girls, man. They're savage. Savagely beautiful. It's not hard to understand how soldiers of the Cirillo Family fell for them.

By the time they finally let up, I'm dripping in sweat, and my chest is heaving so hard I swear my lungs actually hurt, right alongside every other muscle in my body.

"I think you killed me," I groan, staring up at the ceiling above the boxing ring in a daze.

Someone chuckles. I'm not sure which one it is, but really, it doesn't matter.

"You're going to need to build up some stamina if you intend on keeping Alex around."

"I'm not sure I'm the one with the ability to make that call," I say, instantly regretting when their burning stares turn on me.

They're also lying on the sprung floor of the ring with me, but unlike me, they look like they've barely put a workout in.

"You're the one with the pussy. You have all the power," Stella says. "Take it away, and you'll have Alex on his knees, begging to get it back."

"You sound very confident about that."

"We know Alex," Emmie says, joining in. "He doesn't just look at anyone with those puppy dog eyes."

"If you say so," I say quietly.

"We do. And do you know what?" When I don't answer her rhetorical question, she continues. "We're never wrong."

I can't help but laugh. "I can believe that."

A phone pinging stops any further conversation and when I look over, I find Emmie looking up at her screen.

"Where the hell did you get that from?"

"A girl has to have her secrets." She shoots me a teasing wink.

"It's Arch. They're having a party at the den tonight. You in?"

I swallow nervously. "A Wolves party?"

"Yes, a Wolves party," Emmie confirms, barely able to restrain the eye roll I know she's desperate to do.

"I don't know," I say, worrying my lip.

I have never, ever got involved with the Wolves or the Lovell party scene. Both seemed like a really bad idea.

Plus, obviously, I've always been the shy, reclusive nerd who hides in the art department of Lovell Academy. No one in their right mind would ever invite me.

Blakely used to attend them, obviously. She's always been a social butterfly and was always super popular at school. But once her time got swallowed up dancing, among other things. Her free time to party got less and less.

I can't say I was sad about that. I used to be terrified every time I knew she was out partying. There are so many horror stories about what happens when the sun goes down in that place. Hell, it's almost as bad when the sun is up. But I was petrified that one night she just wouldn't return home.

Thankfully, that never happened. But I'm not sure I really want to be picking up where she left off.

"Oh, we should totally go," Stella agrees, sounding all kinds of mischievous. "It's been too long since we really got to party."

"That's what I'm thinking."

"And the guys are working late, right? It'll drive them crazy knowing we're in the Wolves' Den without them." Her eyes dance with mirth as she speaks, her entire body suddenly buzzing with excitement.

"Is that a good thing?" I ask, a little confused.

"Such a good thing." Emmie seems to agree as they both get this far-off look in their eyes.

"Remember the night they dragged us out of The Avenue after serving us house arrest? Didn't you fuck in the back of the car while Alex was driving?"

My chin drops at Emmie's words.

I don't need any kind of confirmation from Stella. The smile that lights up her face says it all.

"Like I said, it'll drive the guys wild. And I think Evie here needs a little experience of just how over the top and possessive our boys can be. Fuck, I'm getting flutters just thinking about it."

"I've already seen it. You're not the only one to be dragged out of The Avenue," I confess, feeling safe to open up a little with these two crazy women.

Stella rolls onto her front ready for the story, and Emmie and I do the same.

"Go on then, spill all the beans."

"Okay, but then I really need to go home."

"You're partying with us though, yeah?" Emmie asks, looking genuinely concerned I might turn them down.

Embracing my new rebellious streak, I turn my smile on her.

"Yeah, I am. I just need a few hours at home first."

"You got it. We'll pick you up en route. Now, give us all of Alex's dirty secrets. We're yet to meet a girl he's hooked up with."

I shake my head at the two of them, but I also can't wipe the smile off my face.

They're... a little bit awesome.

31

ALEX

"Did you get what you needed?" I ask the second I come to a stop inside the Boss's office. My father and Galen stand behind him, as seems to be the norm these days.

There's been no announcement about who's going to take over for Evan, but it'll have to happen at some point.

I'm torn about which way it's likely to go. Either Damien will just pick one of the two standing behind him, or he's using them to keep the position warm until he feels that Nico is ready.

He might look the part sitting before me, beside Theo, looking like he could take over the world. But it's all a front, a front we've been taught to wear since we were kids.

There's a part of me that really wants it for Nico. But there's also a part that's worried it'll be too soon.

Hence the stand-ins, I guess.

Only time will tell. And as of right now, things are calm, and hopefully, we can have a little time to relax before the next big drama kicks off.

"Yes, we did. Great work," Dad praises me, but it falls on deaf ears.

"What was it? Who is he?"

"Sorry, Son. We can't—"

Damien cuts my dad off with a simple raised hand.

"We're working with the Riveras to help with the human trafficking ring they're trying to take down. "

Nico tenses before me, his grip on the armrests turning his knuckles white.

"The one Brianna was almost dragged into?"

"Yes," Damien states.

"Luciana has been working closely with Reid Harris for a while now, trying to take down all the key players. It's led them here."

"So that guy? He didn't seem like he had the backbone to be trafficking anyone."

"No, but we had reason to believe he had intel."

"And did he?" I ask.

"Yes."

I breathe a little sigh of relief, hearing that what I did last night wasn't for nothing. It would have fucking sucked if it was.

"It's given us some leads to look into what we weren't already aware of."

"What do you need us to do?" Theo asks.

"Right now, nothing. My advice from before still stands. Focus on your last exams and take some time. Enjoy yourselves while you can. Things never remain quiet around here for long."

"That's it? That's all you're giving us on this?" Nico snaps. "What am I meant to tell Brianna?"

"That we're working on bringing the men down who were involved in this," Damien says simply. "It's not going to be an overnight thing, but we will ensure it happens. Luciana is out for blood, and so is Reid. Failure isn't an option."

"What about her mum? Will you need to talk to her?"

"Possibly. Although she was young when she went through what she did. This has been going on for twenty years since. The players will be different, the methods completely upgraded. I'm not sure she'll be of much help."

"Good. That's good."

Reaching forward, I squeeze Nico's shoulder in support.

He might not like his one-day mother-in-law, understandably. But he'll also do anything to protect both her and Brianna.

"And Reid, does he know about her yet?" Damien shakes his head. "When she's ready, you can both decide how to handle that."

Nico nods in agreement.

"Theo, Alex, Seb, you're up here on security. Nico and Toby, you're downstairs," Damien says, suddenly cutting off our little rendezvous.

I want to argue and demand the rest of the day off seeing as I had to work last night while these arseholes were loving life at the fight.

If I'm quick enough, Emmie might not have dropped Evie home yet and I could spend the day—

"Did you need something else, Alex?" Damien asks, the deep rumble of his voice dragging me from my daydream.

Glancing over my shoulder, I see the others are already at the door, leaving me standing here like a loon.

"Uh no, sorry. Have a good day," I mumble before rushing to the door. The others openly laugh at me, but fuck them.

Pricks.

"Evie's pussy that good, huh?" Theo whispers as I pass him.

He grunts as I punch him in the stomach then leave him behind as Seb and I go and let the guys currently monitoring the screens off so that they can leave.

"Surveillance. What fun," Seb mutters, echoing my displeasure as he sinks into a chair.

"Could be worse," Theo says after recovering from my hit.

"Really?" I grunt.

"Aw, missing your woman?" he teases.

"Too fucking right," Seb answers, crossing his arms over his chest and huffing out a frustrated breath. "I know we wanted life to calm down, but this? Seriously?"

"You're crabby. Stella's time of the month or something?" I ask. There's usually only one thing that puts him in a bad mood, and it's lack of sex.

"Pfft, as if that stops us."

"Don't know why you even bothered asking," Theo says, his eyes darting around screens as if he actually expects to find any wrongdoings on a sunny Sunday afternoon.

"I'd just rather be fucking her right now than this bullshit."

"Well, we love hanging out with you too, bro," I tease.

"That's not—" He swallows his words when he sees the smile on my face.

"Are you two going to focus or what?" Theo barks, getting into boss mode and throwing two earpieces at us.

Picking it up, I tuck it into place, part wishing we don't need to use them but also hoping for some excitement to help this shift along.

"So, about Alex's girl," Seb starts, no longer able to hide his curiosity.

"She's cool. Emmie likes her."

I stare at Theo, waiting for whatever is going to follow that statement up. But it never comes.

"What?" he asks, sensing my stare.

"That's it?"

"Sure."

"How have you possibly had time to do all your voodoo computer shit to discover all her dark deep secrets and red flags?"

"I'm good. But I'm not that good."

"So I'll wait for you to change your mind then, and warn me off?"

"You sound suspicious," Seb points out. "You think she's hiding something?"

From me, yeah. Her camming job. But from the world?

"No, just cautious. After Bri and her connection to the Hawks, I think we have every right to be."

"Where'd you meet her?"

"Uh…" I hesitate, rubbing the back of my neck.

"Paying for it again, huh?" Theo teases.

"She's not a hooker," I snap, defending her without even realising it.

"Joke, A. It was a joke."

"She was working last night, though. You gotta admit, some of those girls are—"

"She's not like them. It's just a job to get her to uni." Honestly, I have no idea if that's true or not. Until this morning, I had no idea about her plans to get an illustration degree.

"Fair enough. So, back to my original question…" Seb prompts.

With a sigh, I confess the truth. Both of them are aware of how wild my dad's poker nights can get, so it's not going to help with their previous suspicions.

"She was a dancer at Dad's over Christmas."

"You've been seeing her since Christmas and we're only just finding out about it?" Seb asks, looking genuinely hurt that I'd keep something like that a secret.

"No. I didn't see her again until a few weeks ago, and then again Friday night at Paradise."

"Now it all makes sense," Theo says as the pieces slot together. "I couldn't figure out why you wanted to go there. "You've been looking for her."

"Guilty," I confess.

"Well, you've got her now. What are you going to do about it?" Seb asks, making my heart sink.

I shake my head. "I can't. I can't keep her," I say quietly.

"Why the fuck not?" Theo asks incredulously.

I stare between my two best friends who are looking back at me like I've just sprouted a second head.

"I can't have anything serious, and we all know it."

"No, we don't know it," Seb says, his brows pinched in confusion.

"So you think it'll work, having a serious relationship while heading out to seduce who the fuck ever whenever my phone rings with a job?"

Both of them stare at me with blank expressions.

They know what I do. But I've never spoken about it so bluntly before. In fact, I do everything I can to keep it locked down.

"That doesn't have to be forever. It—"

"You think Dad will let me stop?"

"It wasn't him who trained you for the role, A. The man

who decided your fate is long dead. Maybe his wishes for you should be as well," Theo says, as if it'll be that easy.

"And do what? I don't have any skills like you lot do to offer the Family."

"Fuck off," Seb barks. "You're a fucking fantastic soldier and you know it."

"I can't do the tech stuff like you and Toby," I say to Theo. "And I can't shoot like you can," I admit, as much as it pains me to do while looking at Seb. "Without that... I'm... expendable."

"What the fuck, man?" Theo asks. "That is not fucking true. And anyway, who says you can't still do the same job, just not... you know, go all the way? You're fucking killer at seducing intel off our marks."

I shrug, hating how vulnerable I feel with this conversation.

"We'll see. I doubt she'll hang around long enough for me to even worry about it."

"Then I clearly met a different person this morning from the one you're thinking of, because the way she looked at you, bro."

"Don't, I beg.

"Just saying."

Seb reaches over and squeezes my shoulder. "We've got your back, man. You want her, go and fucking get her. The rest will work itself out."

I stare at him, wondering when one of my best friends turned into a fucking relationship guru.

The hours fucking drag as we sit there staring at the rest of the hotel on the screens before us.

As time passes, the casino and bars start to fill up, but it's boring as fuck.

"Someone wanna go and get us some fucking caffeine?" I ask, hoping one of them will volunteer because I'm fucking dead.

Everything hurts. Every-fucking-thing.

"You look wrecked, man," Seb says.

"I'll go. Get you some painkillers while I'm at it," Theo offers.

"Thanks," I mutter, focusing back on the screen again, wondering how I'm going to get through this shift without falling asleep on the job.

I get my answer a few seconds before Theo returns with a whole heap of snacks and the biggest cup of coffee he could find to pick me up.

My phone buzzes in my pocket, and I pull it out, expecting a message from Emmie to tell me that she's delivered Evie home safely and not smashed up Theo's car again. But what I find is a notification from the camming app I downloaded yesterday.

Elite Entertainment: Miss Vixen is now online.

All the air rushes from my lungs before my heart picks up speed.

This could be a really interesting way to keep myself awake for the next few hours.

Reaching for the take-out cup, I take a sip as I hit the button to connect me to her main feed.

"Ow, fuck," I bark the second the coffee singes a layer of skin from my tongue. "That's hot."

"You should have been more specific if you wanted it cold," Theo snarks.

Any response I might have had for him vanishes the second Evie fills my screen.

Holy fuck, she's beautiful.

I zone out as I watch her sitting at what I assume is a dressing table as she applies make-up to her currently bare skin.

Her blonde wig has covered her dark hair, telling me she's in performance mode. It helps me not to see her as the hot girl I had in my bed last night.

I can only hope the same goes for her if the time comes for me to confess my sins.

She talks away as she works, but with my phone on silent, I can't hear a word she's saying. And I can't lip-read for shit, so I focus on looking. I can't see anything from her waist down, but on the top, she's wearing a light pink lace bra that pushes her tits up in the most mouth-watering way. Just remembering how her skin tastes, how hard her nipples get when I brush my lips against her makes my cock swell.

32

———

ALEX

Theo and Seb's stares burn into the side of my face, but even their curiosity isn't enough to pull my eyes away from the screen.

I should know better, but the option to talk one on one that flashes at the top of the screen is too much to ignore, and before I know it, my finger is tapping the button and I'm agreeing to pay for fifteen minutes with my own girl.

Fucking better that than her chatting to someone else.

A few options pop up asking me if I want to give access to my camera or microphone. I decline both in a flash.

I might be willing to monopolise her time, but I don't want her to find out I know about this job of hers by popping up on her screen.

There's a time for surprising people, and right now definitely isn't it.

I get a little loading circle for a few seconds, I guess as the call connects.

Honestly, I've no idea what I'm doing. The only time I talk to people online is either with my friends, or marks. I've been known to do a little sexting in the past to ensure the results I need. I want to say that I'm not ashamed to admit that, but since meeting Evie, I kinda am.

In another life, maybe I'd be the kind of guy that she deserves. But instead, here I am, some fucked-up manipulative gigolo who gets pimped out by his own father.

Christ, thinking about it like that makes it sound even more fucked up than usual.

My heart jumps into my throat when I get a notification that Miss Vixen has joined our chat.

Finally, I glance up, catching the guy's eyes.

"What?" I blurt, sounding guilty as fuck. "TikTok," I say in the hopes it explains if they catch sight of my screen. "Do either of you have headphones on you?"

Sadly, neither of them does, leaving me with few options if I want to see this through.

Movement on the screen drags my attention back down.

One of the guys says something, but I'm too lost to the vision that is Evie to pay them any attention.

Her lips move, presumably asking me a question, but I can't hear her.

"Excuse me," I mumble, dumping my earpiece on the desk and shoving my chair back.

"Where the hell are you going?"

"I... I just need a minute." I wave them off before disappearing down the hall.

I turn to walk into the men's toilets, but at the last minute, I dart toward the disabled one.

No one who ever comes to the top floor of this building is disabled, and as far as I know, all our soldiers who might venture this high are all currently walking on two legs, so I shouldn't be blocking anyone from taking a slash.

The second I'm in the room, the scent of toilet cleaner hits my nose, but it's not enough of a turn-off to stop me.

Shoving the seat closed, I lower my arse and turn the volume up.

Evie is quiet on the other end. She must know I'm here. Maybe she thinks I'm nervous or something. That wouldn't be far from the truth, to be fair.

SinfulPlayer: Sorry, I'm here. Just had to find somewhere quiet to enjoy you alone.

Her eyes dart to the corner of the screen as she reads, then she looks directly at the camera with her big blue eyes.

"Fuck," I breathe. How is it possible that she affects me almost as much through a screen as she does in person?

"Hey. I thought you'd gone all shy on me for a minute then."

SinfulPlayer: Not at all. Just at… work.

"Well, you must have the world's best boss if he lets you slip out to talk to me."

"Or world's most terrifying," I mutter to myself. He would literally have my balls if he knew I was doing this when I should be on duty.

SinfulPlayer: If only he paid better so I could spend more time with you.

"Well, I guess we'll just have to make the most of our time together."

She smiles so sweetly at the camera that it's easy to ignore the blonde hair and the fact we're on a camming site.

"What did you have in mind for these fifteen minutes?" she asks, her voice raspy with need.

I'm sure she's putting it on for the camera, but fuck, my cock really doesn't care.

SinfulPlayer: I just want to listen to you talk.

"You are such a fucking pussy," I chastise myself. *Just tell her you want to watch her and get off imagining she was right in front of you like you would if you were being true to yourself.*

But despite knowing how painfully accurate those words are, I don't say them.

She thinks I'm some random man out there in the world somewhere, getting hard and horny over some young and innocent school girl... if her profile is to be believed.

At least I know she's about to finish her A Levels at LA. I know she's old enough, but the scumbags she talks to don't.

That thought kills my high for a moment, but it soon recovers when Evie continues looking directly at me through the camera while trailing her fingers seductively around the cup of her bra.

"Okay, we can do that? Did you have a topic in mind?"

SinfulPlayer: What made you start camming?

Her lips part to respond, but I quickly add more, concerned I sound like some creepy journo trying to get some inside scoop on a cam girl's life.

SinfulPlayer: A beautiful woman like you must have a queue of men waiting around the block to spend time with you in real life.

She smiles, her cheeks heating at my compliment.

"I'm not interested in the men out on the street."

Thank fuck. I know the area you live in.

"It's hard to know what their intentions are. Here, I don't know," she says thoughtfully. "I guess, I'm a different person here. I can shed my shyness and embrace my inner goddess."

My cock strains against my fly as she continues teasing me with featherlight touches of her own body.

My hand moves of its own volition, rubbing my length through my trousers as my eyes flick between her fingers and her eyes. Something she doesn't miss because her touches get more and more brazen.

My next question should not be asked here. Really, I know the answer. I think I've always known, but I need to hear it.

SinfulPlayer: Are you a virgin?

Her smile is all sweetness, but her actions as she pinches her nipple through the fabric of her bra are anything but.

"Yes."

Spurred on, I continue to undo my fly and shove my trousers and boxers around my hips.

I can't help it.

It's her. She does things to me no other woman has before.

I wrap my hand around myself, groaning at the relief, but it's not enough.

SinfulPlayer: Has anyone ever touched you, Vixen?

She gasps at my question, her eyes darkening and her blush spreading down onto her chest.

Even if she lies, I have my answer.

"Just one person."

SinfulPlayer: Someone important?

"Right now, the only important person in my life is you." I know it's a line and that she's just playing the game, but fuck, it hurts.

SinfulPlayer: You can tell me. I don't mind sharing.

Big fat fucking lie. Any other woman, or man, to be fair, I'd be down for sharing in a heartbeat. But my vixen? No fucking chance.

If I got my way, no other person on this planet would ever get the chance to be with her like I have been. Like I want to be.

She stares at the camera, her eyes searing into mine.

It's fucking unnerving.

She can't see me—I know she can't—but the connection I feel with her sparks through the screen nonetheless.

"How about we focus on why we're really here," she finally says. "Tell me what you're doing right now."

Her heavy lashes bat against her cheekbones and she tilts her head to the side.

My cock jerks in my hand. I don't think I've ever been this turned on without someone else physically in the room.

The power she holds...

Fuck, she's good.

"Or, if you're feeling a little shy, tell me what you'd like me to do."

She smiles. It's so sweet and innocent. But I know the truth.

The image of her legs spread for me, her pretty pink cunt right there for the taking, spurs me on.

SinfulPlayer: Show me your tits. I want to see how pink your nipples are.

She bites down on her bottom lip. I want to believe the shyness, that she's a little hesitant with a new client.

Anger pulses just beneath the surface. I could be any man on the planet right now. And she's about to...

"Fuck," I groan when she pulls the lace cup of her bra down, showing me those rosy buds.

But they're not hard. No like they were for me this morning. And that knowledge sends relief shooting through me.

SinfulPlayer: You're beautiful.

Her blush rises again.

SinfulPlayer: I'm so hard for you.

"Are you playing with yourself?"

"Fuck yes," I grunt, working myself harder, faster. Almost punishing myself for doing this. For being so turned on watching her, for hating what she's doing. I have no right to an opinion on her life. She's allowed to do whatever she wants for money with no judgement.

I'm such a fucking hypocrite.

SinfulPlayer: Yes.

It's all I can manage, my hand trembling with release and my balls starting to draw up.

"Keep stroking your cock," she purrs, her voice like liquid sin and shooting straight to where I need it most.

Her hands move on her breasts, pinching her nipples and letting little moans escape.

They're fake. They sound nothing like the noises she makes when she's actually turned on.

It's another reminder I need that the girl on the screen isn't the girl who was in my bed.

"That's it," she encourages. "You're such a bad boy. I love it."

"Oh, fuck. Fuck," I bark as I spill all over my hand before it drips on my black trousers.

Fucking great.

SinfulPlayer: Fuck, that was good.

A wide smile graces her lips as I confirm that she's done her job.

SinfulPlayer: Thank you.

She chuckles, "You're more than welcome. I'd love to do this again sometime. It's been fun chatting with you."

I don't get a chance to reply because the screen goes blank and a pop-up emerges asking if I want more time. For a price, obviously.

The high I was riding immediately vanishes and the anger that was bubbling takes over.

"Fuck," I roar, swinging my arm around so my clenched fist collides with the wall.

That was my girl.

My fucking girl.

And I loved it. She was so fucking beautiful, so confident, sexy. She fucking owned it. I've never come so hard alone in a bathroom.

But also...

I really fucking hated it.

***

By the time I storm back into the security room, I'm barely keeping a lid on my emotions.

I'm so fucking confused. She has me in a tailspin, and I don't think it's going to slow down anytime soon.

All the things I wish I said to her in that short chat hit me like rocks, one after the other. Regret that I didn't think of them swirls around me like poison.

Both Theo and Seb spin around and look my way when I enter, both with knowing smirks on their faces.

"Oh, look out," Seb says, the amused lilt in his tone making me already hate what he's about to say. "You've got a little..." He wiggles his finger in the direction of my crotch.

"Cum stain," he says, barely keeping a straight face as he says those final two words.

While Theo barks out a laugh, his focus on the job is completely shot.

"Fuck you both," I grunt, marching forward with my head held high.

After I cleaned myself up, I gave my trousers a good mop down. Although, that doesn't mean I did a great job. I'm not going to let these fuckers know I'm not completely confident that there isn't cum on my trousers.

I fall into my chair, surprised the top of my head doesn't just pop right off with the amount of tension within me.

Reaching for my earpiece, my fingers curl tightly around it until I fear it's going to shatter.

I try to focus on breathing, not on my girl practically topless on the internet.

What else does she do?

She asked me to tell her what I wanted her to do. Where would she have drawn the line?

It's her body; it doesn't matter.

She does not belong to you.

And even if she did, there is nothing wrong with what she's doing, you possessive prick.

"You want to talk about it?" Seb offers, any hit of amusement now gone as he studies me with concern.

"No," I grunt. "Let's just do our jobs then get out of here."

I focus on the screens in front of me, but I don't see any of it.

Instead, I spend the next few hours replaying that fifteen minutes online with Evie over and over in my head.

By the time Seb growls in frustration beside me when

our shift is almost over, I'm more than ready to go and find Evie and lay all my cards on the table.

Problem is, they're all so fucking jumbled up, I have no idea what would actually come out of my mouth.

"What?"

"They're in Lovell," he growls.

"They're—"

"At the Den."

I don't need to ask who they're talking about. It's more than fucking obvious.

I might be chastising myself for the level of possessiveness I'm feeling over Evie, but it has nothing on these two wankers.

"Were they on a curfew or something?" I mutter, glad to focus on something other than my own issues for once.

"No, but—"

"So just turn up and surprise them. You know it's what they're expecting."

The two of them share a conspiratorial look.

"You think they've taken your girl?" Theo asks, looking around Seb and right at me.

His words slam into me like a truck.

"I don't have a girl," I snap, fucking hating the truth behind those words the second they fall from my lips. "And if I did, why would they take her?"

"Because they spent the day hanging out? Because she lives in Lovell?" Theo suggests.

"Because neither Stella nor Emmie will ever take no for an answer," Seb adds.

My heart begins to race as I think about her on that call. She was getting ready, putting make-up on. What if she were getting ready for a party, and right this very minute she's standing in the middle of a bunch of fucking Wolves who are looking at her like she's their next meal?

"Let's fucking go," I bark, jumping to my feet.

"Calm down, Casanova. We need our replacements to show up first."

33

———

EVIE

I wasn't expecting to return home to an empty flat. Well, empty aside from my father who was festering away in his room like always. And there was no way I was going to stick my head inside that room to say hello.

I'd messaged Blake and discovered that she'd caved to Zay's begging and had taken him to the skate park, seeing as it was a nice evening. She was happily sitting with her favourite iced latte and topping up her tan. She was probably being ogled by Zay's mates and every horny teenage boy who was hanging out at the park, but she didn't need me telling her that. She was more than used to the attention.

So, I figured I should make the most of my time and earn some money. I showered quickly, washing away the sweat that was covering my skin after the insane workout, and slathered my favourite moisturiser over my body.

Thankfully, my headache from last night has gone. Yes, the spot on the back of my head is still sore, but mostly all that's left of the nightmare is my hazy memories.

I haven't heard anything from Derek, but I can't imagine he has anything good to say about the fact I didn't complete my shift. I guess I can kiss goodbye to that double pay he promised. I doubt I'll even get single pay.

I let out a sigh as I wrap a towel around my body and wash my face.

Despite the memories, I don't miss the way my eyes sparkle with happiness when I look at myself in the mirror. It would be easy to convince myself that it was my time with Emmie and Stella this afternoon that put it there. Part of it is them. Emmie and I might have been at school together for years, although she's a year younger, but we've never really spoken. Honestly, I was a little scared of her. Her and anyone who ran with the Wolves. I'd heard enough horror stories to know the best place to be is as far away from them as possible. But this afternoon, they gave me everything I didn't know I needed. Blake has always been my best friend. Yes, sad, I know. But it's true.

But they're not the real reason for the lightness staring back at me. That's him.

I might have a million and one questions, and he might have just more than a few red flags that should be warning me off. But when we're together... I feel like I've never felt before in my life.

It sounds stupid, but he brings me to life in a way I've only ever seen on TV or read in books. Who knew it actually existed in real life?

I can't lose my head to that, though. The connection is one thing, but I need to get to know him before I can decide if this is actually anything. And getting to know him means confessing what I do in my spare time. He might know about the dancing, but that barely brushes the surface.

When I started camming, I didn't even consider that

there could be a boy that I'd need to think about. Blake and Zay were my only concerns. I had no intention of ever seeing the guy from the poker night again, let alone whatever this is right now.

And how do you even bring it up? *Hey, do you have any hobbies? I do. I talk to horny men online and fulfil some of their fantasies.*

"Ugh," I groan as I apply my cleanser.

I really haven't thought any of this through properly.

But despite that, when I get through to my bedroom, I pull open my underwear drawer and select something I know my clients will like, and then I set myself up with my tablet at the dressing table—after clearing away some of Blakely's shit, obviously.

I log in and set up my live feed, hoping that a few of my regulars might be around to earn me a little quick cash before I have to leave.

Nerves twist up my stomach as I think about this party I've agreed to once more.

I'm heading into the Wolves' Den. Literally.

They're all going to take one look at me, recognise me as the girl who hides from everyone and laugh, I'm sure of it. Of course, that does actually rely on them ever paying me enough attention in the first place.

Once I know I'm streaming, I start chatting away as if it's Blake on the other end of a video call, waiting for someone to join me.

A handful do, so I keep chatting about my party plans tonight and other waffle. Honestly, I don't know how I manage to find anything to say. But thankfully, it keeps bubbling up. And as my viewer number increases, I get more and more motivation to keep going.

Everything is fine. Until I get a request for private time with a username I don't recognise.

Guilt. That's what knots up my stomach to the point that I think I'm going to vomit.

It's ridiculous. Alex and I have promised each other nothing. There is no us. No future.

But it doesn't stop me from considering what he would think. If he would hate me doing this, giving a part of myself to strangers. If he knew, would it turn him off me? Would it be the end? Or would he understand? No, surely no guy would understand this.

But the promise of money, of having a little more in my uni pot is enough to push thoughts of him aside and accept the call.

Plastering on my best game face, I get to work.

After all, I'm a professional.

"Whoa, look at you," Blake says after knocking on the door for permission to enter. That was something we learned very quickly when she did some camming a few years ago and I walked right in in the middle of something I'm never going to be able to unsee.

I shudder just thinking about the man on the screen with a collar and lead on.

I mean, each to their own and all that. But not my thing. Especially when he was alone and having to pretend that my sister was what... walking him?

A wave of apprehension washes through me as she drops her eyes down my body.

"That dress looks insane on you. You can totally borrow it, by the way."

"Thanks," I mutter, my cheeks heating under her perusal.

"So... what's the occasion? Derek doesn't have you doing something you don't want to make up for last night, does he?"

I shake my head. "I'm going to a party," I blurt.

Blake's eyebrows shoot up. "A party? With Alex?"

"Um... no. With Emmie Ramsey and her friend."

Lowering her arse to the bed, she rests back on her palms, silently demanding more information.

Sitting on the dressing table stool opposite her, I slip my feet into my shoes.

"They're Alex's friends. I spent time with them today. They're pretty cool. Archer invited Emmie to a party and she invited me, so..."

Realisation hits her like lightning, her lips twitching into a smile. "You're going to a Wolves party?"

"Apparently so."

"Who are you, and what have you done to my shy little sister?" she jokes.

I shrug, feeling weird about all of this. A lot has changed in the past few months. It's like I spent seventeen and three-quarter years hiding, and then I met Alex. I started discovering I was more than a little mouse who hides in the art department at LA and refuses to speak to anyone remotely popular, excluding my big sister.

"Is it too much?" I ask.

"What? No, of course not. Why would you even think that?"

I shrug again, unable to find the words to express my feelings.

I feel... right. I should be embracing this, enjoying this, but there's still a little part of that old girl still lingering, telling me that I'm not enough to pull off this sexy little black dress, or the heels, or hang out with these people.

"Whatever you're thinking, stop it. Stop it right now," Blake demands. "You're beautiful and sexy and you deserve this. All of this. Friends, a boyfriend, to enjoy yourself. To let go and be a crazy almost eighteen-year-old," she says, raising a brow. "It's like an early birthday party."

"Blake," I warn. "I've already told you that—"

"That we're to let your big day pass without a fuss. Yeah, I heard. Doesn't mean I agree, though."

I glare at her but it doesn't achieve anything. She just grins at me, her eyes silently telling me that she's already organised something that is the exact opposite of what I requested.

"Is Alex going to be there? Vickie told me everything you failed to about what happened last night, by the way. Sounded hot as hell how he came to your rescue and then carried you out of there like a white knight."

"White? Did she fail to mention how much blood he was covered in?"

"He did that for you, Eve. He wants you."

My cheeks heat.

"Have you?"

"No. Still... other stuff," I confess. I've no idea why I get more embarrassed talking about sex with a real-life person when I have no issues discussing camming with Blake.

Because it's real, a little voice says in my head.

"Maybe tonight is the night. Ooooh, or you should wait a few days, do it for your birthday." She wiggles her brows.

"I'm not having sex just because it's my birthday. I want to have sex when—"

"You've got an incredibly sexy mafia man between your thighs who is willing to shed blood to protect you and carry you back to his bed to take care of you?"

"Umm... I was going to say when I'm ready, but—"

"I've got a point, and you know it."

"We'll see. I'm not planning anything." *Because they all go out of the window when we're together anyway.*

My phone starts buzzing across the countertop. "Looks like it's time to go. Do I look okay? I have no idea what to wear to a Wolv—"

"You look perfect. He'll love it."

"Blake."

"Go. Enjoy yourself. Get drunk, dance, laugh. And if you need me, call me. If Alex isn't there to beat someone's arse for you, then I can."

"Don't worry. Emmie and her friend, Stella, are more than capable. They're savages."

"I feel like there could be a story there. But there's no time right now. Go."

She practically ushers me out of the house to the idling car outside.

Sucking in a deep breath, I walk toward the open back door and slip inside.

"You look amazing," Stella says while Emmie shimmies over into the middle seat so I can fit in."

"Thanks. So do you."

Thankfully, they're dressed very similarly to me. Emmie is in a black denim dress with a barely-done-up zip running down the front, exposing her bra, with fishnets and biker boots on her feet. Her make-up is heavy, and her hair is stylishly messy. From what I know of her, it's just... her. And Stella has a shimmery silver dress with spaghetti straps much like mine and what I assume has an open back.

"You two look like twins," Emmie notes.

"I'll take that. Evie is gorgeous," Stella says, giving my confidence a nice little boost.

"Okay, let's get this party started," Emmie says, pulling a little bottle of vodka from her bag and twisting the top.

"Have you told your guys where we're going?"

"Nah, no need," Stella says. "They'll find us eventually."

"Can't wait," Emmie says before swallowing a shot.

"He's gonna be pissed when he sees how much of your knickers you're offering up to the Wolves."

"Pfft, he'll love it. At least I'm not a total ho like some." She jerks her chin in Stella's direction teasingly while the driver coughs. "Are you even wearing *panties?*" she asks, mocking her American accent.

"Of course. I have no plans to pull a Wolf, and I'd prefer if Seb didn't kill anyone tonight."

"That would be ideal," I mumble, wondering what their lives must be like to talk so openly about murder and sex in front of an innocent driver.

The journey is short, and despite not wanting to get drunk, I find myself having more than a couple of shots.

"I'm going to need food," I confess, handing the bottle back.

"We only had waffles a few hours ago," Emmie argues.

"I know, but I don't really drink and—"

"You'll be fine. Just take it slow. The guys will have snacks. It's all good," Stella assures me.

In only minutes, we're pulling up to the Wolves' Den, a warehouse in the deepest and roughest part of Lovell. A place I try really hard not to visit. Ever.

There are people everywhere, and my nerves threaten to get the better of me. But as if they can sense it, the second we climb from the car, both girls flank my sides and thread their arms through mine.

"Ready?" Emmie asks.

"I really don't think I am."

"Good. Out of your comfort place is the best place to be. Look out Lovell, Evie Moore is here," she jokes as the two of them surge forward, giving me little choice but to move with them.

I'm not really sure what I was expecting. A warehouse full of debauchery, drug use, fighting and fucking, maybe. But what I get is... well, a party.

There are people everywhere chatting, laughing and dancing. Some are dressed casually, others more dressed up, mostly the women.

"EMMIE," someone screams, and when we spin around, I find two girls from school bounding our way.

Misha and Low pull Emmie into a group hug, leaving me and Stella on the periphery.

"It's been too long, girl."

"I know. Things have been a bit crazy. You remember Evie, right?"

They both study me for a moment, making me wish the ground would swallow me up.

"Yeah," Low says. "Moore. Blakely's sister, right?"

I internally groan. "Yep, that's me."

"Well, welcome. Grab some drinks and we'll go and find the guys. Arch and Dax were only talking about you the other day."

"All good, I hope," Emmie says with a wide smile.

"Dax loves you. Do you know how much pussy he's got since you gifted him a bad-arse gunshot wound?" Misha says.

My brows shoot up in shock.

Leaning over, I whisper-shout, "You shot Niall Daxton?"

I mean, he's no Archer Wolfe, but he's next in line of importance.

"What? No, don't be stupid," she says, before dropping the truth bomb. "Theo did."

All the air rushes out of my lungs, but I don't get a chance to say anything else before we're steered toward a huge crowd. And front and centre of that crowd is none other than King Archer and his two loyal princes, Dax and Jace, holding court.

"Wow," I breathe. I might have spent years at school with them, but standing there now, leading Lovell's most notorious gang? Well, they're even larger than life than I remember from when they ruled the hallways.

Archer is busy talking to someone, but the second Emmie forces her way through the crowd, he spots her and a wide smile pulls at his lips.

He pulls her into a hug that I'm sure her husband would hate, but he doesn't seem bothered, even if he did shoot his best friend already.

Emmie looks back the second he releases her and gestures me over.

My entire body trembles as I move closer.

Coming to a Wolves party is one thing. But hanging out with Lovell royalty is another entirely.

Emmie introduces us and I wait for the standard 'Blakely's sister' comment, but it never comes.

His eyes narrow a little as he studies me, but he clearly doesn't know who I am.

"Welcome. Any friend of Emmie's is good with us."

And just like that, I'm welcomed into the dark

underworld of Lovell that I never wanted anything to do with.

Weird how life turns out.

34

ALEX

Way too much time has passed since Seb tracked the girls and discovered that Stella and Emmie are in Lovell, or more specifically, at the Wolves' Den.

And unsurprisingly, when I pulled up the tracking app myself and located the tracker I installed in her phone Friday night, I find her in exactly the same place.

Of fucking course they dragged her into this.

It shouldn't bother me. I trust Emmie and Stella; I know they'll protect her just like they would if Calli were partying with them. But while I trust them, I also know what bad influences they are. And Lovell is unpredictable. Or more so the pricks who live there. They'll see her as fresh meat and—

"Will you chill the fuck out?" Seb barks from the driver's seat.

"I'm fine," I lie. He's been getting irritated with how erratically my knee has been bouncing since we left The Empire. Now we're pulling up around the back of the

Wolves' Den, I'm even more restless than I was then. "I just want to make sure she's okay."

"All this time, all the abuse you've given us about protecting our girls. And look at you," Theo says helpfully from the back.

"What?" I ask. "Even you can admit you're both a little OTT at times. Plus, your girls are total bad-arses who could flatten any cunt who tries something. Mine... Evie," I correct, "isn't like them. She's a lover, not a fighter."

"Hey, I take offence to that. Stella is an amazing lover," Seb barks.

"Fucking hell," I mutter, shoving my door open and immediately marching across the pot-holed gravel car park.

Seb's Maserati sticks out like a sore thumb amongst all the old bangers most of Lovell drive around in. The only decent cars here belong to Archer and his boys. And that's only because no one would dare touch them.

The fact that neither Stella's nor Theo's car is here gives a clue as to what state we'll find the girls in when we get inside.

They came with the intention of partying if they organised a driver.

Shaking my head, I think about those two playing my boys to perfection.

I'm sure they're here to get a rise out of them.

They're so predictable, yet Theo and Seb fall for it every time. Not that they don't get anything out of it. If their girls are drunk or high here, they're in for a good night.

The second I push through the main doors and nod at the two Wolves who are guarding the door, I head deeper into the warehouse.

The place is packed. In seconds, sweat makes my shirt stick to my back and beads at my brow.

A few people notice my arrival. Smart ones move out of my way, and the stupid ones just stare as I search for three familiar faces.

"Fuck," I hiss after doing an entire lap of the place without finding them. "Have you seen Archer?" I ask a guy who I recognise as a Wolf.

He's wasted, his eyes barely able to focus on me as he tries to decipher my words.

"Archer?" I bark.

Lifting his hand, he points to the back of the warehouse.

"Fucking great," I mutter, taking off toward his private residence that covers the entire back of the building.

More Wolves stand guard at the door, keeping mere plebs from going back there uninvited.

The guy on my left opens his mouth—to refuse me entry, I'm sure. But then Theo and Seb burst through the crowd and he quickly changes his mind.

"Enjoy your evening, lads."

I glare at him as I pass. The fucking pussy swallows nervously.

I've just passed him when I suddenly dart back and shout, "Boo," in his face.

I swear to God, the prick actually shits his pants.

"Dude, what the fuck?" his mate barks out between his laughter.

"There's a reason why you're out here working and not partying behind the door," I tell him before marching away again.

In here, the music is a little quieter and there are far fewer people crowding the space, meaning that we find the girls we've been hunting for in seconds.

The three of them are standing on top of a table, dancing like no one is watching.

I pause for a moment, just watching Evie move in time with the music. It doesn't matter that she's not at work or locked in a cage; she's just as hypnotising.

Seb and Theo don't seem as thrilled, as the girls provide entertainment for more than a few Wolves whose eyes are locked on their gyrating bodies.

The second Emmie and Stella spot the wild beast heading their way, they exchange a knowing look before jumping out of reach.

Evie throws her head back, laughing at them, her entire face lighting up with amusement. It's fucking breathtaking. So is the little black dress she's wearing that's been revealed now Emmie and Stella have put some space between them.

I see the moment reality hits her; it's at the same time that both Emmie and Stella are manhandled from the table and dragged away. Exactly what they were hoping for, I'm sure.

Evie's head lowers, and she begins scanning the room.

She has to know that if my boys are here, I'm not too far away.

And not two seconds later, she discovers she's right.

Her eyes lock on mine and her chin drops.

A smile pulls at my lips as I stand there watching her.

She looks back, probably wondering why I'm not hauling her over my shoulder and marching her out of here for putting on a show up there.

Little does she know, I fucking love it.

For the first time, I realise that it doesn't matter who's watching her. I'm the only one who's going to be taking her home tonight. It's my bed, and only my bed that she's going to be sleeping naked in.

But she doesn't need to know that. Not yet, anyway.

Taking a step forward, I lift my hand, gesturing for her to continue.

She looks around nervously, feeling self-conscious that she's lost her buddies. But unable to refuse my demand, she slowly starts dancing again.

My cock jerks and my palms begin to sweat.

Fuck me, she's a goddess.

Everyone else in the room blurs into nothing. Even the music seems to evaporate as I watch her.

I've no idea how long I stand there with my eyes locked on her, but eventually, my need to be close gets too much and I stalk forward.

I'm on the table before I've recognised that I've made a decision about what happens next, and I've got one hand around her throat and another gripping her hip, holding her right against me.

"You're a tease, Vixen. You've got all the men in this room wishing you were theirs," I growl in her ear.

She shudders against me as my breath dances down her neck and over her shoulder.

"All of them are imagining what you'd look like if you let this dress drop to the floor."

Releasing her hip, I slide my hand around to her arse.

"They want to know how turned on you are from putting on this little show. Because you love it, don't you? You love pretending to be a dirty slut, you love having eyes on you, experimenting with your exhibitionist side, don't you?"

"Alex," she cries when I latch onto her neck and suck until I break the skin.

"But they can't have you. Do you know why?" I ask.

When she shakes her head, I squeeze her arse hard, punishing her for being naïve.

"Because you're mine, Evie. You can steal all these motherfuckers' attention all night long if you want. But. You. Are. Mine."

Forgetting we're not in a room alone, I slide my hand lower, letting one of my fingers brush against her knickers.

"Fuck, Vixen. You're soaked."

"Please," she whimpers.

"Dirty little thief. It makes me want to steal something from you that you can never get back."

Understanding my words, she grinds against my cock.

"Fucking seductress."

Releasing her throat, I twist my fingers in her hair and drag her head back so I can look at her.

Her eyes are blown and a little bloodshot.

"You drunk or high?"

"D-drunk," she admits with a giggle. "Really drunk. Dance with me," she demands, and just like everything to do with her, I'm powerless but to agree.

Pulling my hand away from the danger zone of her pussy, I grip her arse once more as I roll my hips with her.

"Yes," she sighs before I claim her lips with mine, kissing her as deeply as I can while the world continues around us.

I devour her like it's my last chance to kiss her. It's wet and dirty, and fucking everything as our teeth clash and our tongues duel.

My cock aches to do more, to take her right here in the middle of Archer's living room to prove to every motherfucker who might have been watching her dance that she's mine. That none of them stand a chance because I'd fucking kill them before they got anywhere close.

When someone taps my leg, I almost break their nose when I kick out at them. Thankfully, they predict my move, which gives me a clue as to who it is.

Ripping my lips from Evie's, I glare down at the prick who's interrupted us.

"What?" I bark at Theo, who's staring at us with a shit-eating grin.

"We're leaving. You coming?"

I glance at Evie, wanting her opinion, but the second I find her hooded, drunk eyes, I get my answer.

"Yeah, let's go."

Releasing her, I jump down to the floor and then hold my hands out for her.

Without question, she throws herself into my arms and I stumble back.

"Christ, thief. You trying to kill me?" I joke.

"Nope. I need you too much to kill you."

"Is that right?" I ask as I tuck her under my arm and follow Theo and Emmie out of the room.

"Yep, all I can think about is having your head between my thighs," she admits, making my breath catch.

When I look over, she's got a lazy smile playing on her lips and her eyes are wild with desire.

"How much have you had to drink?" I ask.

"Enough to be really fucking happy, but not enough not to know what I'm doing."

"Right," I laugh, not entirely believing her as she wobbles in her heels.

When we get to Seb's car, we find Seb has Stella pinned against it with her legs wrapped around his thighs.

"You should probably be glad you're drunk. This could be an interesting journey," I whisper in Evie's ear.

"Why?" she asks naïvely.

"Wait and see."

Before Seb has a chance of lowering Stella to her feet, both Theo and I have pulled the back doors open and dropped inside, dragging our girls onto our laps.

The two of us share a look a beat before Seb slams his hand against the window in irritation, making Evie squeal in shock.

"Ignore him. He's just discovered karma."

Her brows pinch in confusion, a look that's entirely too cute. "Come here, Vixen. I'm not done with you yet."

"Fuck my life," Seb grunts as he falls into the driver's seat and looks directly at me in the rear-view mirror.

"What's wrong, Papatonis?" I ask, pulling away from Evie's lips enough to speak. "Can't cope with a taste of your own medicine?"

"I fucking hate you. All of you."

"Aw, poor little Sebby-Webby isn't getting his wiener stroked," Emmie teases in a squeaky voice that has everyone in the car, aside from Seb, falling about laughing.

"Just drive, baby. The sooner we get home, the sooner you can get in the action," Stella says.

"You mean you're not going to blow me as I drive?" he asks, his face dropping in disappointment.

"Nope."

"But it was epic last time," he pouts.

"Aw, you're a big boy, I'm sure you can cope."

"That's what she said," Emmie teases.

Evie snorts a laugh, but it's soon cut off when she looks back at me.

The engine rumbles to life while Seb mutters his irritation at everyone before he backs out of the space.

"I hope your exhibitionist side is also a bit of a voyeur."

"W-why?" she stutters.

I don't need to respond—Emmie does it for me.

"Oh, fuck. Yes," she cries, and when we look over, Theo is attached to her neck with his hands inside her dress, squeezing her tits.

"Oh," Evie gasps.

"Do you remember how long it took to get from our place to yours this afternoon?" I ask.

She nods.

"Plenty of time for things to get a whole lot worse."

"Is this safe?" she asks, proving that she's not as drunk as she could be.

"Hell no. That's half the fun, Vixen."

Threading my fingers through her hair, I drag her lips back to mine and slide her down my thighs, my other hand on her arse.

Her dress rides up, but if she cares, she doesn't say anything.

Her gasp rips through the air when I thrust up, grazing her barely covered clit with my cock.

Taking both of her hips in my hands, my fingertips dig in as I grind her against me.

"Fuck, Evie," I groan, forcing my eyes open as we kiss to meet Seb's gaze that's burning into me from the front.

His eyes narrow briefly before he has to focus on the road once more.

"You think we can make him come in his pants before we get back?" Emmie pants.

"Hell yeah, we can," Stella happily responds.

"Your friends are crazy," Evie almost shouts as I suck on her neck.

"Fuck yeah, we are," Stella agrees. "Welcome to the madhouse, Evie. You'll never forget this ride."

Evie cries out in response as I graze her clit again.

"Fucking hate you all," Seb grunts, taking a corner a little too fast, but Theo are I are ready for it and hold our girls tight.

I glance over and catch his eye, nodding at his silent question.

Let the good times roll.

35

EVIE

"**O**h my God," I cry as Alex works me into a frenzy despite the fact we're fully clothed.

He licks along my collarbone before kissing down my chest while alternating between grabbing handfuls of my braless breasts and pinching my nipples through the thin satin fabric of my dress.

A cry from beside me forces my eyes open.

I shouldn't look, but my curiosity easily wins out.

Looking over, I watch, fascinated as Theo sucks on Emmie's tits. Right. There. In. Front. Of. Us.

A surge of heat rushes straight to my core, soaking my already ruined knickers. I'm pretty sure I'm at the point of creating a damp patch on Alex's trousers, I'm so hot.

"More," she cries. "Theo, more."

"Fucking knew you'd love watching," Alex growls against my skin. "I can feel the heat of your pussy through my clothes. So fucking hard for you."

"Stella, why aren't you wearing any panties under that dress?" Seb bellows.

Emmie and I both look at each other before falling

about laughing as our previous conversation comes back to us.

"Whoops. I must have forgotten," Stella says innocently. Although, something tells me there isn't an innocent bone in her body.

"You were dancing on top of a table with my pussy on display for anyone to see?" The fury in his voice makes me tense, but it seems that Stella is totally unfazed.

Alex's rough knuckles brush over my shoulder, and it's not until a rush of cool air washes over my breast that I realise he's exposed me.

I want to care, to cover up and revert back to my old shy self, but I swallow it down.

I'm no longer her. I'm this new, confident, and sexy version of myself. And if Emmie and Stella can be so brazen, then why can't I?

"Who's seeing it now?" Stella counters.

"Do you want me to kill us all?" Seb growls.

"You won't," she says confidently. "But you will drive faster, because you know you want this."

He growls in frustration. I can only imagine what she's doing to torture him.

"That's it, Hellcat. Take it."

"Oh my God," I scream as Alex wraps his lips around my nipple, sucking it deep into his mouth, and I catch sight of Theo impaling Emmie on his cock beside me. "Please, Alex. I need... I need—"

"I got you, Vixen," he promises, switching to my other side as he shifts us a little so he can get his fingers between my thighs. "So fucking wet for me."

He wastes no time in pushing the soaked fabric aside and plunging two fingers inside me.

"Yes, yes, yes," I chant.

My head spins as he works me hard and fast into what I already know is going to be a mind-blowing release.

The other moans and groans bouncing around the car only spur me on as I shamelessly ride his fingers, desperate for the release that's right in touching distance.

Beside me, Emmie screams out Theo's name as she falls, and I can't help but go right alongside her, my entire body locking up as pleasure slams into me.

"Fuck, Vixen. You just soaked my hand," Alex whispers in my ear so no one else can hear—assuming they have the capacity to hear anything right now.

My heart pounds, and my limbs tingle with aftershocks from the release.

"Can't fucking wait to slide my cock into this tight cunt."

"Yes," I breathe. Honestly, if he took it out right now, I'd have no arguments with sitting straight down on him.

So I guess it's a good thing that the car is suddenly flooded with light before it stops in what I quickly realise is the underground garage of their building.

"Thank fuck for that. You can get your fingers out of your cunt now, Princess. I've got something better for you." Seb is out of the car before he's even finished talking.

"Don't say I didn't warn you," Alex says as Theo grunts his release beside us. "Come on. I'm done sharing you."

After righting my dress, Alex throws the door open and lifts me out.

I stumble the second he releases me, but thankfully, he's out of the car in a heartbeat. He sweeps me into his arms and cradles me against his chest.

I fucking love it.

"Seb," Stella cries.

"Animal," Alex mutters before taking off toward the

door that will lead us to the lift as if I weigh nothing more than a feather and he's not still suffering the effects of last night.

Glancing over his shoulder, my eyes widen as they land on Seb's bare arse as he rails Stella on the bonnet of the car.

A quiet whimper spills from my lips as I watch him loom over her, pinning her wrists above her head, her dress shoved up around her waist.

"Dirty girl," Alex growls, biting my neck.

My eyes don't leave the writhing couple until a wall hides them from me.

I'm too lost in my own head to notice as Alex walks us into the lift. It's not until my back is pressed against the wall and my legs are wrapped around his waist that I return to reality.

He takes my chin in his hand, his grip firm but not painful.

"Do you have any idea how badly I want you right now?"

I swallow nervously but nod. Because, yes. Yes, I do.

He rolls his hips, letting me feel how hard he still is.

Everyone else has either got off, or is getting off, and here he is, trying to be a gentleman.

Fighting to get out of his hold, I put my feet back on the ground and reach for him, grasping his length through the fabric of his trousers.

"Evie," he groans, and I can't help but smile as he thickens even more beneath my touch.

In a rush, I rip open his fly and shove my hand inside, needing more. Needing to make him feel as good as he made me feel in the car.

"Fuck. N-not here—"

But it's too late; the lift dings with our arrival, and the doors open.

I gasp, finding a figure standing there waiting.

His dark eyes meet Alex's, then mine, and then they drop to where I'm still holding him.

"Shit," I hiss, tugging my hand free as heat burns my cheeks.

"It's okay, Vixen. Ant doesn't mind a party," Alex teases, making the poor guy's mouth open and close like a goldfish. "Excuse us, we're in the middle of something," Alex adds before taking my hand and tugging me from the lift, leaving whoever that was standing in the hallway.

"I was just hanging with your brother and Calli," he says once he's recovered, as if his presence needs an explanation. I mean, it might; how the hell should I know?

"Cool," Alex calls back.

"Have a good night." But by the time his words hit us, Alex is already pulling me through his front door and falling back against it.

"Dress off. On your knees. Now."

Shock at the seriousness of his tone renders me useless for a split second before I jump into action.

I push my straps from my shoulders and let my dress pool around my ankles.

His eyes drop, drinking in the sight of me almost naked before him.

His fists curl, his chest heaves, and his cock strains against the fabric of his trousers.

"I said, get on your knees," he demands.

His tone is dark and his eyes are deadly glittering grey orbs as he stares me down.

This is the man I first met.

The one who had me bending to his will, doing things

I'd never done before and breaking down barriers I didn't even know existed.

My body moves on instinct, and my knees sink to the wooden floor before I finish the job I started with his trousers and tug both them and his boxers over his hips.

His cock immediately springs free.

Without wasting a second, my fingers wrap around his thickness and my tongue sneaks out to lick the tip.

"Fuck," he grunts, his hand twisting my hair. But it's not as tight as I remember from that night.

He's holding back. Because of last night maybe, or because he knows me now, I've no idea, but I fully intend to get back to that night.

I want him to lose control.

I tease him by only sucking and licking the head. My hand works the rest, but it's slow, nothing like what he wants.

"Vixen," he warns, his cock jerking in my grip with his need for more.

Rolling my gaze up his shirt, I find his eyes.

With my mouth full of his cock, although not as much of it as he'd like, I silently challenge, *Make me.*

His fingers tighten, finally starting to pinch as his hips lift from the wall.

"You're going to regret that," he groans before his hips thrust forward, forcing his cock deeper into my mouth.

Sucking in a breath through my nose, I force myself to relax.

He hits the back of my throat, making me want to gag, but I manage to stop it.

In only seconds, tears are stinging my eyes, threatening to spill over, but I don't care.

Watching him come apart before me is the most mind-blowing thing I've ever experienced.

Deep groans of pleasure fall from his lips as he uses me to take what he needs. I give back everything I can while I'm mostly immobile.

"Vixen, shit. Your mouth. Never. Anything like it," he forces out between thrusts.

Finally, my tears spill over, racing down my face and splashing onto my bare thighs.

Reaching out, he wipes his thumb through the little river of wetness and brings it to his mouth, tasting me.

His punishing thrusts never stop, and nor do I.

Humming around his length, he groans once more, his fingers tightening just like I remember, sending pain shooting down my neck.

"Fuck. Yes. Yes," he chants as his cock thickens even more with his impending release. "Vixen. Fuck. Evie." And as my name falls from his lips, he crashes, shooting hot ropes of cum down my throat.

I swallow him down as he pulls his dick from my mouth. He stares down at me for a beat, complete awe and adoration in his eyes.

It's a look that makes my heart ache in the best kind of way. But also a dangerous kind of way.

I'm still lost in my own head, my own fears when I'm lifted from the floor. My arms rest over his shoulders and my legs wrap around his waist before he pushes from the wall and carries me to the bedroom, kissing me every step of the way.

He lays me down like I'm the most delicate thing he's ever seen. I want to scream at him to be rough, to throw my body around like a rag doll and take what he still needs. But

I can't. The alcohol, the exhaustion, they both hit me like a freight train and I start crashing hard.

Slipping my shoes off my feet, he quickly massages my soles like he did last night and I moan in delight. The second he's finished, he kisses up the length of my thigh until he gets to my hips. Tucking his fingers beneath the side of my knickers, he whispers, "When you're in my bed, nothing but me and the sheets touch your body."

I somehow find the energy to lift my arse from the bed so he can pull them off me.

My legs fall open in offering, but I can't open my eyes to watch his reaction.

I hear it though, the sharp breath that's sucked in through his teeth.

"Vixen, you're a tease, showing me everything I want but can't have."

"Alex…" His name is nothing but a whisper as darkness begins to suck me under.

"Tomorrow," he promises. "I'll give you anything you need tomorrow. I'm not doing anything more to you when you're too drunk to remember."

He moves me, although I can't register how, before something soft covers my body.

"I'll be right back," he says, but it's too late. I'm gone, sinking into slumber with his taste still on my tongue and memories of his touch tingling through my body.

36

ALEX

When I wake the next morning, Evie is still out cold, but my phone is buzzing somewhere in the room.

I glance at the time, not surprised in the slightest that it's lunchtime. My stomach growls loudly at the confirmation we've missed a meal as I push up on my elbow to search for my phone.

My trousers are in a heap on the floor, the corner of my phone sticking out of the pocket.

As gently and as quietly as I can, I slip from bed and pull it free.

Walking naked through my flat, I turn the coffee machine on and then stand in front of the floor-to-ceiling window that looks out over the city beneath me.

There's a little part of me that likes the idea of people looking up here to find me baring all, maybe even scratching my balls if they're lucky. But I know it's impossible. We're too high up. I should know, I've been out there in all lights trying to find out if I can see into my flat. Call it morbid fascination.

My phone rings off, but no sooner does it still, it starts up again.

Swiping the screen to answer Nico's call, I press it to my ear.

"What fucking time do you call this?" I groan, my voice still rough from sleep.

"I've been trying to get hold of you for hours," he complains.

"You know where I live."

"I'm not home. I'm out... planning something."

I take a moment to digest that.

"Nico Cirillo is planning something. Shit, what century did I wake up in?"

"Fuck off. Listen, I've already secured it with the boss and whatever, but I need to know if you're available to fuck off for the rest of the week?"

"Depends where we're fucking off to."

"It's a secret."

"You're shitting me?"

"Nope. Doing something special for my girl, and you fuckers are coming along for the ride."

"You know I'm good with secrets, right? Daemon and Calli ring any bells?"

"Don't care. This information is classified until the very last moment."

"Fine," I sigh, already scheming up ways to get the truth out of him. Although, in all honesty, he's probably decided that we can all spend the week at his Dad's cabin. Which I am so not against. Although...

I look back over my shoulder with a heavy heart.

I'd fucking love to take her out there. But while she might have already met some of my friends, can I really allow her to spend any more time with them? What if she gets attached? What if the girls drag her deeper into this little fucked-up family we've got going on? How would I ever be able to set her free then?

"Fuck," I hiss, scrubbing my hand down my face.

"What's wrong?" Nico asks, sounding slightly panicked that I might be about to put a spanner in his plans.

"Nothing. When are we going?"

"First thing in the morning. Four AM."

"Four AM?" I echo.

"You'll need clothes for five days and your passport."

"My passport?'

"Are you just going to repeat everything I say?"

"When it's so surprising? Yes."

"I can organise shit," he grunts.

"I guess we're about to find out," I tease.

"Everything is sorted. I've got it all under control. Just be downstairs tomorrow morning, four AM."

"You got it."

"You gonna be able to leave your girl for five days, lover boy?"

"Fuck you." I hang up before he gets another word in. I already knew that Theo would have told him about Evie. But fuck, he's right. Leaving her for five days...

No. This is a good thing.

We'll have today, then I can do the right thing.

She'll have forgotten all about me in five days... right?

I can delete the app, put everything since meeting her behind me. I found her. I had a taste of the girl that drew me in that night at my dad's. More than just a taste, if we're being honest. I got what I wanted. Now, I need to figure out how I'm going to refocus on my life, my job, my future.

I grab the coffee that's rapidly cooling in the kitchen before falling back on the sofa, my eyes locked on the blue sky outside as I continue to try and convince myself that I'm doing the right thing.

Evie is too sweet, too innocent to be dragged into the life I'm forced to live.

I've no idea how much time passes as I lie there lost in my own fucked-up head, but eventually, movement on the other side of my flat catches my attention and I find her walking toward me wearing the shirt I discarded last night before I climbed into bed with her.

She's only done up a handful of buttons, so as she moves, she exposes the swell of her breasts and the soft flesh of the tops of her thighs.

Her hair is still a mess from sleep, her eyes and lips both a little puffy, but for entirely different reasons.

"Hey," she says shyly as she bites on her nail while her eyes trek down my body.

"See something you like?" I tease.

Her cheeks redden, making the pillow creases in one more obvious. So fucking cute.

"How are you feeling?"

"Surprisingly good," she confesses, moving closer and stealing my half mug of coffee that I abandoned on the side.

She takes a sip before I can tell her it's probably freezing.

"Ugh," she complains, pulling it away and scowling at it.

Unable to stop myself, I hold my hand out for her.

"Come here, Vixen."

She threads her fingers through mine the second she's in touching distance and I help her climb on top of me.

Her bare pussy hits my quickly growing cock, and I bite back a groan.

It's better you don't sink inside her before you set her free.

She deserves for someone else to take that.

But that doesn't mean I'm not going to take whatever else I can get until our time is over.

With one hand tangled in her hair and the other on he arse, I drag her mouth toward my lips.

She opens for me instantly, letting me taste my own minty toothpaste and coffee on her tongue.

A needy groan rumbles in my chest as she rocks her hips over my length.

"You're already wet for me," I mumble into our kiss.

"I was dreaming about you," she confesses.

The words are like a punch to the heart.

I love them as much as I hate them.

Stop burrowing your way in, little thief.

I kiss her deeper, harder, wishing that things could be different. That I could be a better man. Her man.

But I never will be.

No matter what, I'll always have certain things expected of me. And if that's not seducing the truth out of anyone who comes my way, it's dirty, dangerous and violent. All the things that have no place in Evie's life.

She deserves a bright future. One where she can go to uni and study and make a better life for herself.

Needing more, I drag her head back, parting our lips.

"Get up here and sit on my face."

Her chin drops in shock. "W-what?"

"You heard me. I want your cunt on my mouth. Now."

"But—"

I slide down the sofa a little, giving her knees some space before grabbing her arse and hauling her up my body.

"Oh my God," she gasps, staring down her body at me beneath her.

"Bad view?" I hold her eyes for beat before focusing on her pussy. "Because mine is fucking fantastic."

Lifting my head up, I run my tongue up the length of her, savouring her taste.

She cries out, trembling from that touch alone.

"You really did wake up horny, huh?" I ask, wrapping my hand around her thighs and dragging her closer. But she's resistant.

"I said, sit on my face, Vixen. Not hover."

"B-but, I might—"

"I won't let you suffocate me with your pussy. Although... I can think of worse ways to go. I can almost picture my headstone now... *Alexander Deimos, died doing what he loved. Eating Evie's pussy.*"

She snorts a laugh but, thankfully, does as she's told and lowers herself onto my face. I'm not sure if she's being a good girl or terrified of what might come out of my mouth next.

Either way, I'm not complaining, because I get what I want. And I fully intend on making the most of it.

She watches me as I eat her, her pupils dilated with need as I suck, lick and nip at her sensitive flesh until she can't keep them open any longer.

"Eyes," I demand.

They pop open again.

"Watch me make you fall," I command against her.

Releasing her thighs, I slide my palms up her stomach, cupping her heavy breasts.

"Oh God," she moans when I pinch her nipples.

"Come, Evie," I demand.

I've no idea if she can hear the words I say into her pussy, but she definitely feels the vibrations.

"Yes, yes. ALEX," she screams, her body quaking as she shatters so beautifully for me.

"More," I demand, "But this time..."

Wrapping my hands around her hips, I flip her around so her back is to me before pressing my hand between her shoulder blades, forcing her face toward my aching dick.

"Oh," she gasps.

Dragging her back a little, I latch onto her over-sensitive clit and suck hard.

"OOOOOH," she screams.

"Suck me, Vixen. And if it's good, I'll reward you. How many do you think I can drag out of your body before I shoot my load down your throat?"

I don't get an answer. It was a rhetorical question anyway.

Instead, I just indulge in these last few moments with my little thief.

Turns out, the answer was four.

Although, obviously, I was happy to round it up to five, but Evie wriggled away from me, claiming she couldn't go again.

I wanted to disagree, especially when I saw the state of her beautiful face with tears staining her cheeks from choking on my cock.

Fuck. She really was everything.

After I made us fresh coffee and gave her some time to recover, I dragged her into the shower and told her to get ready, until she pointed out the fact that she only had a sinful little black dress to her name.

I had a few options, five of them to be exact, but the flat next door and the girl who owed me more than a few favours was the best of them.

After demanding a set of clothes from Calli without explaining why, I returned to my girl with something for her to cover up her delicious body with.

And then, I set about giving her what I hoped was a perfect day to leave her with a few good memories.

We hit up Nina's café for breakfast before taking her on a tour of all my favourite places in the city.

We didn't do anything flashy, and I barely spent any money, but it was perfect.

Borough Market, Camden, Soho, China Town, Trafalgar Square, Leicester Square. And we finally finish the day with a picnic of all the things we'd picked up in Green Park, lying out in the early evening sun where a mix of the city's commuters rush along around us and young families play and laugh.

"Today's been amazing," she says from her spot beside me on the grass.

When I look over, I find her already studying me.

"Who knew the wealthy mafia man could find so much enjoyment in the little things?"

"Isn't it all about the little things? Money is great. The flat, the cars, the clothes. But they don't make anyone happy, not really."

Her eyes go all soft as she listens to me.

"Tell me something," she whispers. "Something real that not many other people know."

I pause, fear assaulting me.

All the things I keep hidden aren't things I'd ever want her to hear.

"I'm a pretty open book, Vixen," I say, looking back up at the sky once more, unable to look into her eyes as I lie so easily.

"Hmm... Okay, I'll let that go. Hopes for the future?"

"Same as what everyone wants. Love, a family. To be happy in whatever form it comes in."

"The bad boy is a little bit romantic," she teases.

A smile twitches at my lips.

"What about you? Famous illustrator?"

"I mean, yeah. Don't we all want to be successful? Not sure about famous, though. Mostly, I just want to help my brother and sister. Give them a better life."

"Parents?" I ask.

She pauses. "Mum died a few years ago."

"Shit, I'm sorry."

"Why? Were you driving the car that slammed into them?"

"Uh... no."

"Then you have nothing to be sorry for. It is what it is. Dad, he's... a waste of oxygen, mostly. He was injured in the accident and is now in a wheelchair, but he was pretty shitty before all that, to be honest."

Another apology sits on the tip of my tongue, but I bite it back.

"He's always just wanted an easy life, will do anything for a quick buck, even if it's at our expense. My sister, though... she's an angel."

"Blakely, right?"

"Yeah, sorry about her meddling."

Rolling onto my side, I reach out and tuck a lock of Evie's hair behind her ear.

"She cares about you. You've nothing to apologise for."

"I told her that you hadn't—"

"Neither of you had any reason to believe me. I could have just as easily as I didn't."

She swallows, accepting the truth behind my statement.

"And your brother?" I ask, getting back on track.

"Zayden." A bright smile lights up her face at the mention of him. "He's eleven. Going to be starting at LA in September. He's... going to be the most incredible man. He's kind and sensitive, sporty. He's pretty incredible on a skateboard."

"He sounds awesome," I say honestly. Anyone who makes her eyes go all soft with love like they are now is good with me.

"What about you? Parents? Siblings?"

"Divorced parents. I'm sure you've already formed plenty of opinions about my father," I tease, seeing as we only met because of his poker nights. And they're always... interesting events. "He's... set in his ways. My grandfather instilled the ways of the Family in him to the point that he struggles to see another way. It can make things... challenging. Mum is amazing. She's a nurse and just wants to help people. I'm not really sure how the two of them ended up together, but whatever." I lose myself in my thoughts. It's been a while since I saw Mum. I miss her. "Oh, and one brother."

"Nice afterthought there," Evie laughs.

"He's... well, him. We're very similar in some ways and yet night and day in others. Makes things interesting."

"Close in age?"

"Very," I say with a smirk. I don't know why I withhold

the truth, but I do. None of it really matters if it ends here, anyway.

"So your mum and dad got along at some point then?"

"Yeah," I agree lightly as a football rolls between us.

Looking up, I find five boys all staring our way, panicked looks on their faces.

Climbing to my feet, I dribble the ball away from Evie and then kick it back to them.

I stand there for a few minutes with the sun sinking into the trees behind the boys and just watch them play.

Not so long ago, that was us. To the outside world, we looked like average little boys. No one would have any idea watching us what our lives were really like. The secrets we were hiding, even back then. The ugliness we'd experienced and how much worse it was going to get as the years went on.

A small dark figure in the treeline catches my eyes, and it makes my heart bleed.

"Hey, you okay?" Evie asks, pressing her warm hand against my lower back and stepping into my side.

"Yeah, I'm good. I should probably get you home. Your sister will be worried."

I look over just in time to catch the disappointment on her face before she wipes it away with a stunning smile.

"Yeah, probably. She's a bit of a mother hen."

"Ah, and here I was thinking that she'd want all the details."

"Oh, there's that too."

"Come on then," I say, leading her back to our picnic to clear up. "All good things have to come to an end eventually."

If she hears me, then she doesn't respond.

37

───

EVIE

The tension is palpable as Alex pulls up outside my building. And it's not just because he sticks out like a sore thumb driving his fancy Audi around the streets I grew up on.

Since he watched those little boys playing football in the park, there's been a sadness in his eyes that I haven't seen before.

I don't like it, but I also don't know what to do about it.

I don't know him well enough to be able to guess, and I also don't really know if we're at a point yet that I can even ask.

"Thank you for today. It's been incredible," I say after we've been sitting here silently for a few seconds too long.

Finally, he turns to look at me. There's a darkness in his features that I don't like, but he quickly covers it with his signature smile. It's not his real one, though. That seems to be non-existent right now.

"You're welcome. It was pretty epic, huh?"

"You and your ego," I joke, hoping to lighten the mood.

He shakes his head. "I... uh..." he starts, glancing down at his lap as if he's unsure of himself. Which surely can't be the case? I've never met anyone who's as confident as he is. It's more proof that a handful of orgasms don't mean you know someone. I only know what he wants me to. That much was obvious when he evaded some of my personal questions earlier. "I'm going to be out of town for a few days."

"Oh, okay. Business or pleasure?"

"Uh..."

"It's okay," I say in a rush. "You don't need to answer that. I understand the things you do are... I don't know, secret or something."

A soft smile pulls at his lips as he reaches out to cup my cheek.

"Thank you," he whispers. "For everything."

I narrow my eyes at him, sensing many unspoken words teetering on the tip of his tongue.

"Call me when you get back, maybe?" I ask hopefully, but it doesn't stop the sinking feeling in my stomach. "You're going to miss my birthday," I blurt like an idiot. Normally, I like the day to pass without anyone noticing. Clearly, I'm clutching at straws like a loser right now.

Stage-five clinger sitting right in his passenger seat.

"I'd better give you your present now then."

His hand slips into my hair, pulling me over the centre console, then he presses his lips to mine.

His kiss is different from all the times before. It's slower, deeper. Less rushed, although it's as all-consuming and passionate as ever. But it's like he's saying everything he refuses to with words with his lips and tongue instead.

When he pulls back, we're both breathing heavily.

Forcing myself to be normal, I twist around and pull the door handle.

"Enjoy your trip," I say, climbing out.

"Enjoy... your birthday."

"Thanks. See you soon?"

His response is a nod.

A fucking nod.

Sucking in a deep breath, I will the tears to stay inside as I wave him off.

"Fuck," I breathe once his car has disappeared around the corner.

"You okay?" Blakely asks, appearing from the shadows behind me. "I wasn't stalking, I promise. I was leaving, and I didn't want to interrupt."

"I-I—" One look in her eyes and I crumble.

"Oh shit. It's okay. I've got you."

I'm in her arms in a heartbeat and guided upstairs for privacy.

"Happy birthday," Blakely sings when I finally haul my arse out to the kitchen for a cup of very strong caffeine.

"Thanks," I grunt.

"Nice to see you're going into your eighteenth year of life with a positive attitude," she teases. Her joy soon dies when our eyes collide. "Oh, sweetie."

"It's okay. I'm okay," I lie.

Truth is, he's been gone two days, and all I've had is radio silence.

I've messaged him twice. I refused to send any more than that and look desperate. And by some kind of miracle, I've only checked his Instagram once since. But that is just as inactive.

It makes me think that wherever he is, he's working and he can't reach out.

At least, it's easier to tell myself that. The alternative hurts too much.

I wasn't meant to fall for him. But...

At some point, it happened. And clearly, it happened fast. Because after only spending a few short days with him, the void he's left in my life is large and unignorable.

"Here you go. I got your favourite pods and did it just as you like it," Blake says, pushing a fancy-looking salted caramel latte toward me with my favourite biscuits sitting on the saucer.

I look up at her through watery eyes.

"Don't give me that look. One coffee does not equal too much effort. It's your big day. You deserve it."

"Happy birthday," Zay shouts, running at me at full speed. "Just so you know, I still think you're young and fun, even if you technically are an adult now."

That finally brings a real smile to my lips.

"Thanks, little man. I appreciate that."

He hops up on a stool next to me and Blake slides him a hot chocolate that matches mine with whipped cream, sprinkles and biscuits.

"Have you given it to her yet?" he asks Blake.

"Guys, I told you not to—"

"We didn't spend any money, if that's what you're going to whine about," Blake says with a roll of her eyes.

Reaching into one of the cupboards, she pulls a gift out and passes it over.

"Thank you," I say, swallowing my argument about no presents.

Ripping open the paper, Zay bounces in excitement for me to see whatever is hiding inside.

My brows narrow when I find an old jewellery box. Flipping the lid, I gasp.

"Is this...?"

"Mum's locket, yeah. She'd have wanted you to have it, Eve."

Those tears I was fighting come rushing back full force.

Reaching into the box, I run my finger over the delicate floral design engraved into the silver. Mum was given this by her parents when she was eighteen, and she never took it off. Not until...

"Don't you want it?" I ask, assuming she would.

"I have what I need to remember her. This is yours."

Clutching it in my fingers, I let my tears flow.

A small pair of arms wrap around my waist, his head snuggling my arm.

"We didn't mean to make you sad."

"Aw, Zay. It's okay. They're happy tears." Mostly. "I love it so much."

"Open it," he encourages.

So I do. The photograph staring back at me does little to stem the flow of tears.

Inside is the very last photo that was taken of the four of us together. And opposite, a recent one of the three of us.

Oh, my heart.

"That one is just for now," Blake says, pointing at the newest photo. "Figure you might want to replace it with your own family one day."

"I love it so much."

"Okay, now drink up, go and get dressed. We have a whole day planned."

"Guys," I warn.

"We listened. No crazy surprise birthday party or anything. Just a day of fun with your two favourite people."

God, I'm an emotional wreck today.

After enjoying my coffee and giving each of them a tight hug, I head back to our bedroom with the locket clutched in my fingers.

Hopelessly, I check my phone. But there are no messages.

I let out a pained sigh before getting ready to go out, hoping that by the time I return, I'll have forgotten all about him.

We have the best day. Blake and Zay had decided on London Zoo, and we spent almost all day there going to each of the animals, reading all the information about them and watching them go about their lives. We stopped for more ice cream than anyone should consume in a day, and we had waffles, with more ice cream for lunch. Then we went to a dessert-only restaurant for dinner.

It was perfect. And by the time we got back to our flat, the three of us were purely running on sugar.

Blakely looked exhausted, but she's doing so much better than she was just a few weeks ago. It gives me hope that she might one day soon be able to dance again, and not just around our flat.

We all put pyjamas on and flopped on the sofa to watch a film that Zay chose on Netflix.

At some point, Dad rolled through the living room and surprised me with a card.

"Happy birthday, kid," he grunted. It was more effort than any of us had seen him make in a long time, and I can't deny it had my hackles rising.

But really, what harm was there in a card?

Maybe he was going to start trying.

I also started laughing at that thought alone. Hell is more likely to freeze over.

That was confirmed when I opened it. Narrowing my eyes, I stared at the heartfelt wording on the front about daughters being priceless. I guess someone else chose this then. Someone who for some reason thinks he actually gives a shit about my existence.

When I fall into bed later that night, although my phone was still quiet, and the ache in my heart was still there, I had a wide smile on my face.

Dad aside, I really do have the best family.

The flat is in silence when I wake the next morning, and when I head out to find out where everyone is, I find a note on the kitchen counter.

Evie,

I've taken Zay to Josh's on my way to work. I'll collect him again later.

Have a good day.

Call me if you need me!

B xxx

With a sigh, I pad toward the coffee machine for a caffeine fix.

I stare out the window while it works its magic, taking

in the dark and dingy view before me despite the summer sun. You'd think it should make this place look better, but sadly, it has little effect.

I think about the view from Alex's fancy flat. It's like looking out at an entirely different world.

It's just another example of the vast differences between us.

I let out a sigh. I didn't check my phone when I woke. I couldn't cope with the disappointment.

A crash from the other side of the flat makes me tense before Dad rolls out of his room.

"Morning," he says. "Any chance of one of those?" He nods at my brewing coffee.

"Sure," I mutter, while silently imagining throwing the whole thing at him.

Every time I see him, it makes me wonder how any of us can be related to such an apathetic human being.

I don't remember him so bad when Mum was alive. He's always been cold and a little detached, but I'm sure he used to care, even just a little bit. Or maybe my imagination has made that up to make my life a little less depressing.

"Did you have a good birthday?" he asks.

"Yep."

"It's all downhill from here, you know?"

"I'll keep that in mind."

"You know, all I ever wanted was a better life for my family," he confesses.

"How did that work out for you?" His right eye twitches as I talk back to him.

A few years ago, I wouldn't have dared. But since Alex, and seeing as I'm an adult now and everything, I figure I can let my mouth run away with itself more than ever.

"I hoped to be able to give Blakely a better life, but she screwed that up for herself long before I even realised. But you, my sweet girl. I can give you everything."

I narrow my eyes at him.

"Are you seriously drunk at ten AM?"

"I'm not drunk," he scoffs as if the suggestion is ludicrous.

"Okay, sure."

"You're going to be a beautiful wife for someone," he says, confusing me all over again.

"Okay, old man. Take this, it might sober you up a bit."

He smirks at me as I pass over my own coffee before starting on another one for me.

"Are you going out today?"

"Uh... probably not, no. Why?"

"Derek wants to see you."

My stomach drops. I still haven't heard anything from him since my disaster at the fight. He isn't going to have anything good to say to me, that's for sure.

"Great. I'll be in my room working."

"Be good," he says, wheeling away. He's almost gone before I hear him mutter, "Your innocence is where the money is."

I shake my head and let his weirdness go. He knows full well what Blake and I both do. Hell, he was probably the one who put the idea into Derek's head to bring us under his wing. What better way to help fund his alcoholic lifestyle? It's not like his incapacity benefit and child support get him very far. Even less now he's lost money for me.

My heart bleeds for him.

I shut myself in my room, aware that I should probably

log into the app and do some actual work that's going to keep my bank balance rising. But I feel about as sexy as a dead fish. I have done since Alex drove away from me. It's stupid, but I feel like he took a piece of me with him, wherever he is.

With a sigh, I grab my tablet, but I don't open the camming app. Instead, I find my favourite drawing one and open up a new canvas.

I lose hours sketching, and I both love and hate my result. Alex and I tangled together in his bed. The sheets are all twisted up, and pillows have fallen to the floor in our passion.

Need pulls at my muscles, but it's still not enough to convince me to start working.

I'm still sitting there staring at my creation when the front door slams and a deep voice booms, "Evie?"

My heart jumps into my throat. It's like I'm a little girl all over again, and the headmaster has just walked into the classroom and called my name.

But, sir. I didn't do anything wrong.

Unable to hide from him, I lock my tablet and throw my legs off the edge of the bed.

When I pull the door open, I find him pacing back and forth through the living room while Dad wheels toward him.

"Sorry, I'm late. I was held up at— Evie," he says, his eyes locking on mine as a wicked smile pulls at his lips. "Just the girl I've come for."

My stomach knots so tight it's hard to breathe.

"Derek, I'm sorry for the other night. I totally understand that you won't—"

"It's okay," he says, his leery smile growing as his eyes

drop down my body, making me regret the shorts and tank I step out here wearing.

Man, this guy is a creep.

"It's in the past. We need to focus on the future now. Isn't that right, Jeremy?"

Dad nods in agreement. He looks weirdly excited about something that doesn't help to squash my unease.

"Are you ready?" he asks me.

"Ready for what?"

"Your birthday present."

I take a step back, not liking any of this.

There's something in his dark eyes and amused smirk that's different to all the previous times he's been here.

"What's going on?" I ask, my voice giving away my nervousness.

"You're eighteen now, Evie. I've got a new position for you."

"W-what is it?" I stutter, my hands trembling as I wrap my arms around myself.

"Come with me, and I'll make sure everything is explained on the journey."

I shake my head. "I-I don't want to go anywhere."

"That's a shame, it really is," Derek says, taking a step closer. "Unfortunately, you no longer have a choice. Someone has paid a pretty penny for your innocent cunt, and your job is to do as you're fucking told."

One second, I stare into the eyes of a monster who's always demanded I call him uncle, and the next, everything goes black.

The only person I see is *him*, and the last thing I remember thinking is that it's too late. He's not going to rescue me this time.

Want to see where Alex disappeared to?
Sign up to Patreon for early access to the bonus novella that
explains it all!

More Alex & Evie are coming!
Pre-Order Sinful Princess now!

ABOUT THE AUTHOR

Tracy Lorraine is a *USA Today* and *Wall Street Journal* bestselling new adult and contemporary romance author. Tracy has recently turned thirty and lives in a cute Cotswold village in England with her husband, baby girl and lovable but slightly crazy dog. Having always been a bookaholic with her head stuck in her Kindle, Tracy decided to try her hand at a story idea she dreamt up and hasn't looked back since.

Be the first to find out about new releases and offers. Sign up to my newsletter here.

If you want to know what I'm up to and see teasers and snippets of what I'm working on, then you need to be in my Facebook group. Join Tracy's Angels here.

Keep up to date with Tracy's books at
www.tracylorraine.com

<u>Trick You</u> #2

<u>Defy You</u> #3

<u>Play You</u> #4

<u>Inked</u> (A Rebel Ink/Driven Crossover)

<u>Rosewood High Series</u>

<u>Thorn</u> #1

<u>Paine</u> #2

<u>Savage</u> #3

<u>Fierce</u> #4

Hunter #5

Faze (#6 Prequel)

<u>Fury</u> #6

Legend #7

<u>Maddison Kings University Series</u>

<u>TMYM: Prequel</u>

<u>TRYS</u> #1

<u>TDYW</u> #2

<u>TBYS</u> #3

<u>TVYC</u> #4

<u>TDYD</u> #5

<u>TDYR</u> #6

<u>TRYD</u> #7

<u>Knight's Ridge Empire Series</u>

<u>Wicked Summer Knight</u>: Prequel (Stella & Seb)

Wicked Knight #1 (Stella & Seb)

Wicked Princess #2 (Stella & Seb)

Wicked Empire #3 (Stella & Seb)

Deviant Knight #4 (Emmie & Theo)

Deviant Princess #5 (Emmie & Theo

Deviant Reign #6 (Emmie & Theo)

One Reckless Knight (Jodie & Toby)

Reckless Knight #7 (Jodie & Toby)

Reckless Princess #8 (Jodie & Toby)

Reckless Dynasty #9 (Jodie & Toby)

Dark Halloween Knight (Calli & Batman)

Dark Knight #10 (Calli & Batman)

Dark Princess #11 (Calli & Batman)

Dark Legacy #12 (Calli & Batman)

Corrupt Valentine Knight (Nico & Siren)

Corrupt Knight #13 (Nico & Siren)

Corrupt Princess #14 (Nico & Siren)

Corrupt Union #15 (Nico & Siren)

Sinful Wild Knight (Alex)

Sinful Stolen Knight (Alex & Vixen)

Sinful Knight (Alex & Vixen)

Ruined Series

Ruined Plans #1

THE REVENGE YOU SEEK
SNEAK PEEK

Chapter One

Letty

I sit on my bed, staring down at the fabric in my hands.

This wasn't how it was supposed to happen.

This wasn't part of my plan.

I let out a sigh, squeezing my eyes tight, willing the tears away.

I've cried enough. I thought I'd have run out by now.

A commotion on the other side of the door has me looking up in a panic, but just like yesterday, no one comes knocking.

I think I proved that I don't want to hang with my new roommates the first time someone knocked and asked if I wanted to go for breakfast with them.

I don't.

I don't even want to be here.

I just want to hide.

And that thought makes it all a million times worse.

I'm not a hider. I'm a fighter. I'm a fucking Hunter.

But this is what I've been reduced to.

This pathetic, weak mess.

And all because of *him*.

He shouldn't have this power over me. But even now, he does.

The dorm falls silent once again, and I pray that they've all headed off for their first class of the semester so I can slip out unnoticed.

I know it's ridiculous. I know I should just go out there with my head held high and dig up the confidence I know I do possess.

But I can't.

I figure that I'll just get through today—my first day—and everything will be alright.

I can somewhat pick up where I left off, almost as if the last eighteen months never happened.

Wishful thinking.

I glance down at the hoodie in my hands once more.

Mom bought them for Zayn, my younger brother, and me.

The navy fabric is soft between my fingers, but the text staring back at me doesn't feel right.

Maddison Kings University.

A knot twists my stomach and I swear my whole body sags with my new reality.

I was at my dream school. I beat the odds and I got into Columbia. And everything was good. No, everything was fucking fantastic.

Until it wasn't.

Now here I am. Sitting in a dorm at what was always my backup plan school having to start over.

Throwing the hoodie onto my bed, I angrily push to my feet.

I'm fed up with myself.

I should be better than this, stronger than this.

But I'm just... I'm broken.

And as much as I want to see the positives in this situation. I'm struggling.

Shoving my feet into my Vans, I swing my purse over my shoulder and scoop up the couple of books on my desk for the two classes I have today.

My heart drops when I step out into the communal kitchen and find a slim blonde-haired girl hunched over a mug and a textbook.

The scent of coffee fills my nose and my mouth waters.

My shoes squeak against the floor and she immediately looks up.

"Sorry, I didn't mean to disrupt you."

"Are you kidding?" she says excitedly, her southern accent making a smile twitch at my lips.

Her smile lights up her pretty face and for some reason, something settles inside me.

I knew hiding was wrong. It's just been my coping method for... quite a while.

"We wondered when our new roommate was going to show her face. The guys have been having bets on you being an alien or something."

A laugh falls from my lips. "No, no alien. Just..." I sigh, not really knowing what to say.

"You transferred in, right? From Columbia?"

"Ugh... yeah. How'd you know—"

"Girl, I know everything." She winks at me, but it

doesn't make me feel any better. "West and Brax are on the team, they spent the summer with your brother."

A rush of air passes my lips in relief. Although I'm not overly thrilled that my brother has been gossiping about me.

"So, what classes do you have today?" she asks when I stand there gaping at her.

"Umm... American lit and psychology."

"I've got psych later too. Professor Collins?"

"Uh..." I drag my schedule from my purse and stare down at it. "Y-yes."

"Awesome. We can sit together."

"S-sure," I stutter, sounding unsure, but the smile I give her is totally genuine. "I'm Letty, by the way." Although I'm pretty sure she already knows that.

"Ella."

"Okay, I'll... uh... see you later."

"Sure. Have a great morning."

She smiles at me and I wonder why I was so scared to come out and meet my new roommates.

I'd wanted Mom to organize an apartment for me so that I could be alone, but—probably wisely—she refused. She knew that I'd use it to hide in and the point of me restarting college is to try to put everything behind me and start fresh.

After swiping an apple from the bowl in the middle of the table, I hug my books tighter to my chest and head out, ready to embark on my new life.

The morning sun burns my eyes and the scent of freshly cut grass fills my nose as I step out of our building. The summer heat hits my skin, and it makes everything feel that little bit better.

So what if I'm starting over. I managed to transfer the

credits I earned from Columbia, and MKU is a good school. I'll still get a good degree and be able to make something of my life.

Things could be worse.

It could be this time last year...

I shake the thought from my head and force my feet to keep moving.

I pass students meeting up with their friends for the start of the new semester as they excitedly tell them all about their summers and the incredible things they did, or they compare schedules.

My lungs grow tight as I drag in the air I need. I think of the friends I left behind in Columbia. We didn't have all that much time together, but we'd bonded before my life imploded on me.

Glancing around, I find myself searching for familiar faces. I know there are plenty of people here who know me. A couple of my closest friends came here after high school.

Mom tried to convince me to reach out over the summer, but my anxiety kept me from doing so. I don't want anyone to look at me like I'm a failure. That I got into one of the best schools in the country, fucked it up and ended up crawling back to Rosewood. I'm not sure what's worse, them assuming I couldn't cope or the truth.

Focusing on where I'm going, I put my head down and ignore the excited chatter around me as I head for the coffee shop, desperately in need of my daily fix before I even consider walking into a lecture.

I find the Westerfield Building where my first class of the day is and thank the girl who holds the heavy door open for me before following her toward the elevator.

"Holy fucking shit," a voice booms as I turn the corner, following the signs to the room on my schedule.

Before I know what's happening, my coffee is falling from my hand and my feet are leaving the floor.

"What the—" The second I get a look at the guy standing behind the one who has me in his arms, I know exactly who I've just walked into.

Forgetting about the coffee that's now a puddle on the floor, I release my books and wrap my arms around my old friend.

His familiar woodsy scent flows through me, and suddenly, I feel like me again. Like the past two years haven't existed.

"What the hell are you doing here?" Luca asks, a huge smile on his face when he pulls back and studies me.

His brows draw together when he runs his eyes down my body, and I know why. I've been working on it over the summer, but I know I'm still way skinnier than I ever have been in my life.

"I transferred," I admit, forcing the words out past the lump in my throat.

His smile widens more before he pulls me into his body again.

"It's so good to see you."

I relax into his hold, squeezing him tight, absorbing his strength. And that's one thing that Luca Dunn has in spades. He's a rock, always has been and I didn't realize how much I needed that right now.

Mom was right. I should have reached out.

"You too," I whisper honestly, trying to keep the tears at bay that are threatening just from seeing him—them.

"Hey, it's good to see you," Leon says, slightly more subdued than his twin brother as he hands me my discarded books.

"Thank you."

I look between the two of them, noticing all the things that have changed since I last saw them in person. I keep up with them on Instagram and TikTok, sure, but nothing is quite like standing before the two of them.

Both of them are bigger than I ever remember, showing just how hard their coach is working them now they're both first string for the Panthers. And if it's possible, they're both hotter than they were in high school, which is really saying something because they'd turn even the most confident of girls into quivering wrecks with one look back then. I can only imagine the kind of rep they have around here.

The sound of a door opening behind us and the shuffling of feet cuts off our little reunion.

"You in Professor Whitman's American lit class?" Luca asks, his eyes dropping from mine to the book in my hands.

"Yeah. Are you?"

"We are. Walk you to class?" A smirk appears on his lips that I remember all too well. A flutter of the butterflies he used to give me threaten to take flight as he watches me intently.

Luca was one of my best friends in high school, and I spent almost all our time together with the biggest crush on him. It seems that maybe the teenage girl inside me still thinks that he could be it for me.

"I'd love you to."

"Come on then, Princess," Leon says and my entire body jolts at hearing that pet name for me. He's never called me that before and I really hope he's not about to start now.

Clearly not noticing my reaction, he once again takes my books from me and threads his arm through mine as the pair of them lead me into the lecture hall.

I glance at both of them, a smile pulling at my lips and hope building inside me.

Maybe this was where I was meant to be this whole time.

Maybe Columbia and I were never meant to be.

More than a few heads turn our way as we climb the stairs to find some free seats. Mostly it's the females in the huge space and I can't help but inwardly laugh at their reaction.

I get it.

The Dunn twins are two of the Kings around here and I'm currently sandwiched between them. It's a place that nearly every female in this college, hell, this state, would kill to be in.

"Dude, shift the fuck over," Luca barks at another guy when he pulls to a stop a few rows from the back.

The guy who's got dark hair and even darker eyes immediately picks up his bag, books, and pen and moves over a space.

"This is Colt," Luca explains, nodding to the guy who's studying me with interest.

"Hey," I squeak, feeling a little intimidated.

"Hey." His low, deep voice licks over me. "Ow, what the fuck, man?" he barks, rubbing at the back of his head where Luca just slapped him.

"Letty's off-limits. Get your fucking eyes off her."

"Dude, I was just saying hi."

"Yeah, and we all know what that usually leads to," Leon growls behind me.

The three of us take our seats and just about manage to pull our books out before our professor begins explaining the syllabus for the semester.

"Sorry about the coffee," Luca whispers after a few minutes. "Here." He places a bottle of water on my desk. "I know it's not exactly a replacement, but it's the best I can do."

The reminder of the mess I left out in the hallway hits me.

"I should go and—"

"Chill," he says, placing his hand on my thigh. His touch instantly relaxes me as much as it sends a shock through my body. "I'll get you a replacement after class. Might even treat you to a cupcake."

I smile up at him, swooning at the fact he remembers my favorite treat.

Why did I ever think coming here was a bad idea?

Chapter Two
Letty

My hand aches by the time Professor Whitman finishes talking. It feels like a lifetime ago that I spent this long taking notes.

"You okay?" Luca asks me with a laugh as I stretch out my fingers.

"Yeah, it's been a while."

"I'm sure these boys can assist you with that, beautiful," bursts from Colt's lips, earning him another slap to the head.

"Ignore him. He's been hit in the head with a ball one too many times," Leon says from beside me but I'm too enthralled with the way Luca is looking at me right now to reply.

Our friendship wasn't a conventional one back in high school. He was the star quarterback, and I wasn't a cheerleader or ever really that sporty. But we were paired up as lab partners during my first week at Rosewood High and we kinda never separated.

I watched as he took the team to new heights, as he met with college scouts, I even went to a few places with him so he didn't have to go alone.

He was the one who allowed me to cry on his shoulder as I struggled to come to terms with the loss of another who left a huge hole in my heart and he never, not once, overstepped the mark while I clung to him and soaked up his support.

I was also there while he hooked up with every member of the cheer squad along with any other girl who looked at him just so. Each one stung a little more than the last as my poor teenage heart was getting battered left, right, and center.

With each day, week, month that passed, I craved him more but he never, not once, looked at me that way.

I was even his prom date, yet he ended up spending the night with someone else.

It hurt, of course it did. But it wasn't his fault and I refuse to hold it against him.

Maybe I should have told him. Been honest with him about my feelings and what I wanted. But I was so terrified I'd lose my best friend that I never confessed, and I took that secret all the way to Columbia with me.

As I stare at him now, those familiar butterflies still set flight in my belly, but they're not as strong as I remember. I'm not sure if that's because my feelings for him have lessened over time, or if I'm just so numb and broken right now that I don't feel anything but pain.

It really could go either way.

I smile at him, so grateful to have run into him this morning.

He always knew when I needed him and even without knowing of my presence here, there he was like some guardian fucking angel.

If guardian angels had sexy dark bed hair, mesmerizing green eyes and a body built for sin then yeah, that's what he is.

I laugh to myself, yeah, maybe that irritating crush has gone nowhere.

"What have you got next?" Leon asks, dragging my attention away from his twin.

Leon has always been the quieter, broodier one of the duo. He's as devastatingly handsome and as popular with the female population but he doesn't wear his heart on his sleeve like Luca. Leon takes a little time to warm to people, to let them in. It was hard work getting there, but I soon realized that once he dropped his walls a little for me, it was hella worth it.

He's more serious, more contemplative, he's deeper. I always suspected that there was a reason they were so different. I know twins don't have to be the same and like the same things, but there was always something niggling at me that there was a very good reason that Leon closed himself down. From listening to their mom talk over the years, they were so identical in their mannerisms, likes, and dislikes when they were growing up, that it seems hard to believe they became so different.

"Psychology but not for an hour. I'm—"

"I'm taking her for coffee," Luca butts in. A flicker of anger passes through Leon's eyes but it's gone so fast that I begin to wonder if I imagined it.

"I could use another coffee before econ," Leon chips in.

"Great. Let's go," Luca forces out through clenched teeth.

He wanted me alone. Interesting.

The reason I never told him about my mega crush is the fact he friend-zoned me in our first few weeks of friendship by telling me how refreshing it was to have a girl wanting to be his friend and not using it as a ploy to get more.

We were only sophomores at the time but even then, Luca was up to all sorts and the girls around us were all more than willing to bend to his needs.

From that moment on, I couldn't tell him how I really felt. It was bad enough I even felt it when he thought our friendship was just that.

I smile at both of them, hoping to shatter the sudden tension between the twins.

"Be careful with these two," Colt announces from behind us as we make our way out of the lecture hall with all the others. "The stories I've heard."

"Colt," Luca warns, turning to face him and walking backward for a few steps.

"Don't worry," I shoot over my shoulder. "I know how to handle the Dunn twins." I wink at him as he howls with laughter.

"You two are in so much trouble," he muses as he turns left out of the room and we go right.

Leon takes my books from me once more and Luca threads his fingers through mine. I still for a beat. While the move isn't unusual, Luca has always been very affectionate. It only takes a second for his warmth to race up my arm and to settle the last bit of unease that's still knotting my stomach.

"Two Americanos and a skinny vanilla latte with an extra shot. Three cupcakes with the sprinkles on top."

I swoon at the fact Luca remembers my order. "How'd you—"

He turns to me, his wide smile and the sparkle in his eyes making my words trail off. The familiarity of his face, the feeling of comfort and safety he brings me causes a lump to form in my throat.

"I didn't forget anything about my best girl." He throws his arm around my shoulder and pulls me close.

Burying my nose in his hard chest, I breathe him in. His woodsy scent mixes with his laundry detergent and it settles me in a way I didn't know I needed.

Leon's stare burns into my back as I snuggle with his brother and I force myself to pull away so he doesn't feel like the third wheel.

"Dunn," the server calls, and Leon rushes ahead to grab our order while Luca leads me to a booth at the back of the coffee shop.

As we walk past each table, I become more and more aware of the attention on the twins. I know their reps, they've had their football god status since before I moved to Rosewood and met them in high school, but I had forgotten just how hero-worshiped they were, and this right now is off the charts.

Girls openly stare, their eyes shamelessly dropping down the guys' bodies as they mentally strip them naked. Guys jealousy shines through their expressions, especially those who are here with their girlfriends who are now paying them zero attention. Then there are the girls whose attention is firmly on me. I can almost read their thoughts— hell, I heard enough of them back in high school.

What do they see in her?

She's not even that pretty.

They're too good for her.

The only difference here from high school is that no one knows I'm just trailer park trash seeing as I moved from the hellhole that is Harrow Creek before meeting the boys.

Tipping my chin up, I straighten my spine and plaster on as much confidence as I can find.

They can all think what they like about me, they can come up with whatever bitchy comments they want. It's no skin off my back.

"Good to see you've lost your appeal," I mutter, dropping into the bench opposite both of them and wrapping my hands around my warm mug when Leon passes it over.

"We walk around practically unnoticed," Luca deadpans.

"You thought high school was bad," Leon mutters, he was always the one who hated the attention whereas Luca used it to his advantage to get whatever he wanted. "It was nothing."

"So I see. So, how's things? Catch me up on everything," I say, needing to dive into their celebrity status lifestyles rather than thinking about my train wreck of a life.

"Really?" Luca asks, raising a brow and causing my stomach to drop into my feet. "I think the bigger question is how come you're here and why we had no idea about it?"

Releasing my mug, I wrap my arms around myself and drop my eyes to the table.

"T-things just didn't work out at Columbia," I mutter, really not wanting to talk about it.

"The last time we talked, you said it was everything you expected it to be and more. What happened?"

Kane fucking Legend happened.

I shake that thought from my head like I do every time he pops up.

He's had his time ruining my life. It's over.

"I just..." I sigh. "I lost my way a bit, ended up dropping out and finally had to fess up and come clean to Mom."

Leon laughs sadly. "I bet that went down well."

The Dunn twins are well aware of what it's like to live with a pushy parent. One of the things that bonded the three of us over the years.

"Like a lead balloon. Even worse because I dropped out months before I finally showed my face."

"Why hide?" Leon's brows draw together as Luca stares at me with concern darkening his eyes.

"I had some health issues. It's nothing."

"Shit, are you okay?"

Fucking hell, Letty. Stop making this worse for yourself.

"Yeah, yeah. Everything is good. Honestly. I'm here and I'm ready to start over and make the best of it."

They both smile at me, and I reach for my coffee once more, bringing the mug to my lips and taking a sip.

"Enough about me, tell me all about the lives of two of the hottest Kings of Maddison."

"Okay... how'd you do that?" Ella whispers after both Luca and Leon walk me to my psych class after our coffee break.

"Do what?" I ask, following her into the room and finding ourselves seats about halfway back.

"It's your first day and the Dunn twins just walked you to class. You got a diamond-encrusted vag or something?"

I snort a laugh as a few others pause on their way to their seats at her words.

"Shush," I chastise.

"Girl, if it's true, you know all these guys need to know about it."

I pull out my books and a couple of pens as Professor Collins sets up at the front before turning to her.

"No, I don't have diamonds anywhere but my necklace. I've been friends with them for years."

"Girl, I knew there was a reason we should be friends." She winks at me. "I've been trying to get West and Brax to hook me up but they're useless."

"You want to be friends so I can set you up with one of the Dunns?"

"Or both." She shrugs, her face deadly serious before she leans in. "I've heard that they tag team sometimes. Can you imagine? Both of their undivided attention." She fans herself as she obviously pictures herself in the middle of a Dunn sandwich. "Oh and, I think you're pretty cool too."

"Of course you do." I laugh.

It's weird, I might have only met her very briefly this morning but that was enough.

"We're all going out for dinner tonight to welcome you to the dorm. The others are dying to meet you." She smiles at me, proving that there's no bitterness behind her words.

"I'm sorry for ignoring you all."

"Girl, don't sweat it. We got ya back, don't worry."

"Thank you," I mouth as the professor demands everyone's attention to begin the class.

The time flies as I scribble my notes down as fast as I can, my hand aching all over again and before I know it, he's finished explaining our first assignment and bringing his class to a close.

"Jesus, this semester is going to be hard," Ella muses as we both pack up.

"At least we've got each other."

"I like the way you think. You done for the day?"

"Yep, I'm gonna head to the store, grab some supplies then get started on this assignment, I think."

"I've got a couple of hours. You want company?"

After dumping our stuff in our rooms, Ella takes me to her favorite store, and I stock up on everything I'm going to need before we head back so she can go to class.

I make myself some lunch before being brave and setting up my laptop at the kitchen table to get started on my assignments. My time for hiding is over, it's time to get back to life and once again become a fully immersed college student.

"Holy shit, she is alive. I thought Zayn was lying about his beautiful older sister," a deep rumbling voice says, dragging me from my research a few hours later.

I spin and look at the two guys who have joined me.

"Zayn would never have called me beautiful," I say as a greeting.

"That's true. I think his actual words were: messy, pain in the ass, and my personal favorite, I'm glad I don't have to live with her again," he says, mimicking my brother's voice.

"Now that is more like it. Hey, I'm Letty. Sorry about—"

"You're all good. We're just glad you emerged. I'm West, this ugly motherfucker is Braxton—"

"Brax, please," he begs. "Only my mother calls me by my full name and you are way too hot to be her."

My cheeks heat as he runs his eyes over my curves.

"T-thanks, I think."

"Ignore him. He hasn't gotten laid for weeeeks."

"Okay, do we really need to go there right now?"

"Always, bro. Our girl here needs to know you get pissy when you don't get the pussy."

I laugh at their easy banter, closing down my laptop and

resting forward on my elbows as they move toward the fridge.

"Ella says we're going out," Brax says, pulling out two bottles of water and throwing one to West.

"Apparently so."

"She'll be here in a bit. Violet and Micah too. They were all in the same class."

"So," West says, sliding into the chair next to me. "What do we need to know that your brother hasn't already told us about you?"

My heart races at all the things that not even my brother would share about my life before I drag my thoughts away from my past.

"Uhhh..."

"How about the Dunns love her," Ella announces as she appears in the doorway flanked by two others. Violet and Micah, I assume.

"Um... how didn't we know this?" Brax asks.

"Because you're not cool enough to spend any time with them, asshole," Violet barks, walking around Ella. "Ignore these assholes, they think they're something special because they're on the team but what they don't tell you is that they have no chance of making first string or talking to the likes of the Dunns."

"Vi, girl. That stings," West says, holding his hand over his heart.

"Yeah, get over it. Truth hurts." She smiles up at him as he pulls her into his chest and kisses the top of her head.

"Whatever, Titch."

"Right, well. Are we ready to go? I need tacos like... yesterday."

"Yes. Let's go."

"You've never had tacos like these, Letty. You are in for a world of pleasure," Brax says excitedly.

"More than she would be if she were in your bed, that's for sure," West deadpans.

"Lies and we all know it."

"Whatever." Violet pushes him toward the door.

"Hey, I'm Micah," the third guy says when I catch up to him.

"Hey, Letty."

"You need a sensible conversation, I'm your boy."

"Good to know."

Micah and I trail behind the others and with each step I take, my smile gets wider.

Things really are going to be okay.

DOWNLOAD NOW TO KEEP READING

www.ingramcontent.com/pod-product-compliance
Lightning Source LLC
Chambersburg PA
CBHW031003190726
48285CB00004BB/1448